PRAISE FOR STINA LINDENBLATT

Tell Me When

TELL ME WHEN is a heartbreaking and emotional story. Be prepared to do nothing else but read once you start this book!
—*Fresh Fiction*

"I felt that even though the subject matter is a little over used, Tell Me When did it in a way that was rawer, darker and more realistic and that made it feel fresh and unique."—*Bookish Treasures*

"If you're looking for an exciting read, filled with secrets, mystery, danger, and realism, this story is a perfect match! I give, Tell Me When, by Stina Lindenblatt, 4 Intense, Powerful, Healing, and 'Falling in Love' filled Stars!"—*A bookish Escape*

"I. LOVED. THIS. BOOK!!!!"—*Seeking Book Boyfriends*

"If you are looking for well written story that will take you on a ride of highs and lows of our human emotional states and of the good and the bad of what life is willing to offer, then I highly suggest you read this fantastic story!"—*Biblio Belles Book Blog*

Let Me Know

"I love Stina's writing style. It's very emotive, and flows beautifully. I felt connected to the characters from very early on and cried several times at the pain these characters go through"—*Reading Realm Blog*

"Overall, I think Ms Lindenblatt did a phenomenal job writing this series. From the intriguing plot, interesting and unique characters, to the overall well written storyline, this series is a must read"
—*Tyhada Reads*

"This was an amazing read, I could not out this down. The author really wrote this one so beautifully. Let me say that the author's writing bought out so many emotions from me, I just loved it"
—*Lustful Literature*

This One Moment

"A thrill ride that kept me on the edge of my seat, *This One Moment* is hot, intense, and filled with emotion—contemporary romance at its finest. Nolan stole my heart from page one, and Hailey was a heroine with whom I could truly identify. I was in reader heaven!"
—*New York Times* bestselling author Rachel Harris

"A well-written story that kept me entertained from start to finish."
—*Harlequin Junkie*

"I loved this book; this is romance at its best, this is that perfect ending we all read romance for, this is an absolutely beautifully told love story."—*Guilty Pleasures Book Reviews*

"Very satisfying . . . Stina Lindenblatt is a new author to me and a very good one I may add. . . . I will sure keep an eye on her in the future. She is really worth it!"—*Collector of Book Boyfriends & Girlfriends*

"The story is amazing and the suspense is thrilling."—*Just One More Chapter*

"Filled with emotion, intensity, a lot of sexual tension and the perfect amount of heat."—*About That Story*

My Song for You

"Romantic angst powers this fast-paced novel, and readers will return to the series to learn more about the enigmatic side characters whose own stories are waiting to be told."—*Publishers Weekly*

"The author has an amazing and deep connection with her characters. . . . I loved every single page."—*Extreme Damage Blog*

"From the first to the last page—greatness unfolded."—*Ellie Is Uhm . . . A Bookworm*

"Filled with romance, misunderstandings, lies and a whole lot of heat . . . [*My Song for You*] has everything to satisfy the romance itch in all of us."—*Twin Spin*

"Six stars—Stina Lindenblatt has a skill to write heroes with some depth like few can."—*Collectors of Book Boyfriends & Girlfriends*

"Oooh, a secret baby story with a twist . . . and I liked that twist. I also really liked that this was somewhat of a friends-to-lovers story. . . A really good, entertaining read and I enjoyed it a lot. I'd definitely recommend it."—*Smitten with Reading*

I Need You Tonight

"Ms. Lindenblatt has penned another remarkable read for this series. . . . Full of exquisite heat and passion, and the ending brought happy tears to my eyes. . . . I would highly recommend *I Need You Tonight*."—*Book Magic*

"*I Need You Tonight* is one of those books that you go into thinking one thing and end up getting your mind blown because you were not expecting the emotion that this made you feel. Honestly, this had to have been the best book of the series because of that."—*Life of a Crazy Mom*

"[Stina Lindenblatt's] writing shows superb talent and care for both the storyline and her characters. This is not a book you want to pass the chance at reading."—*Ellie Is Uhm . . . A Bookworm*

"There are so many, many things that I loved about this story. . . . I hadn't realized I'd been missing and I was craving the Pushing Limits boys until this one came along. And it came with a bang!" —*Collectors of Book Boyfriends & Girlfriends*

ALSO BY STINA LINDENBLATT

CONTEMPORARY ROMANCES

Carson Brothers Series

One More Chance

One More Secret

One More Betrayal

Pushing Limits Series

This One Moment

My Song For You

I Need You Tonight

Lost in You Series

Let Me Know

ROMANTIC COMEDY NOVELS

By The Bay Series

Decidedly Off Limits

Decidedly with Baby

Decidedly with Love

Decidedly with Mistletoe

Decidedly by Chance

Decidedly with Luck

Decidedly with Wishes

Visit stinalindenblattauthor.com for more books

TELL ME WHEN

LOST IN YOU DUET, BOOK 1

STINA LINDENBLATT

NOTE FROM AUTHOR

Dear Reader,

When I first decided to write *Tell Me When*, I thought back to when I was in university and became the target of a stalker. I met the guy at a nightclub and told him too much about myself. I'm not sure why I did that. I wasn't interested in him. He ended up stalking me. It was a terrifying ordeal, especially since I had to deal with it on my own. I thought no one would take me seriously because he hadn't tried to physically harm me. His persistence resulted in my quitting my part-time job so I could escape him. My personal story is, unfortunately, all too common in college-aged students.

Prior to the original release of *Tell Me When*, I organized a blog hop focused on stalking. The release date coincided with National Stalking Awareness Month, and I wanted to increase awareness of the problem in this age group. Numerous participants involved in the blog hop shared their personal experiences, as did those who commented on the posts. The majority, both males and females, had been victims of stalking while in high school or college, or had known someone who was a victim during this time period. Those who wrote about their personal stories survived. Not all the victims were that lucky.

Everyone is at risk of becoming a target of stalking, regardless of your age or gender, but there are things you can do to decrease the chance of it happening to you. I invite you to visit https://www.rainn.org/articles/stalking to learn more.

Stay safe,

Stina Lindenblatt

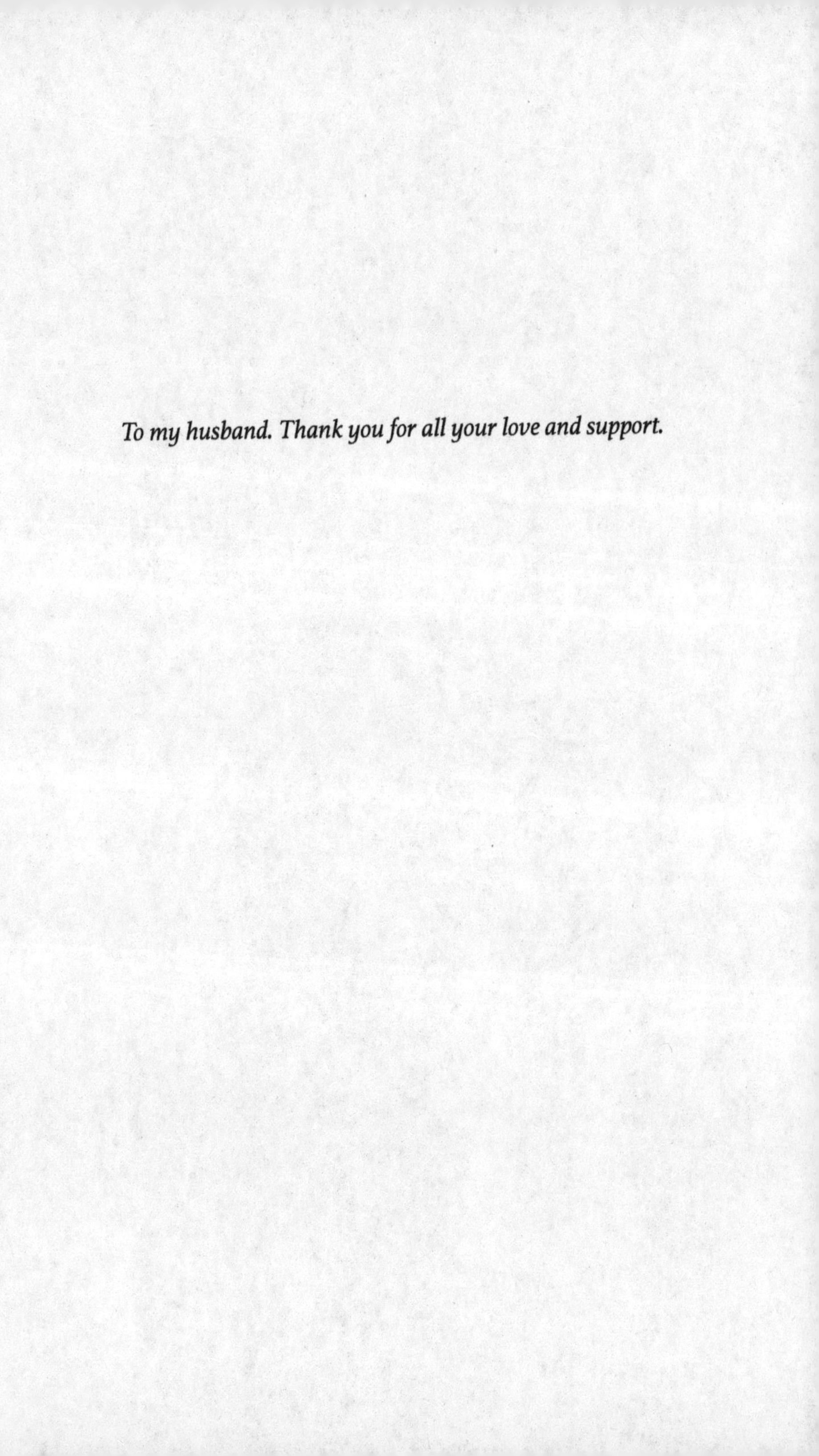

To my husband. Thank you for all your love and support.

TELL ME WHEN

1

AMBER

My windshield wipers squeak as I pull into the empty parking spot in front of Your Designs. Rain pelts my window. My heart pounds along with it.

I can do this. I need to do this.

A mother and her toddler dash past the car as I pull the hood of my rain jacket over my head. He stops, a mischievous smile on his face, and leaps into a puddle. His red rubber boots splash water in every direction. I can't help but laugh at his expression. At least *he's* not afraid of the weather.

Before I can change my mind, I grab my purse from the passenger seat and make a break for the store. Once inside, I fish through my purse for the picture I found on the Internet, after hours and hours of research.

"Hi, Amber," Kathy says from the counter. Her long, curly blond hair is pulled back in a ponytail, and she's wearing skintight jeans and a black T-shirt that reads Rock On.

"You're finally going for it?" She's referring to the five other times I've been here, checking the place out, but never quite having the courage to go through with it.

An oversized jar with a hole in the lid and a picture of a lotus flower on the side sits on the counter. Above the flower is the message: Please donate and help victims of sexual assault and abuse become survivors. I poke a five-dollar bill through the slot like I've done every time I've come here.

"You're the one giving me the tattoo, right?" I ask.

"That's right. Do you have an idea of what you want?"

Swallowing hard, I unfold the picture of a dozen small blue flowers floating on a breeze. Forget-me-nots. I hand it to her. "I want it here." I indicate the inside of my left forearm, which is hidden under my jacket sleeve. "And I also want it to say 'Trent and Michael.'"

Kathy pulls out a book with different fonts and I pick an elegant script. It's perfect.

"Just let me set up, and we'll get started." She heads to the back of the store and disappears down a hallway.

I wander over to a wall of tattoos. I've seen them each time I've been here, but that doesn't stop me from marveling over the more intricate designs. Until now, I've never been impressed by tattoos. It was my ex-best friend who wanted one. Funny how things change.

I'm inspecting a delicate fairy with wings like autumn leaves when the chimes above the door ring. Two guys, maybe twenty-one or twenty-two, enter. Both are good-looking and have the tall, muscular bodies of basketball players. That's where the similarities between them end.

The dark-haired guy has that bad-boy vibe some girls find appealing, with his military boots, jeans, and black leather jacket. His blond-haired friend is the kind of guy most girls feel safe with. He's wearing sneakers, jeans, and a blood-donor T-shirt. The clothes and his friendly expression make him appear trustworthy. Like he won't break your heart or your body or your soul.

But I've long since learned that appearances are never what they seem. Either man could be sweet, or he could be dangerous. The trick is to never let them get close enough for you to find out the truth the hard way.

Blond guy walks to the counter and chats with the store owner, a man not much older than us, with tattoos covering his arms. Neither pays attention to me. I resume studying the wall.

From the corner of my eye, I notice the black-haired guy walking toward me. Instead of checking out the designs on the wall, his gaze roams over my body, taking in the view. *Jerk.*

A one-sided smile slides onto his face. He's the kind of guy who uses his good looks to his advantage, the kind of guy whose sole mission in life is getting laid.

My hand tap-tap-taps my right thigh, keeping pace with my heart, which has picked up speed as the jerk continues staring at me. I narrow my eyes at him, silently telling him to find another girl. He's wasting his time with me.

The men at the counter laugh.

"Dude, that's the first time I've seen you get shot down by a female," blond guy says, still chuckling.

Dark-haired guy flips him the finger and points to the fairy. "This would look hot on you right"—he strokes his finger against my lower back—"here." His voice is low, the words slow and practiced.

I jerk away and stride to the rear of the store. The other two men laugh even louder.

"Give up, Marcus," blond guy says. "She's a lot smarter than your usual girls. I like her already."

Kathy reappears from the hallway as blond guy and tattoo guy high-five. Dark-haired guy shrugs with an easy grin and walks over to join them.

"I'm ready for you now." A reassuring smile curves on Kathy's face.

She leads me into another room and gestures to a padded chair with a moveable armrest. "Sit down, please, and remove your jacket."

Relieved to have escaped the guys, I make myself comfy on the chair.

After gathering her supplies, Kathy sits on the chair next to me and examines my wrist. Her thumb brushes against the thick scars, as if she's a fortune-teller reading my past, present, and future. Hope she has a strong stomach.

"It's horrible what he did to you." She gives me the sad look, the one I witnessed too often last spring. A combination of horror, disbelief, sympathy.

I nod, frantically figuring out a way to change the topic. I wasn't prepared for this. No one on campus has recognized me yet as the girl whose tragedy was splashed across the front-page news...and I want to keep it that way.

I focus on my breathing to keep from flashing back to that nightmare. To keep from thinking about what I'm doing. To keep from answering questions I'd rather avoid.

Kathy wipes my forearm with a warm, disinfectant-smelling liquid. "I'll warn ya now. It's gonna hurt like hell."

Good. "I'll be fine."

2

AMBER

"**W**ake up, bitch!"

Someone—my roommate, I think—shakes me. I open my eyes to find a pair of dark ones glaring at me.

"What the hell's your problem?" Miss Sunshine says. "It's five fucking o'clock in the fucking morning."

"Sorry." I blink, eyes slowly adjusting to the darkness. I'm safe. In my dorm room. The fire has long since been extinguished, and Paul's touch can only haunt me in my dreams. The cops, the DA, my mom, they all promised he can't hurt me anymore.

If only they could convince my subconscious.

"That's the third fucking time you've woken me up with your fucking nightmares this month."

Three? That's all? She's lucky.

I shove away the memory of the dream and sit up. Even though the darkness prevents Brittany from seeing the scars on my wrists, I grope around the mattress until my fingers brush the soft fleece of Trent's hoodie. I yank it on, hiding the scars. All of them. Inside and out.

A soft knock at the door distracts Brittany. I scramble out of bed, desperate to escape before she turns me into a lump of ice with her wonderfully warm disposition.

She grunts and opens the door. "What do you want?" she snaps, her voice quiet so as not to wake everyone else, in case I haven't already.

A tall, dark figure pushes past Brittany. I can't see her face, but I'm sure Jordan's smiling. We've been friends only since the beginning of term, when I helped open her mailbox because her arms were overloaded with books, but every time I see her, she's smiling. Like she doesn't know how not to smile.

I used to be like that.

The light from the hallway spills into the room. It's not enough for either girl to see my leg clearly. I grab my sweat pants from the bed and pull them over my sleep shorts before one of them spots the scars.

"Since you're up, you can come with me to the gym." Jordan's voice is a welcome warmth against the chilled air known as Brittany. Not that I can blame her. I'd be cranky too with me as a roommate.

"Okay. Let me get changed."

Brittany mumbles something about Jordan and I both being screwed-up in the head, which in my case is probably true.

I return from the bathroom a few minutes later, dressed in yoga pants and a long-sleeved T-shirt. My ponytail is hidden under the hood of Trent's dark-gray hoodie.

"Okay, let's go," I whisper to Jordan, who's waiting for me outside my door. Her long brown legs appear even longer in her shorts. She's an inch shorter than me, but as far as I know, she doesn't play any sports. I haven't asked because I don't want her asking me the same question. I want to avoid the topic of why I lost the chance to be recruited in my senior year of high school, like everyone had expected.

"You wanna talk about your nightmare?" she asks. Her tight, shoulder-length corkscrews are pulled back with a colorful scarf.

"It's no big deal. Sorry if I woke you."

"You didn't. I was already up texting Garrett before he left for practice."

We walk toward the Sports and Fitness Center. Every couple of seconds, I peer into the darkness beyond the lit paths. Even with Jordan beside me, I can barely breathe. Someone could be watching me, studying me, stalking me.

The rustle of leaves whispers from the direction of a shadowed bush near the path. I freeze, my body unwilling to obey even my simplest command. A branch moves and the leaves rustle again. My heart careens into my throat.

"What's wrong?"

I feel Jordan's puzzled gaze on me as I search the shadows, unable to speak.

Just as I'm about to back away from the bush, a ginger cat appears from between the foliage. Crouching, I let out a slow breath, and stretch my arm in front of me, letting him know I won't hurt him.

The cat trots over, and I stroke his soft fur. "Hey, boy."

"You know," Jordan says. "You really are like Snow White. You call, and all the animals flock to you."

I laugh. "Flock?"

"You know what I mean. Animals love you. At least they love you until you stick them in the butt with a needle." She shudders. Since I was three years old, all I've ever wanted to be is a vet.

"How are you gonna be a physician if you can't stand the sight of needles and blood?" I press my lips together to keep from smiling at the irony. It's not the first time I've pointed this out.

She shrugs. "Try telling that to my parents. Because they're surgeons, they think I live for blood and gore."

As I straighten, the cat rubs against my legs, then wanders off to chase a mouse or whatever else hangs out on campus.

It's still early, so the gym isn't busy by the time we arrive, which is why I usually come early, just not this early. I'm not quite the morning person like Jordan. But I'm definitely more of one than Miss Sunshine, my roommate.

I climb on a treadmill next to one marked Out of Order, and program it to go I'm-training-for-the-Olympics fast, even though I'm not training for anything. Jordan takes the one on my other side. We've only worked out together a few times, but she knows I'd rather not talk while I run. Not that it's easy to talk when you're trying to suck in enough oxygen to keep going. That's challenging enough without throwing in a side of conversation.

Before my thoughts drift to a terrifying memory I want to leave unexplored, I adjust the pace so that I'm running so fast I can barely think. Jordan does a double take. I pretend not to notice and focus on the pounding of my sneakers against the surface. *My fault. My fault. My fault.*

"I'm done." Jordan's voice jerks me back to the moment. She slows the speed of her treadmill.

According to the glowing red numbers on my console, we've been running for thirty minutes. Careful not to trip on the fast-moving belt, I glance around. Most of the treadmills aren't being used.

I ignore my body's screams that it's had enough. "I'm gonna run a little longer." I tug at the black cotton of my yoga pants clinging to my sweaty legs. Sweat drips down the side of my face. What I wouldn't give to wear my old Lycra shorts and tank top. The ones that used to turn Trent on whenever I wore them. I push away the thought and pick up my pace to a near sprint.

Jordan walks to the dumbbell rack. I run until my legs feel like mush, which doesn't take long, and slow the treadmill to a stop. I climb off and walk over to join Jordan.

"You know you're insane."

I let out a short laugh, which sounds a little forced. "Maybe. But I love running. And I love running fast." If only I could run fast enough to escape my memories. Now that would be something. I select two dumbbells. They're a lot heavier than what Jordan's using.

"I heard there's a party this weekend at a frat house," Jordan says as I lie back on the padded workout bench. I used to bench-press barbells, but I don't think Jordan knows anything about spotting. And I don't want to ask one of the guys to help me and give him the wrong idea.

I push the weights away from my chest. "There's always a party at some frat house."

"I know. But I've never been to one, so I thought we could go. Have fun. Take a break from studying for once."

The weights I'm lifting freeze midair. "You've seriously never been to a party before?"

"Never." She makes a face. "I guess in high school I just figured they weren't worth the effort. I was too busy with other things. But that was in high school. I'm in college now."

"I'll pass, thanks." I lower the weights to my chest.

Jordan flashes me her puppy-dog eyes. "Please!"

I shake my head and lift the weights again, gaze focused on the high ceiling, and the strong metal beams straining to keep the roof from caving in. Anything to avoid the pleading in her eyes. "Sorry. Can't. I need to study for my math test."

"Maybe you can meet a cute guy who can help you. Maybe a hot math geek."

I laugh and almost drop the weights on my chest. I'm about to tell her there's no such thing as a hot math geek, but I choke on the words. "Not interested, thanks." My arms quiver as I push the final rep.

"What? You're not interested in finding a guy to cuddle with who can also tutor you in math?" She raises and lowers her eyebrows suggestively.

I want to tell her, "Been there, done that," but I don't want to talk about my past, and answering that question will lead to ones

I'd rather avoid. I've had that guy, and it didn't end well for either of us.

"I don't have time to get all cuddly with a guy. Besides, what are you supposed to do while I'm cuddling? Your boyfriend lives in Texas." I flash her a smile. Point for me.

She looks as if she plans to argue but shakes her head and goes back to lifting weights. *Thank God.*

I do the same, pushing my body as I did on the treadmill.

A weird feeling prickles me while I do seated biceps curls. Like someone is watching me. I glance around and spot the black-haired guy from Your Designs studying me from across the gym. My heart speeds up, and not in a good way.

Jordan returns from the warm-up mats. "You almost finished?"

"I'm done," I say a little too hastily, but Jordan doesn't seem to notice. Normally I stretch before I leave, but the way the guy watches me warns me I need to escape. Now.

3

MARCUS

Careful not to disturb Tammara, I slide out from under her covers and grope for my clothes on the floor. My fingers touch the rough fabric of my jeans at the same moment the bedside light pops on. *Crap*.

"Don't leave," Tammara purrs, wild red curls tumbling over her naked shoulders. The sheet fortunately still covers her breasts, hiding one of her best assets. My cock twitches at the memory of my tongue flicking against her nipples last night.

Knowing I don't have time for an encore, I snatch up my jeans and drop onto the edge of her bed. "I have to."

She knows my rules, but that doesn't stop her from crawling over to where I'm sitting. Her large breasts press into my back, the sheet no longer covering them. *God dammit.*

Her arms start to snake around me. I leap out of the way and scramble to pull on my jeans before my cock decides it wants to play some more.

She pouts. "You know, you don't have to go so early. I'm not one of those other girls. You don't have to leave in the middle of the night with me."

I glance at the alarm clock. "It's five in the morning." And five fucking hours later than it should be. I should have left last night when I had the chance, but I figured it wouldn't be a big deal. She knows our relationship is purely about the benefits.

"I was thinking," she continues, sliding off the bed, "I haven't been with another guy since we began hooking up, and I know I make you feel good. And you definitely make me feel good. So I thought maybe it's time we become exclusive." Her gaze trails down my body and settles on where my cock is—in my jeans.

I kick my T-shirt off the floor with the top of my foot and catch it, eyes still focused on Tammara and the jungle painting behind her with the fast-flowing river plummeting over a cliff.

She pouts again. "How come I never get to go to your place?"

"Because you and Chase hate each other."

She takes a step closer. Never thought I'd say this, but I wish she'd put on some damn clothes. Seeing her naked like this is crushing my self-control. If it weren't for the direction this conversation is headed, I'd have her back in bed, so we can do what we do best.

"I don't hate him."

"You just don't see eye to eye." Massive understatement of the year. I know Chase won't be too disappointed that the friends-with-benefits deal I had going with Tammara is over. The last thing I need or want is a girlfriend, especially one that irritates the hell out of my best friend.

I yank the T-shirt over my head and turn to leave.

"You don't have to go." Her tone is seductively smooth, confident. She knows this works on most guys.

I'm not most guys.

"I have an early class." We both know that's a lie, but hell if I'm telling her I need to go to the gym. Restlessness gnaws at me, and I only know how to deal with it physically. Since I don't want to stick around any longer, I need to get physical another way.

The gym isn't busy when I arrive, with a few guys in the weight area and two girls running on the treadmills. And damn are they hot, especially the blond who was at Your Designs the other day. Even though she's hidden under her dark clothing, I can tell she's got a tight bod. She has to, at the speed she's running. It's like she's trying to escape from something. Maybe the same feeling that likes to sink its teeth in me.

I watch her for a minute, mesmerized by her speed, then move so she can see me. But her attention is locked on the treadmill console. She doesn't notice me. Since watching her won't chase away the restless feeling, I head over to the weights and pretty much forget her. When I take a break between my two sets of dead-lifts, she's with her friend in the weight area. But while her friend lifts wimpy-girl weights, she lifts more serious ones, even though she's slightly on the skinny side, judging from how her clothes hang off her body. She's both strong and sexy as hell.

I wait for her to turn in my direction. She finally does and I smile. *C'mon, babe. I've got time before my first class.*

She doesn't return my smile or giggle or do any of those other things girls do when they flirt. She just glares at me like she did the other day. Looks like I'll have to deal with the restlessness in a less fun way.

She and her friend both leave. Neither spares me a second glance. I consider going after them, to see what her problem is, but I hold myself back. Maybe she's acting that way because our pasts have crossed during some party, and she's pissed because I never called her. Not that I ask for girls' numbers. Most just give them to me. And I figure I'm doing them a favor by not calling them. Calling them only makes them think there could be something between us beyond them screaming my name when I make them come.

After my final class of the day, I head over to the engineering building, where my car is parked. Chase has already left for the day, so I'm on my own.

Forty minutes later, I pull into the familiar parking lot near my old neighborhood, steer around several potholes, and park as far from the other vehicles as possible. I don't see *their* car, but that doesn't surprise me. I doubt they ever visit. They didn't care about him when he was alive. Why would they care now?

The sky is free of clouds, much like the day he died. I wish it had been stormy instead. It's easier to hate the storm for bringing pain than to blame the sun. But the truth is, neither is at fault for what happened. The fault is all mine.

From the passenger seat, I remove the worn copy of *Harry Potter and the Sorcerer's Stone* and stride along the path between the rows of graves.

4

AMBER

I squeeze through the tide of students as I walk to my math class and the test we'll be taking. I don't mind the closeness of everyone packed together. It makes it harder to follow or see me. Like camouflage.

The cool September air brushes my cheeks, and I hit the speed dial on my cell phone. It rings a few times before someone answers.

"Amber!" Grandma says, a smile in her voice. "Are you doing okay?"

I smile back even though she can't see me. A guy headed in my direction grins, apparently thinking I smiled at him. I avert my eyes and walk as fast as the flow of students will allow. "I'm fine, Grandma. I miss you and I wanted to say hi."

"How are classes?"

"Good. I have a math test next." I can almost see her cringe. She knows math was never my best subject, even if I did usually get As. They didn't come without a lot of hard work and Trent tutoring me.

"I'm sure you'll do well, sweetie. You always do."

"How's Smoky doing?" I ask, changing the topic, hoping she'll fall for it.

"He's fine. I reckon he misses you as much as you miss him."

I do miss him. More than he can ever imagine. "Can you give him a hug from me?" I ask.

"I sure can. And I think he has something to tell you. Hold on a second."

The phone goes quiet; then Smoky's rumbling purr comes on. "Hey, boy. I miss you. You keep Grandma safe like you did me, all right?"

Smoky meows into the phone and I laugh, tears blurring my vision.

"See, told you he misses you," she says.

"I have to go now."

"Good luck on your test."

I hang up and put the phone back into my pocket. My fingers wrap around the familiar chain I keep hidden there. It's broken, but it still has my half of the Best Friend charm. I hold on to it tightly.

When I glance up again, it's as though the charm has conjured the owner of its other half. Emma's standing several yards ahead of me. Her body is facing me, but she's looking around, craning her neck to see past everyone.

Before I can spin around and take a different route to class, her gaze lands on me and her lips part, a silent gasp falling from them. She takes a hesitant step toward me.

I turn abruptly and slam into someone. I try to keep from falling, arms flailing, but since I wasn't expecting anyone to be that close, I stumble. My ankle twists as I struggle to regain my balance. Both my hand and hip hit the concrete hard, knocking the air out of my lungs. My hand stings, my hip aches, and my ankle grumbles in protest.

Good thing I'm not superstitious, or else I'd see this as a bad omen for my math test.

Emma's already gone by the time my gaze jerks up again. Not that I'm surprised. Nothing could atone for the pain I've caused her and her family.

Heaviness fills me, making it hard to breathe. I miss her and would do anything to take the past year back if I could.

"You okay?" The dark-haired guy I've seen twice in the past week bends down next to me.

Up close, he's even hotter than I first realized, with his hazel eyes scanning my face and his full lips that beg to be kissed. Trent had kissable lips. This guy puts Trent's lips to shame.

A sudden dizziness fills me, and I scoot away. "Why are you following me?" The words barely squeeze past the tumor-sized lump in my throat.

"Following you? I'm going to class. Why would I be following you?"

Because that's what stalkers do. I push myself up and test my weight on my foot. My ankle isn't too impressed, but it'll survive.

Jordan rushes to my side. "Are you okay?"

It takes a lot of will to get my lips to bend into a smile. "I'm fine. I wasn't looking where I was going." I start to limp toward my classroom, to quickly put space between me and the guy. I don't have to say anything to Jordan. I know she'll come after me.

"Thank you for helping her." Jordan doesn't say it in a flirty voice. If I turned around to check them out, I would almost expect her to be shaking his hand.

"Okay, first. Wow, who was he?" she asks once she catches up with me. "And second, you're hurt. You shouldn't be walking." She glances back in the direction we came from.

"I'm fine, really. But I have a math test and I don't wanna be late."

"I'm sure he'd be happy to carry you to class." She jerks her head toward where the guy was standing.

I don't turn around to see if he's still there. "No, thanks."

"So how come you're going the long way to class?"

"I, er—I got lost." *Right.* Like she'll believe that.

She shakes her head, the usual smile gone. Her gaze drops to my ankle. "Are you gonna be okay?"

"I'll ice it once I've finished my math test." If there's one thing I've learned from varsity basketball, it's how to deal with a sprained ankle. This one isn't too bad.

I enter the building where my math class is located. Jordan has already scurried off to the library to work on her sociology paper, and the hallway is almost deserted except for a few stragglers. I open the classroom door and the entire class turns to look at me, test papers on desks.

The instructor holds out a test booklet. "You're late."

I limp to the front of the class and take it from him without an explanation for my tardiness. Quietly, so as not to annoy anyone, I remove my backpack and jacket and settle in an empty seat.

For the first time since the incident with Emma, I realize I'm shaking. God, what is she doing here? She, Trent, and I had planned to attend the University of Chicago. That's where we had wanted to play for as long as I can remember, and our varsity coaches told us we had an excellent shot at being recruited. So why did she change her mind?

Maybe for the same reason I changed mine. I knew she would be there. I didn't want to cause her more pain than I already had. And I knew I'd never play basketball again, but she would. So I took the easy out and applied to the University of Illinois at Chicago, figuring the chance of seeing my former best friend in a city that huge was a big fat zero.

Some big fat zero. Of course if I were still on Facebook, and she hadn't unfriended me yet, maybe I would know all of this. I would have known she'd changed her plans. But I deleted my account after what happened. I didn't want anyone else to have that kind of access to my life again.

I read the first test question, but it's like the numbers are performing acrobatics on the page. If Trent were here, he'd tell me to take a deep breath and let the numbers talk. "Math is easy once you let the numbers into your heart," he once told me, his soft lips brushing against the side of my neck. I'd leaned my head toward my shoulder, giving him easier access, and closed my eyes. Forget math, this was so much better.

A loud cough behind me snaps me back to the present, and I yawn. I fight the urge to lay my head on the desk and close my eyes for a second. They feel scratchy and dry, making it hard to focus on the test.

My eyes drift shut. *Trent. Emma. Test.* I jerk awake. Everyone else is busy, heads bent over their papers. What the hell is wrong with me, other than not sleeping much lately? That's nothing new. I should be used to working on only a few hours of sleep a night. I've been doing that since spring.

I take a deep breath and concentrate on the numbers in front of me as I try to forget about Emma, try to forget about Trent, try to forget that my ankle's throbbing.

Just get through this. I need at least a C. I can do it. I used to get As in math all the time. I push away the voice in my head that whispers, *Because Trent helped you study. But there is no more Trent.*

I blink back the tears and work through the test, doing the best that I can even if my best might not be enough. For me. For the university. For my future.

"It's time." The instructor's voice breaks through the silence, and I startle. *It's time, Amber.* This time the voice in my head isn't mine. It's a voice I still fear.

The voice that wakes me at night and leaves me screaming.

5

MARCUS

Chase slams shut the hood of the truck he's been working on for the past hour. We're the only two people here since his dad and the other mechanic had to leave early.

"Watch this bitch purr." Chase climbs into the driver's seat. I'll give it to him; he knows how to make an engine respond. Not that I've heard his past girlfriends complain, either.

"So ya wanna shoot hoops after we're done here?" he asks, appearing a little too comfortable behind the wheel. If his old man didn't frown on it, Chase would give that baby a test drive to make sure it really is running smoothly, even though it obviously is. But his dad doesn't like us driving the vehicles we fix. I think he's scared we'll drag-race them.

"I can't. I have to go see my mom. Maybe she'll change her mind."

Chase snorts. "As if that'll ever happen. Look, dude, I can lend you the money, so you don't have to go back there."

"I have to. And you know I can't take your money."

"Well, it's sure the hell better than going back home. What about Frank?"

My stomach turns at the name. "What about him?" I slap the

20

wrench down hard on the tool bench. Why did he have to bring up that asswipe?

"Isn't he gonna be there?"

"No. It's Wednesday afternoon. I'm pretty sure he's off gambling and getting drunk." The two things he excels at, if you call losing every time "excelling."

"Shit, man, you're crazy." Chase wipes the grease off his hands with a rag. "How about after that, then? I can meet you at the court when you're done. You're gonna need to blow off steam anyway."

I laugh. "There're other ways to blow off steam."

He groans and tosses the rag at me. "You mean Tammara. Why do you put up with that bitch? And don't tell me it's because she's a great lay."

"Then I won't." Even though it's true. "But she did donate money to the youth center for a new water heater." I skip the part where it was technically her family who donated the money, at her suggestion. But it's how I first hooked up with Tammara. She saw me playing ball with some of the kids who hang out there. "Anyway, you won't have to put up with her anymore."

"Why not?" It's almost as if he's holding his breath, hoping I'll give him the answer he's been praying for since I first hooked up with her a few months ago.

"She's starting to get clingy."

"Dude, she's been clingy all this time. You just refused to see it."

I guess if you call her almost clawing another girl's eyes out for talking to me at a party "clingy," he has a point. Now I have to figure out how to end our little arrangement without risking my package.

Another reason I avoid relationships: too messy.

I remove my greasy overalls and hang them on a hook at the back of the garage. It's not a large place, but it's done well for Chase's dad. Just not enough for him to want Chase to take over the business one day. That's why his dad pushed him into going to college and studying engineering. An opportunity made possible by a trust fund from Chase's grandparents on his mom's side.

Guilt money, as Chase calls it, because they wanted nothing to do with him, at least not until they found out their daughter had died, and they wanted to make up for not being there for her at the end.

Now if only my mom would feel a hint of remorse and give me the money I need. But that would involve her becoming something she's incapable of being.

Human.

I drive to my old home. The neighborhood hasn't changed. Same shit hole it's always been. The house isn't much better. The white paint has long since flaked away, leaving the building as tired-looking as my mother. The porch resembles some sort of death wish for anyone crazy enough to risk the stairs. Step the wrong way and chances are good you'll fall through. Only Frank is stupid enough to believe he can sue the person because they broke the step. Maybe that's why he hasn't bothered fixing it.

I park my piece of crap on the street. Mom's rusty blue Ford Mondeo sits in the driveway. I stare at the house for a minute or two but then realize I'm not ready just yet to deal with the ghosts that haunt the place. My ghosts. Ryan's ghosts. They're all the same.

I stride down the street and find a spot to sit under a tree not far from the playground.

"In nineteen eighty-two, who was the finals MVP?" Alejandro says behind me. I turn and smile at the sight of the tall fourteen-year-old and his not-so-tall friend. They drop their asses on the ground next to me.

I fist-bump them. "Magic Johnson for the Lakers. What are you doing here?"

"Why else would we be here?" Juan pipes in. "We're looking for some sexy *mamacitas*."

"At the playground?"

Juan scans the area, and his hopeful grin vanishes. The only girls here are the little kids and their moms. "Well, maybe not now. But you should see some of the girls who hang out here when they're babysitting." His eyebrows raise and lower in a comical dance.

Alejandro snorts. "And they shoot you down every time."

Juan lifts his chin, undeterred. "They're just playing hard to get. You just wait, dude. Soon they'll be begging me to show them how a real man kisses."

Alejandro glances away, then laughs. "Sure, you keep believing that."

We talk for a few more minutes before Alejandro has to leave. Juan goes with him. Not ready to face Mom quite yet, I stay under the tree and watch the kids on the equipment. Their squeals of laughter fill the air as they play tag. A toddler points to a baby swing and holds his arms up to his mother. Smiling, she slides him into the seat and pushes him from the front. He giggles every time the swing moves toward her.

I don't have to scour my memories for a similar moment between me and my mom. It doesn't exist.

The mother removes the toddler from the swing. He wraps his arms around her neck. She probably can't breathe but doesn't seem to care. She kisses his head and places him on the ground. His small hand disappears in hers and they walk away.

With a sigh, I return to the house belonging to my mom and the shithead she married when I was eight.

Mom's car hasn't moved from where she left it. I let myself in with my old key. Neither Mom nor Frank has remembered to ask for it back, though I suspect that's because Frank was drunk the few times I've come over. It's definitely not because I'm welcome here, unless Frank is looking for a punching bag. Then I'm welcome anytime.

It doesn't take long to find her sitting at the table, a cigarette in one hand and a coffee mug in the other.

"Hey." I flip my old seat around and straddle it. "Tough day?"

Her head snaps up. "What are you doing here?"

Glad to see you too, Mom.

I glare at the bullet hole in the wall behind her, my hands tightening on the back of the chair. *Christ*. They haven't fixed it. What is it? A fucking memento?

I tear my attention away from it and look at Mom, releasing my grip on the chair. Bringing it up won't help me. Just the opposite.

Her gaze fixates on my biceps. "You got a tat?"

I want to say, "You like it? I got it for Ryan." If she were any other mom, she would care that I wanted to honor her son, my brother.

If she were any other mom…but she's not.

"Yeah, I did."

"You better not let Frank see that."

"Why? What's he gonna do? Hit me?" The piece of crap's been doing that for years.

"He don't like tats," she says to no one in particular. Her eyes narrow. "You join a gang?"

Somehow I keep from rolling my eyes. "No, I didn't. I'm too smart for a gang." I have no idea where I got my smart genes. Not from her, that's for sure.

She takes a moment to digest that I'm not in a gang, no doubt disappointed at the truth. What better way to get rid of an unwanted son than for him to get involved in a gang fight?

"So what are you doing here?"

"You know why. The same reason I came last time."

She slams her mug down. "Then you know the answer's the same."

My hands clench into tight fists against my knees. "He was your son."

"Makes no difference. I ain't got the money." She jerks her chin at me. "You're the one with a job, a scholarship. Gonna be some fancy engineer someday. You don't need my money. And I ain't got any to waste on either of you boys."

I open my mouth for a comeback but never get that far. The front door clicks open and bangs against the wall. *Shit*.

"What the hell is Marcus's car doin' on the street?" Frank booms.

Why the hell aren't you getting drunk and losing all your money? I want to reply.

I push myself to my feet instead.

Mom throws me a look that says it all: *Screw up and it's your funeral.* As if I need to be reminded. I know what happens when you rub Frank the wrong way. I have the scars to prove it.

Frank staggers in, face red. "Who invited you here?" He doesn't bother to glance at Mom for confirmation that she did. He knows she doesn't give a damn about me unless she's figured a way to get money out of me.

I step closer. The pungent smell of beer, smoke, and sweat rolls off him. "I came to talk to my mom," I say in what I hope is an intimidating voice. I easily out-muscle him, but I doubt he cares much about that when he's this drunk. To him, I'm the same twelve-year-old he used to show who's boss.

"In case you haven't figured it out yet, you ain't welcome here." *Yeah. Got that.*

6

MARCUS

Mom doesn't move from her seat as Frank stumbles toward me. Her face lacks any hint of concern, which is no different than it's ever been, even when Ryan was around. My brother and I realized at a young age that we were nothing more than an inconvenience. A mistake. Only she didn't learn enough from her first mistake. She went on to have me.

"I said, you ain't welcome here," Frank slurs. He must have lost a lot of money today. His drunkenness is usually tightly correlated to his losses. And his anger is directly proportional to his drunkenness. Fortunately there's a diminishing point of return, where his drunkenness makes him weak. But right now, he's not at that point. Right now, he's at his most dangerous.

I cross my arms. "So how much did you lose today, Frank?"

He tightens his hand into a fist, and I know in an instant what's coming next. I step away and barely avoid getting tangled with my chair. I duck my head to the side as his fist slams into my jaw. The move lessens the power of his blow, but the impact still hurts and sets me reeling.

Fingers brush above the waistband of my jeans and I jerk away, mind fuzzy. I shake my head clear, and having no intention of being his punching bag, ram my shoulder into his chest. Frank stumbles back into the wall.

"Step away from him, Marcus." Mom's tone is deadly calm. "Step away or I'll shoot."

I take a cautious step back and turn around to find a handgun pointed at my chest. *Shit.*

For several long moments, no one speaks or moves. "Get out of my house, Marcus," Mom says. "I don't ever want to see you again. Do I make myself clear?"

I move away from Frank and the kitchen, then storm out of the house. Even if Mom hadn't turned the gun on me, Frank would never give me the money, because no matter what I say, he knows I'll never betray my brother's secret.

He knows he wins.

Needing more than ever to burn off excess anger, I drive to the youth center. The sun is low in the horizon, but there's still enough light to get in a few quick games. Chase's car is already here, which is surprising since he's notorious for losing track of time.

I check the clock on my dashboard. Okay, maybe I'm wrong and he wasn't on time after all. I'm fifteen minutes late.

I park next to his car and climb out. Chase, dressed in shorts and a red T-shirt, is sitting on his hood, forearms resting against the ball on his lap.

"Hey, dude," he says as I approach. A police siren wails from several blocks away. "Was starting to wonder if you were gonna show." He tosses me my gym bag.

"Sorry. Had a run-in with Frank."

"You okay?"

I grin, not wanting to tell him what happened and give him the satisfaction of knowing he was right. "Will be once I wipe your ass all over the court."

He slaps me on the back. "You wish."

I return a few minutes later, ready to work my ass off in a game of one-on-one.

"So did you get the money?" Chase asks, trying to distract me.

It doesn't work. I dribble past him, missing the crack in the concrete, which would have sent the ball off course, and do a perfect lay-up.

The ball shoots through the large hole in the side of the net. Chase catches it and dribbles to the three-point line. I steal it from him.

"No. Not even close," I say. "She wasn't going to bend even before the asswipe showed up." I bounce, bounce, bounce the ball, then push past him.

Chase blocks me, forcing me out of the zone. "What are you gonna do now?"

"I don't know. Earn it somehow."

He smirks. "Maybe instead of dumping Tammara, you could sell her to the highest bidder."

Bounce. Bounce. Bounce. "I'm pretty sure that's illegal."

"You have a point. Besides, I wouldn't want to be the guy who ends up with her. She's likely to claw his eyes out."

Seeing that I'm not going to get past him easily, I go for the jump shot. The ball arcs gracefully in the air and swooshes through the net. Chase groans.

"What about your father?" I ask as he jogs after the ball. "Can he give me more hours?"

He swoops down and scoops up the rolling ball. "I doubt it. As it is, he should be cutting back our hours. Business is slow these days." No thanks to the gang activity in the neighborhood. While the gang has left Tony alone, which still surprises me, it's driven a lot of his old clients away. They now go to the mechanic favored by the turf gang, if they know what's good for them. Which means I could be facing fewer hours soon, instead of more.

"Maybe you could try tutoring," Chase suggests, bouncing the ball. "You're good at math. And you're a great basketball coach." He aims the ball and sends it soaring toward the hoop. It bounces off the backboard and ricochets past the rim.

I laugh and snatch the ball from the air as it flies overhead. "Apparently not."

Chase wipes the sweat off his forehead with his hand. "Just think about it."

"There's nothing to think about. I'm not a teacher and I don't wanna be one." I dribble the ball, hinting that I want to play, not talk.

"Not if it meant tutoring some hot babe and getting to screw her?"

I smirk. "I hope you don't kiss your aunt with that mouth." That doesn't sound like Chase talking. That sounds like me. Chase is more the relationship type than the defender of one-night stands.

"Speaking of my aunt, she's been asking 'bout you."

"How so?"

"She's worried about you." He gives me the look that says he worries about me, too.

"Tell her I'm fine." Bounce. Bounce. Bounce.

He shrugs. "She wonders when you're gonna settle down with a nice girl."

Okay, that does sound like his aunt. She's asked me the same question several times in the past few years. Apparently she reads way too many romances for her own good.

I stop bouncing the ball. "You can tell her I'm good." The last thing I need is to get caught up in some sort of relationship crap.

A Lincoln pulls into the parking lot. The steady bass beat vibrates through the car. The doors open and rap music spills into the cool air. Four men step out and my entire body tenses, each muscle on high alert. "What the hell do they want?"

"I guess it's too much to hope that they're just searching for the bathroom," Chase says, body as still as mine. We've both had more run-ins with these guys in the past few years than we would like.

Carlos leads the way, his moves smooth and lethal like a panther. A bald-headed panther. Following close behind are his cronies. None I recognize. They must be new recruits.

Carlos stops in front of us and smiles, but there's nothing friendly about it. " 'Sup?"

"What are you doing here?" My voice is somehow steady, considering he's packing heat and we aren't.

"I'm looking for Alejandro."

I clench my hands, the movement not missed by the other shit-heads. One, with tattoos covering his arms, steps closer. I can tell he's itching to take a slice out of me.

"Leave him alone," I snap at Carlos. "He's just a kid." I make a move toward him, my blood boiling fierce.

Chase grabs my arm. "Don't do anything stupid."

Carlos laughs. "Listen to pretty boy. You don't wanna mess with us. Not if you value your life."

And with that he walks away, his goons close behind.

"Fuck." I start pacing. "What the fuck am I going to do? It'll destroy his family if Alejandro gets sucked into that life."

Chase shakes his head. "You can't help everyone, Marcus."

I stop abruptly. "Everyone? I haven't been able to save *anyone* who matters to me. Not one person."

7

AMBER

"**W**ould you fucking wake up!"

Something soft covers my mouth and nose. Oh God, I can't breathe. Paul's finally going to do it. He's going to kill me.

Screaming, I flail my hands in the air. All I find is emptiness. Whatever is covering my face is yanked away, revealing the overhead bedroom light and a scowling Brittany with a pillow in her hand. *Oh.*

My arms dart under the covers. "Sorry," I whisper before checking my alarm clock. It's only 2:00 a.m., which means if I go back to sleep, I can look forward to an encore of nightmares.

Brittany glances away and gives me the precious seconds I need to grab Trent's old hoodie off the bed and snuggle into it. The dark-gray fleece is soft against the secrets I hide beneath it. When she turns back to me, her face gives no indication that she saw either the tattoo or the scars. She does, though, return to glaring at me as if that's enough to make me go away.

Outside, the rain pounds on the windows.

"My tire's flat," I say on the phone. A flash of light fills the night sky followed by the loud rumble of thunder.

"Don't worry. I'm on my way."

I blink and I'm in the room. I grab my sweat pants and wiggle into them while still under my covers.

"I'm not a lesbian, if that's what you're thinking," Brittany snaps.

Huh? "Yeah. Okay." Not that it changes anything. If she wants to freak because she thinks I believe she's something she's not, that's fine. Anything's better than the truth.

I climb out of bed and pick up my biology textbook. "I'm going to the common room."

She mutters something about me maybe moving there permanently. I don't stick around long enough to ask.

I limp down the hallway, the overhead light guiding the way. No one's in the common room, and part of me is relieved I don't have to socialize with anyone.

The other part wishes there were someone here to talk to. I miss being that girl. The girl who had lots of friends. The girl who didn't have secrets. The girl everyone cheered for when she was on the basketball court. The girl who never gave the wrong guy the wrong idea and now has to pay a horrendous price for it.

I make myself comfy on the tacky orange couch and pull the old afghan on it around my shoulders. Anything to keep the storm from getting inside me. To keep it from making me feel worse than I already do.

The wind whistles outside the window. I pull my feet onto the couch and wrap my arms tightly around my knees.

"Do you need help?"

My body shakes. I don't want to remember. *Please don't let me remember.* I can't be normal if I do, and I so want to be normal again.

I open the textbook and read ahead. Why didn't I grab my phone before I left my room? Loud rock music usually helps. As long as I can't hear the storm, I'm fine.

I turn on the TV and find a cooking show. That's always a safe bet. I return to my textbook.

Several hours later, I'm still awake, but I'm not sure how much longer I can last. My eyelids feel like stones have been attached to them, and gravity is weighing them down. I yawn, stretch out on the couch, and pray the nightmares stay away this time.

When I wake up, again, the sunlight is streaming into the room, and two guys are watching the news from the other couch. I sit up, and the afghan slides off my shoulders and pools around me.

"Sleeping Beauty awakens." The guy returns his attention to the news. The second guy glances over at me, as if he hadn't noticed me before, and also goes back to watching TV.

A familiar voice on the news steals my attention.

"The real victim in the crime is my client," Mom says, and a mix of pride and pain and longing ping-pongs through my body at the sound of her voice. *"He was in the wrong place at the wrong time and was framed by the police and the woman."* The TV flashes to a picture of her "innocent" client, who was charged with drug possession and physical assault.

Not wanting to hear any more, I pick up my textbook and leave. God, does she seriously believe he's innocent? That *he's* the victim?

I want to call her and scream into the phone that she's wrong and ask her how she can defend guys like that after what happened to me. But good girls never scream. Paul taught me that.

My body aches at what else he taught me.

Brittany's not in our room. I grab my clothes and toiletries and head to the bathroom. Luckily, there's no line to use the showers. I turn on the water as hot as it will go, which isn't as hot as I would like. How can Mom defend jerks like that? I know the whole spiel about how everyone deserves a fair trial, but where's the fairness in what he did? The woman didn't ask for that to happen to her. Why should she be made to feel like the criminal?

I bounce my fingers against my thigh before catching myself. Unlike usual, it does nothing to drive away the agitation. There's only one thing that can do that, and I don't play it anymore.

Brittany still isn't in our room when I return. My side is slightly messy, my bed unmade and books scattered on my desk. Her side is beyond neat, everything lined up and her bed made with hospital corners. Mom would love Brittany.

I squash the temptation to sit on her bed to see if Brittany notices. She hates me as it is. Violating her personal space would push her over the edge. And the old Amber would never do anything as risky as that.

But the old Amber never said no, and look where that got me.

Someone knocks at the door. "Amber, it's me," Jordan says. "You ready?"

I open the door and wave her in. "I just need to wrap my ankle first."

"How's it doing?"

"Better. At least I can walk without crutches. That's saying something." In the grand range of ankle sprains, this one's minor.

As I wrap my ankle with the elastic bandage that Jordan bought for me yesterday, even though I don't really need it, my cell phone plays a few bars of classical music. For a fleeting second I consider letting Mom's call go to voice mail.

With a sigh, I turn away from Jordan and answer the phone. "Hi, Mom."

"Amber. I'm glad I reached you." Her tone isn't warm and motherly. It's professional, as if I'm a client instead of her daughter. "How are you doing?"

Not too great. I'm having nightmares and flashbacks. You know, the usual. "Good."

"And your classes are going well?"

"Yes." *No.*

"That's good. Is there anything you need?"

Yes. For you to tell me you love me. "No. I'm good, thanks."

"All right. I'll let you get to class now. And Amber"—*I love you and miss you and don't blame you for what happened even if you do,* I want her to say—"I'll be busy with a new case. So if you need anything, let my assistant know. Okay?"

"Okay." The word cracks, but I doubt she notices. She hangs up before I can. I turn back to Jordan, a smile pasted on my face. "Ready to go?"

"Is everything okay?"

I try to turn my smile into a real grin to reassure her; I have a feeling it resembles a grimace. "Everything's fine. My mom is busy, but she just wanted to make sure I didn't need anything." And really I can't complain. Those are the most words she has said to me in a while.

Biting her lip, Jordan studies my face. She opens her mouth to say something.

I don't give her the chance. "We should go. I wanna get a coffee on the way."

Jordan frowns. "Since when do you drink coffee?"

"Since I decided it's part of the college experience, and since I decided I need caffeine to keep awake." Lots of caffeine.

"You had another nightmare last night, didn't you?"

Knowing there's no point in lying, I nod. She waits for me to elaborate. I don't want to tell her everything, but I don't want to lose her as a friend, either, because she thinks I can't be honest and open with her.

I take a deep breath. "I was trapped in a burning building last spring. That's why I have nightmares."

"Were you hurt?"

"I was treated for smoke inhalation and that's it....I just don't like talking about it. That's why I haven't mentioned it before."

Her frown shifts into an understanding smile. "Well, I'm here if you ever need to talk about it."

We walk to The Coffee Shack. It's still raining but not as hard as last night. The sun eagerly breaks through the clouds, creating a rainbow ahead of us. The agitation from earlier fades like early morning fog in the sun.

"Hey, isn't that the guy who helped you yesterday?" Jordan asks while we wait for our coffees. I'm busy inhaling the caffeine-scented air in case it gives me an extra boost.

She nods toward the door.

Standing next to the wall are the guys I first saw at Your Designs. And we aren't the only ones who've noticed them. Most of the twentysomething females are checking them out.

"Maybe you should go over and say hi." Jordan gives me a nudge in their direction.

I look back at her, frowning. "Why would I do that?"

She grins. "Oh, I don't know. Because maybe he'll ask you out."

Forget medicine. She should go into the matchmaking business.

I'm saved from having to respond when they call out our order. By the time we turn around again, the guys have left. Problem solved.

The day creeps by, and the caffeine perks have long since faded by the time I walk in the rain to math. I consider buying another coffee, but there's not enough time. After being late for my last math class, I don't want to be late again and interrupt. The fewer people who notice me, the better.

Because I'm not going the long route this time, I arrive with several minutes to spare and sit at the rear of the room.

"I have your test marks," the instructor announces when the class begins, his tone menacing. Or maybe it's just me who feels that way because I've been dreading this moment. "Some of you will need to put in a lot more effort if you hope to pass the course." He calls out names and one by one everyone goes to the front and collects their test. "Amber Scott."

I want to tell him not to say my name out loud, where everyone can hear it. I'd rather be anonymous and not have to worry about anyone recognizing it or thinking it's a great idea to memorize it, fantasize about it, cover a wall with it.

I want to say that, but the words stay stuck in my throat as I make my way to the front, legs trembling. I take the test booklet and breathe in deeply before daring a glance at the grade.

The page is covered with red and a big fat forty percent stares back at me.

I dig my fingernails into my palm to keep from crying and return to my seat. *Shit.* I'm screwed. Unless I can figure this stuff out, there's no way I'll pass the class.

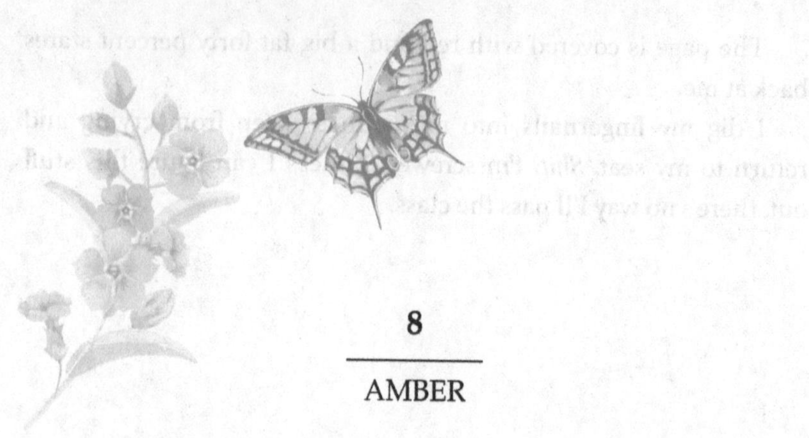

8

AMBER

A week after receiving my disastrous math grade, I sit cross-legged on my bed, math book and notes in front of me, and close my eyes. I can almost imagine Trent next to me, his familiar scent of lemons and sunshine lingering in his hoodie. He forgot it the night he rushed out of my house, angry at what I had said. Words I've wished a million times I could take back. Then he would still be with me. Things would never have changed.

Neither Emma nor his parents realized the hoodie was missing. That, or they never bothered to ask for it back. It's all I have left of him, other than his old basketball T-shirt and the photos of us together.

Abandoning math for a moment, I remove a small scrapbook from my desk drawer. I return to the bed and leaf through the pages. They're pictures of happier times, before any of this happened. When the worst thing I had to worry about was if Trent would be healthy in time for the homecoming dance, because he had the stomach flu.

I brush my fingers over the picture of us camping with our

friends, the summer prior to when I started volunteering at the animal shelter.

"I talked to a woman at the shelter today," I say, the campfire crackling and popping in front of us, Trent's arm around me, keeping me close. I've known Trent forever, and we've been best friends for just as long. Even though we've officially been boyfriend and girlfriend for over a year, some days I still can't believe it was real. Him and me.

"What did she say?" he asks.

"That she would love to have me help out."

He hugs me tighter and kisses me. "I'm so proud of you."

"How much is she paying you?" Emma asks.

"She isn't. It's a volunteer position. But the money isn't important. It'll look good on my college application." I sound like Mom, but she has a point. Plus it would look good for when I applied to veterinarian school. A means to the end, as Mom always says, even though she'd prefer I follow her path and study pre-law, like Michael.

"How many hours a week is it for?"

"Until basketball season starts, I'll be working there an hour or two every day after school." With my high grades, I can handle it. More than handle it. I'll be around animals. That's all I've ever wanted, but Mom doesn't like pets. They're messy and expensive, in her opinion. The closest thing I've come to having a pet is Dragonfly, Trent and Emma's cat.

Emma pouts. "Now I'll never see you."

I close the scrapbook and slip it inside my desk drawer. Regret claws at me like a rabid raccoon. If I hadn't taken the position, Trent and Michael would be alive.

Lying down, I pull two old T-shirts from under my pillow and hug them, hard, the comforting scents of Trent and Michael long gone. I want to roll up in a tight ball and fall into a dreamless sleep, but that's impossible. My sleep is never dreamless, never free of darkness. I burrow the T-shirts under my pillow, hiding them from Brittany, hiding them from Jordan, hiding them with a piece of me wrapped securely inside—and return to my math.

An F. I've never received an F in my entire life. Not even a C or a D. A tired voice reminds me of what I could lose if I don't smarten up. I need to pass the course as part of my pre-vet requirements. If I don't, I'll have to repeat it. Sitting through it the first time is bad enough. Sitting through it a second time will be hell.

A sharp knock on the door intrudes on my thoughts.

"Coming." I scoot off the bed. Most people in the dorm don't bother locking their doors when they're in their rooms. I'm not most people. I unlock the door and open it.

Becca, the RA, gives me a sad smile. "Hi, Amber. I need to talk to you for a moment. Is this a good time?"

Not really. "Sure, what's up?" I open the door wider and let her in.

"It's been brought to my attention you're having nightmares and waking your roommate. She put in a request for a room change, but unfortunately nothing's available. Is there something you'd like to talk about? Maybe it would help."

I cross my arms, then uncross them and let them drop to my sides. "No, I'm fine."

"Well, my door is open any time you need to talk."

"Thanks." *Only weak people admit they need help, Amber.*

Jordan walks into my room and freezes when she spots Becca. The grin on her face falls away. "Hi."

As if the conversation between us never happened, Becca exchanges a few words with Jordan about one of their courses and leaves. I shut the door behind her.

"So what did Becca need to talk to you about?" Jordan asks. "I bumped into her earlier, and she asked if I knew when you'd be around. She looked pretty stressed about it."

"Oh, it's nothing. Brittany asked to be switched out of this room because of my nightmares, and Becca wanted to see if she could psychoanalyze me instead."

Jordan grimaces. "Did she?"

"Nope. There's nothing to analyze." Before she can voice a few suggestions, I add, "So what's up?"

The grin returns, her usual enthusiastic energy pouring off her in waves. I let some of it in and feel better. Almost normal, but not quite.

"I just talked to some guys in the common area, and they told me about a major party tonight off campus. We have to go."

I shake my head, the almost-normal feeling ripped away. "I'm sorry, J. I don't do parties." Anymore. Or anything else where I'll be noticed.

She looks at me with her puppy eyes. "Pleeeease. I just want to experience a real party once in my life."

"You aren't missing anything. Just a bunch of drunk people going crazy and puking."

"We wouldn't have to stay long. I promise. I just want to see how the other half lives."

I squish my lips to keep from laughing. I guess she means parties that don't involve polite conversation, waiters, and appetizers passed around on silver serving plates.

I want to say no, but it's a word I've never been good at until recently. And I owe Jordan a lot. She's the only person who hasn't been put off by my need to maintain a wall. Not that you can maintain a wall with Jordan for long. And since she knows nothing about my past, I almost feel normal when I'm with her. What more could I want?

"Hey, what's this?" Jordan reaches for the card on my desk and reads it before I can stop her. On the front is a picture of a lotus flower. It's one of Grandma's favorite plants. She often bemoans that it doesn't thrive in Illinois; otherwise, she would grow them in her pond.

I cringe as Jordan reads it, hoping she doesn't ask what Grandma meant by "You're stronger than you realize." I knew it was a mistake leaving it on my desk, but I do love the picture.

"It's your birthday? Why didn't you tell me?" Jordan scans the room for other cards.

There aren't any, other than the one that my mom forwarded to me from Emma, which I've hidden in my desk. It's too painful to look at, but I don't want to get rid of it, either.

"I kinda forgot about it. You know, what with studying for exams and writing term papers." I pause, searching for a way to distract her from this conversation. "Okay," I say before I can yank the word away. "I'll go with you to the party, but I need to study math first."

She returns the card to my desk, beaming brighter than the summer sun. "I promise you'll have fun. It'll be like a birthday party."

"Give me till nine and then we'll go, okay?"

"Sounds good. Can't wait to see what you're wearing." A not so subtle hint she wants me to wear something other than my usual jeans, T-shirts, and hoodie.

I bounce my fingers against my thigh. I used to wear dresses and skirts to parties. The kind that showed skin, just not too much. But that was in my previous life, when I had Trent at my side and no one dared bother me. Heck, that was when I wasn't afraid to tell a guy where to go if he touched me.

I can't wear those outfits anymore.

I want to tell her I've changed my mind, that I don't want to go, but she's already left my room, excited for what she perceives to be her next great adventure.

I wish I felt the same way.

I'm halfway through the third math question when the door opens. Brittany. I swear ice forms on the windows the moment she steps into the room.

"Hi," I say. *Are you staying long?*

Without a word—not that she has to, the glare says it all—she sits at her desk and pulls out a sketch pad from her bag. She then removes a small metal box filled with pencils. She draws? All I know about Brittany is that she's either studying pre-med or criminology. Or both.

"Can I help you?" Her tone suggests she'll be anything but helpful.

"No." I pick up my math book and notes and slip them into my backpack.

I arrive at the library to find it quiet, with only a few other students studying in the cubicles against the walls. I sit at a table where it's easy to spot anyone watching me. It's harder to study here than in my room because I have to be alert to everything around me. But this is better than nothing, and it's better than being in the same room as Brittany.

I open my math book and study the example, again. I can do this. *Take a deep breath, Amber, and let the numbers talk to you,* Trent's voice says in my head. I work through the problem once more, but it feels as though all my energy has drained into my chair. All that's left of me is the lifeless shell of a rag doll.

My eyelids drift closed, my fight to keep them open lost in the pointless battle.

"WAKE UP, AMBER." SOMEONE TENDERLY TOUCHES MY CHEEK. "TIME TO wake up. I have a surprise, and I know you love surprises."

He's wrong. I hate surprises. Everyone knows that, but it doesn't stop Trent from surprising me. He says it's more romantic that way.

Inwardly I smile. When did my best friend become such a romantic?

I feel funny. Groggy. Drunk. I don't remember getting drunk. I remember driving and getting a flat tire. I remember Paul showing up and offering to help. I don't remember much else.

I open my eyes. I'm in a fun house, mirrors everywhere I look. I stagger up and sway on my feet as I turn around, searching for an exit. Fun house? There are no fun houses in Crossfields.

"Am-ber. Wake up." The voice booms through the room. I cover my

ears, trying to block out the deafening noise. My heart slams against my ribs, a frightened bird trapped in a cage, desperate to escape.

"Am-ber," the voice taunts. "You're mine forever. And I'll love you in a way your boyfriend never could."

"Go away," I scream. "Leave me alone."

This is met with a laugh that sets the mirrors shaking. Thick cracks split across them like a network of branches. One by one, the mirror fragments fall free of the walls. I drop to the ground and cover my head with my arms. Glass cuts into my back and I scream, the sound masked by the shattering of glass against the cold concrete ground.

"Hey, wake up," a male voice says, and someone nudges my shoulder.

I jerk awake and sit up abruptly, heart still slamming into my ribs. Only instead of a fun house, I'm in the library.

The black-haired guy I first saw at Your Designs, now with a faded bruise on his jaw, crouches next to me. The movement does nothing to slow my speeding heart.

"That must have been some dream." He watches me with a mix of concern and curiosity, head tilted to the side. "You were screaming." He checks out the book in front of me. "Math not your thing, huh? Well, that would explain the nightmare." A cocky smile spreads on his face, setting off alarms in my head.

"Look," I say, still shaken at seeing him here, "if you don't stop stalking me, I'll report you to the cops."

"Whoa"—he unfolds himself and steps away from the table in a fluid motion—"what the fuck are you talking about? I'm not stalking you." The smile is back on his face. "I don't need to stalk women. They tend to stalk me."

"Well, unless you can help me get an A in my class, get lost." This guy doesn't appear as though he gets As in any of his classes, let alone in math.

His smile widens. "I can tutor you, Kitten."

I narrow my eyes. What kind of idiot does he think I am? "And how much would that cost me?" I ask, not seriously considering his offer.

His gaze roams over my body, his message quite clear.

"Go to hell!"

9

AMBER

Two hours. That's all I have to stay here for, and then I can leave.

Jordan's face lights up as she takes in what could easily be a small mansion. The loud music. The dancers in the middle of the room, pressed together, some practically having sex on the dance floor. The smell of booze, sweat, perfume. Everything, without a doubt, forbidden by her parents. She's like a little kid on Christmas morning.

"So, what do you want to do now?" I ask. *Escape? Go home?* I scan the area, searching for anyone I recognize. If I'm lucky, I won't see anyone I know from high school. They know I was responsible for the death of their golden boy. I can't bear seeing the blame in their eyes, too.

I spot one guy from high school, one I didn't know very well. He was in my AP physics course. I check out the other partiers. There are a few people from my college classes, but no one I've talked to. Not that I've talked to many people.

"I want a drink." Jordan says it with such awe and determination, I'm positive she's never drunk alcohol before tonight, other than maybe a few sips of wine.

46

She asks someone holding a beer where he got it from. He directs her to the kitchen, pointing the way we need to go. We make our way through the throng of sloshed students. The heat of their bodies and the room close in on me.

Jordan's dressed for this in a miniskirt, tank top, and thigh-high boots. It's a version of her I've never seen, and I'm sure it's one her parents have never seen. But it makes me proud since I get the feeling taking charge of her own life is a new experience for her.

A jealous sensation snakes its way in. Not because of how the guys are drooling over her. And they are. But because a year ago I would have dressed the same way for parties. I wouldn't be wearing jeans and a long-sleeved T-shirt—and melting.

We locate the keg and grab plastic cups from the guy manning it. I've never been a huge fan of beer, but I'm hot and the drink is cold, and that's all that matters. I gulp some down.

Jordan takes a tentative sip and screws up her face.

"You've never had beer before, have you?" I ask, laughing.

She shakes her head. "My parents don't drink beer."

"Don't worry. You'll get used to it."

She nods, but I'm not sure if she believes me.

We move toward the living room where the dancing is. My palms grow sweaty, and my heartbeat kicks up a few notches. Neither has anything to do with the heat.

It's all right. It's just a party. He didn't like parties. You're safe.

I used to go to parties all the time. That was normal. I want to be normal again. How hard can this be?

I take another gulp of my beer. And freeze.

Emma's standing near the makeshift dance floor, wearing a strapless dress that shows off her athletic body and tan. She's not looking in my direction. She's talking to some girls and smiling at whatever they are saying.

"How 'bout we go over there?" I point to the opposite side of the massive room, where Emma won't be able to see me. I don't explain why I want to move, and Jordan doesn't ask.

We weave between several small groups until we reach the other side of the room. Jordan gazes longingly at the dance floor. *Do you want to dance?* Those words used to slip painlessly from my mouth. Now they're glued at the back of my throat.

"You wanna dance?" The words didn't come from me. They're from a tall, hot guy who's grinning at Jordan.

Grinning back, she nods, then turns to me. As much as I don't want to be abandoned here, I'm not about to prevent her from having fun. And it's not like she'll disappear with the guy. She has a serious boyfriend. She just wants to dance. Though from the way this guy's checking her out, he might have other things in mind.

They walk to the edge of the dance floor, where I can keep an eye on her. For a girl who's never been to a party, she sure knows how to dance, and lover boy's appreciating it. His hands slide all over her. She doesn't push him away. Instead, her moves intensify. She could easily be a dancer from a music video. Looks like I'm not the only one with secrets.

"Hey, babe," a blond guy says, breath reeking of stale beer. "You're in my biology class. I thought maybe you and I could study bio together." He runs his hand down my arm. My body tenses.

I yank my arm away and glance over at Jordan. She's too busy having fun to notice I'm not. "Not interested."

"Why not? You don't have a boyfriend."

"Sure I do. H-he's with his friends at...at his brother's football game."

"I know you're lying, Amber."

"I know you're lying, Amber. I've seen how you look at me when you're not with your boyfriend. It's me you've always wanted."

I suck in a sharp breath. "What makes you think I'm lying?"

A blush creeps onto his face. "O-one of my friends lives in your dorm. He said you're single. And...just give me a chance."

I check the dance floor again. Jordan is still dancing, and it doesn't appear as though she's going to stop anytime soon. I step away, ready to make a hasty escape.

The guy grabs my arm. "Hey, where you goin'?" His gaze drops to my chest.

"Bathroom."

"I'll come with ya."

I pull away. "Don't bother. I'm a big girl. I can go on my own." I squeeze past some guys who could play collegiate football, then disappear into the crowd, avoiding the direction where I last spotted Emma.

With a quick glance behind me to ensure the creep's not following, I enter the kitchen. It's just as crowded as the rest of the house. A large group of people are hanging around a table, playing a game of quarters. No one pays attention as I slip out the door.

The party has spread into the backyard and around the swimming pool. The chill in the air hasn't turned off a few partiers from wearing swim trunks and bikinis, with leis around their necks. A couple makes out in the shallow water. The way they're going at it, I wouldn't be surprised if they have sex in the pool.

No one seems to notice me as I rush past.

I find a quiet corner and sit on a short wall overlooking a large heart-shaped pond with a tall waterfall made of rocks in one corner. I picture Grandma's beloved lotus flowers floating on the water, with goldfish darting in between.

I close my eyes and the sound of the partiers takes me back to when I used to hang out at the lake with my friends. Back when they were certain I would play collegiate basketball, become a vet, and marry Trent. Back when I was living day-to-day when it came to our relationship. Anything could happen. My father walked out on my family when I was young. Maybe Trent would walk out on me, too.

And he did. He walked out the night we had an argument. He died, crushing my heart the way the tree crushed his car.

"There you are, babe." Annoying Guy yanks me back to the present. He stands in front of me, blocking my escape.

"When are you going to get the hint? I'm not interested!" I stand

and fake a move to the right, but he doesn't fall for it. That, or he's so drunk, he thought he was going my right and went left instead. "But I like you." He leans in and traps me, his lips close to mine.

10

MARCUS

I study the girls in the crowded room. Most are already drunk —easy lays with no commitment. I feel off-balance again, and I don't know why. It's been this way since the library, when I heard the girl cry out in her sleep. And then her reaction when I woke her. She was genuinely scared. Not scared because of her dream. Scared because someone has hurt her.

I may be an ass, but I would never hurt a girl. Use them, yes, by mutual consent, but never hurt them.

"You still angry 'bout Carlos?" Chase asks.

"Wasn't till you brought him up."

"So why do you look ready to screw half the girls here?"

"It's nothing."

Chase rolls his eyes. "Yeah right, dude. I know you. Something's bugging you."

I chug my beer, stalling. No way am I mentioning the girl from the library. A girl having the power to unnerve me would make his day. "Like I said, it's nothing. But you are right about me wanting to get laid." I go back to scanning the possibilities and catch the eye of a tall blond nearby. Her strapless dress shows off her tan and hot bod. She tilts her head to the side, obviously checking me out.

51

She glances away, though I can tell she's still interested. This is all part of her game.

She's the type I usually go for—hot and willing—but for some reason, I can't make myself go over to her. "You want another beer?" I ask Chase instead.

He chuckles. "You're blowing off that girl for a beer. Now there's a first."

I shrug. "What can I say? My priorities might be a little screwed tonight." All I can think about is the girl in the library. The same girl I've seen three other times, who thinks I'm stalking her, who's made it quite clear she's not interested.

"You sure you haven't changed your mind about Tammara?" Chase asks.

I don't get the chance to answer as I spot the girl from the library talking to a guy who reminds me of an overgrown ape. And from where I'm standing, she looks happier talking to him than she did talking to me, though that's not saying much.

I try pushing away the image of my body pressed against hers, my lips exploring her mouth, her neck, her breasts, continuing south until I reach the part of her that will leave her screaming my name. I try to push the image away. But as hard as I try, I don't succeed.

"Hey, Marcus. What's up?"

I tear my gaze from her and turn to find a guy from one of my engineering classes. Chase disappears into the crowd. I'm not sure if he's even noticed I'm not with him.

"Hey, Todd."

"I see you're checking out Amber." He nods toward several people, including the girl from the library.

"Which one's Amber?"

"The girl in the pink long-sleeved T-shirt." Library Girl.

"You know her?"

He nods. "She was in my AP physics class last year." He looks at her and an odd sort of pain twists onto his face. "I wouldn't waste your time with her."

A pretty red-haired girl slips past several people, her face flushed. "Todd, I'm not feeling good. Can you drive me home?"

He brushes his hand against her cheek and frowns. "You're really hot."

She nods and leans into him.

"See you in class," he says to me before they walk off, his hand on her lower back.

I glance at Amber, then head toward the kitchen. The other girl, the one with the light-blond hair, is sounding more appealing by the second. She should help me forget about the girl who reminds me of a kitten: soft and vulnerable, and ready to scratch your eyes out if you aren't careful.

In the kitchen, I grab some beer from the keg and join Chase at a table where he's watching a heated game of quarters.

"Any other takers?" a guy who could play football or hockey asks.

I'm about to volunteer when Amber walks into the kitchen and hurries out the back door. She's not rushing to be somewhere else. It's more like she's trying to escape, but whoever was following her must have given up the chase. No one else enters the room after her.

I miss my chance to play. A girl who looks like she's had one too many beers goes against Chase and two other guys.

The guy Amber was talking to stumbles into the kitchen. He scans the room, frowning, and leaves out the same door she escaped through a few minutes ago. A prickly feeling in my gut warns me something's not right.

I push past the crowd around the table and follow him out the door. I can't see either of them when I step outside, due to the number of partiers around the pool. I'm surprised the cops haven't been called yet. It's as loud out here as it is in the house.

I walk around, scanning drunk, grinning faces for Amber. Shit, where'd she go? A voice in my head whispers that maybe I'm jumping to conclusions. That maybe they're making out somewhere, not wanting to be found by me or anyone else.

Just as I'm about to ignore my gut and return inside, I see them by a large pond. Amber looks annoyed, her lips squeezed in a tight line. She jerks to her right, then moves to the left, but Ape Man isn't fooled and blocks her. I'm already stalking toward them as he leans in, ready to kiss her. It's clear to anyone but this idiot that she's not a willing participant. Anyone but this idiot can easily recognize her expression for what it is: a mixture of shock and fear.

She turns her head to avoid his kiss, hands pushing against his chest. Undeterred, one of his hands grabs her behind the neck and forces her face to his. His other hand cups her breast, ignoring that she's squirming to get away.

A fiery protectiveness scorches within me. I snatch hold of his shoulder and whip him around. Amber slips past, and I slam my fist into his face.

He stumbles back and his hand snaps to his jaw, to where my fist made contact. "What the fuck is your problem?" he growls.

"You, shithead. She doesn't want you kissing her."

"S-says who?"

I want to slam my fist in his face again, to jump-start a few of his brain cells. "She did. Or do you usually kiss girls who look scared shitless?"

He sways on his feet. "She wasn't scared. She wanted me." Only now he doesn't appear so sure. He glances over my shoulder. I don't have to turn to know we've got an audience.

"The only thing she wanted was for you to leave her the fuck alone." I step closer, trapping him, giving him a taste of how she felt. "And if I catch you near her again, I'll beat the shit out of you."

He holds up his hands. "Okay, I got it." He doesn't stick around to see if I have anything more to add. He stumbles toward the house.

I follow, ignoring the curious gazes watching me. Once inside, I search for Amber. Her friend is dancing with a guy, but I have no idea if she and Amber came here together. If they did, Amber has to be here, somewhere.

I continue searching for her but give up after scouring the place for fifteen minutes. She either doesn't want to be found or she's fled the party.

The restless feeling from earlier intensifies.

"You looking for me?" a girl asks as I scan the living room. I turn to find the blond who flirted with me before, her mouth curved in a seductive smile. She places her hand on my arm, eyes focused on my lips. "Hi, I'm Emma." She lifts a plastic cup to me. "You look like you could use another beer. So I got you one." Her words are slightly slurred, but she doesn't seem overly drunk. All bets are off when the girl's too drunk to know what she's doing.

I take the cup from her. "Marcus." She's even prettier up close, with blue eyes that want to devour me and a body made for action.

She might not completely take the edge off how I'm feeling, but it'll be enough. And sex with Emma is a much better option than tracking down Tammara.

I brush my thumb against her cheek, and she leans into me. I breathe in her coconut scent. My junk tightens in my jeans, and I push away all thoughts of Amber. If she doesn't want to be found, then this girl will most definitely do. And I'd be crazy to go after a girl like Amber. It's the last thing either of us needs.

My lips caress Emma's, and she moans. "Do you live near here?"

"I live on campus. Can we go back to your place?"

"Sorry. No one's allowed there. My mother's sick. With cancer." The first part's right, even though I don't live with my mom. She is sick. Sick enough not to stop Frank from hurting me and Ryan. Sick enough to have babies and not care about them.

I gulp down the beer. "Do you have a roommate?"

"Yes. But she's away for the weekend."

"Will you be able to sneak me in?"

She nods, confident, as if she has sneaked plenty of guys into her room without getting caught, though I can't help but notice a thread of sadness in her eyes.

Not wanting to dwell on that and miss out on this opportunity, I say, "Okay, let's go." I place my beer on a coffee table that's been pushed against the wall and remove my phone from my back pocket.

Mission in motion, I type, letting Chase know I'm leaving. Although he doesn't openly judge me for sleeping with so many girls, it doesn't mean he thinks it's a good idea. One day he'll let his opinion be known, and I'd rather he didn't do that in front of a girl I plan to screw.

Since Emma came to the party with her friends, I drive us both to the university and park near her dorm.

"Give me a few minutes and I'll let you in," she says outside the emergency exit.

I examine the door. "The alarm won't go off?"

"Hasn't yet." Further proving she's done this with other guys, which is a good thing. It means she won't expect anything between us beyond tonight.

Five minutes later I'm still waiting for her to let me in. *Shit*. How long's this going to take? There's always the chance she changed her mind and went to bed without bothering to tell me first. I pace back and forth, deliberating whether to give it another minute or two, or just bail and return to the party. It's still early. I can find another warm, willing body to take her place.

As I'm about to walk away, the side door opens. "Coast is clear," Emma slurs, a little more than before.

I nod and quietly follow her into the building, up three flights of stairs, and down the hallway. She needs to work on her spy skills. She giggles for no reason every so often, setting me on edge. I hate gigglers.

Except for one other guy wandering the hallway, we don't bump into anyone. Which is lucky, since there are a couple of parties going on. A battle of loud music—pop versus rock—and giggling spill into the hallway.

"This is it." She opens the door and motions me into a room that can only be described as an orange-and-pink explosion. I pull her into my arms and kiss her. Rum and coke. She didn't taste like this earlier when I kissed her. So that's what took her so long.

I deepen the kiss and slide my hand to her ass. She moans.

I pull away slightly. "Which bed's yours?"

She points behind her. I walk her backward to it.

A photo on her desk catches my attention. In it, Emma and Amber are standing with a good-looking guy, his arm around Amber's waist. I pick it up. "Who are they?"

"That's Trent. My brother." She leans over and pukes in the trash can.

"You okay?" I ask, which is obviously a dumb question. Clearly she isn't. I put the photo back on the desk.

She straightens. "Yeah, I'm good. Just give me a second. I have to go to the bathroom." To puke some more, no doubt.

Which means she's too drunk for this to be consensual. Which means if we have sex, it's rape.

She's barely gone a minute before I slip away. But as easy as it is to leave Emma, it's not so easy to stop thinking about Amber. The girl in the picture looked happy, but the girl I've met doesn't look like she's done much smiling lately.

11

AMBER

The red numbers on my alarm clock glow 6:00 a.m. I might as well go to the gym. After last night, I need to work out more than ever.

Brittany snores softly from her bed. I guess I wasn't screaming in my sleep this time. That, or she drugged herself so she doesn't have to worry about me accidentally waking her with my dreams.

Dawn stretches across the sky as I jog toward the kinesiology building, my eyes and ears open to anything unusual. And not for the first time, I wish I could run outside instead of being forced to use the treadmill. I used to do it all the time. This was my favorite time to run, when the world is fairly quiet, and it was just Emma and Trent and me.

Since it's Saturday morning, the gym is quieter than normal. I select a treadmill and start running, pushing myself harder than usual, if that's even possible. After a few minutes, sweat drips down my face and back. My legs and lungs burn, a sensation I welcome. It means I'm alive.

"Hey, you're here early." Even at six in the morning, Jordan's smiling.

"I woke...up early." I attempt a smile of my own. I really am happy to see her. It's just my brain, as well as my leg and face muscles, are all fighting for the same limited supply of oxygen. "Figured...you'd sleep...in."

Jordan's smile vanishes and her gaze drops to my treadmill console. "What's going on?"

"What...do you mean?"

"You're supposed to be able to talk when you run. Why are you running so fast?"

"I just...felt like it." *And I don't want to stop.*

"I can tell when you're upset. You always push yourself way too hard on the treadmill. So what gives?"

And once again, I'm shocked that this girl, who I haven't known for long, whom I'm keeping secrets from, cares enough about me to notice something's wrong. And that makes me smile inside, even if my muscles can't replicate the effect on my face.

"It's...nothing. I was...thinking about...math test."

Jordan climbs onto the treadmill next to me. I slow my pace. She'll want to talk while running, and I can't do that, breathe, and run at the same time. I'm having a hard enough time with the last two as it is.

"Wish I could help you with your math." She lets out a long, loud breath. "But I can't."

"Why not?" I ask. She's never mentioned that she's struggling in her course. And if she's pre-med, she must have the same math requirements. It would only make sense.

She focuses her attention on the treadmill, pretending it's the most fascinating thing around. She presses Start and increases the speed until she's running just a pace slower than me. "I told you I want to be a child psychologist, right?"

I nod. "You did, but you said your parents want you to be a physician."

"A surgeon," she corrects.

"O-kay. So what does that have to do with you not being able to help me with math?"

She shrugs, a sheepish expression on her face. "I can't help you 'cause I'm taking algebra, not pre-calculus."

"What, you don't need calculus for pre-med?" I don't see the fairness in that if I require it for pre-vet.

She shrugs, again. "I'm not exactly taking pre-med courses. I'm taking courses for a psych degree."

I almost stop running and fall off the treadmill. "Do your parents know?" From the first day we met, she'd told me she was going into medicine, like I told her I was going to be a vet.

She shakes her head.

"Are you planning to tell them?"

Again, she shakes her head.

"Never? Won't they figure out you're not a physician at some point?"

"Yeah, I guess. But you don't know my parents, Amber. My family. Everyone, including my brother and sister, went into medicine. My parents will be furious."

"Even if it means you're doing what you want to do?" Something that won't cause her to faint or puke, which isn't the case with medicine.

"My parents aren't like yours," she says, oblivious to the truth about mine. "Mine will be disappointed in me, and I can't handle that."

"I know what you mean. My mom wanted me to enter the family business, too, and be a lawyer." But surely Jordan's parents wouldn't turn their backs on her. Not if they know how much child psychology means to her. At least Mom didn't say I *couldn't* be a vet. She just pointed out that corporate lawyers make more money.

"She knows you're not studying pre-law, right?" Jordan asks.

I nod.

She looks thoughtful for a moment, but I get the idea it doesn't change anything. She still plans to keep the secret from her parents for as long as possible. "Anyway, we're not discussing my math grade. We're discussing yours. You could get a tutor."

Inwardly I roll my eyes at her attempt to change the topic. But I can't complain since I'm just as bad. "Except I don't know any."

"What about him?" She jerks her chin at the dark-haired guy who just entered the gym. The same dark-haired guy who offered to tutor me in math. Who's she kidding? I doubt he even knows what pre-calculus is. Sex seems to be his subject of choice.

"Wouldn't it be better if the tutor actually knows something about math?" I ask.

"I'm guessing he knows a thing or two, considering he's an engineering student."

I let out a choked laugh. "Where did you hear that?"

"From the guy I was dancing with last night. He and Marcus are in a class together."

"You talking about Marcus Reid?" a girl on the treadmill next to me says, loud enough to be heard by half the people in the gym. Including Marcus.

I shoot her a look at the same time Jordan replies, "Yes." Just what I don't need—Marcus thinking I'm interested in him. Which I'm not.

"Do you know him?" Jordan asks, her voice competing with the loud hum of the treadmill and the pounding of our feet while keeping quiet enough so Marcus can't hear her.

"I'd say." The girl's expression hardens. "He's amazing in bed, but don't expect more than that. The guy's got a reputation a mile long. He's not looking to settle down."

"Then he's perfect," Jordan exclaims.

I stare at her, mouth open. "Perfect for what?"

"Tutoring you. A hot tutor who's great in bed—what more could you want?"

"You're not serious, are you?"

Jordan laughs at my no-doubt-shocked expression. "Of course not. You need a tutor who can help you with math, not one who's so hot he'll distract you from learning anything."

Oh, good. She hasn't gone completely insane.

"What about Brittany?"

I take it back. She is insane. "You've gotta be kidding me, right?"

"She's pre-med and I've seen her calculus text in your room."

"You're forgetting she hates me."

"No, she—okay, maybe she does a little."

"She tried to be transferred to a new room because of my nightmares. I'm pretty sure she hates me more than just a little." I press the speed button and up my pace. "Any other suggestions?"

"Sleep with your teacher."

She laughs at my expression. The same one I had when she told me a tutor who's hot in bed is a great idea. I'm tempted to lean over and increase her speed just so she can't keep talking.

"I'm kidding," she says, laughing again. "But you have to admit, being tutored by Marcus is better than sleeping with your instructor." Especially since the guy is like fifty. I shudder at the thought.

"Maybe I could study harder," I suggest.

"You're already studying harder. How's that going for you?"

I pretend I didn't hear her. "There must be someone else who can tutor me. What about the tall, redhead girl on our floor? What's her name?"

"Ann. And she's poli-sci. So that would be a big no."

"There has to be someone who can..." *Only the weak ask for help, Amber. Wasn't that what Mom always said? The strong help the weak, not the other way around.*

"There isn't anyone. Not unless your instructor can suggest someone."

Marcus selects a barbell and performs a combination of squat and overhead press. His shoulder muscles ripple under his gray T-shirt when he pushes the weight upward. The hem rises, revealing his taut stomach.

"I'll ask him."

She nods at Marcus. "Go now before he leaves."

I snort. "I meant my instructor. I'll ask him if he can recommend somebody."

She lets out a disappointed huff. Not giving her a chance to voice her opinion, I ask, "So what happened with you and the guy you were dancing with?"

"He asked for my phone number and I told him I have a boyfriend, and that was it."

You're my forever. And I'll love you in a way your boyfriend never could.

I increase the treadmill speed, again, chasing away the words. "And he was fine with that?" Of course he was. He wasn't Paul.

"Sure, why wouldn't he be?" She slows her treadmill. "Speaking of boyfriends. I need to call mine. He should be up by now." She steps down. "I'll see you at the dorm."

"Okay."

As soon as she's out of view, I increase the speed until I'm running at my previous pace. As long as I'm pushing myself this hard, the memories of last spring stay away.

Sweat streams down my back and the gym spins around me. I stumble and catch myself in time to avoid a face-plant. I don't stop. I can't stop yet.

I run past trees, the buds not fully formed. My bare feet slip on the muddy ground. Branches reach out to grab me.

A hand touches my lower back and the ground stops moving under my feet. A subtle spicy scent embraces me. I'm safe. It's not Paul.

I snap to the present, to the gym.

"Fuck," Marcus says, hand still on my back. "I didn't hit a guy yesterday just so you could kill yourself on the treadmill."

I shake away my uneasy feeling and grab the treadmill side rails, steadying myself. "I wasn't trying to kill myself. I was working out."

His eyebrows draw together. "Didn't look like it from where I was standing."

My mouth flaps open and shut as Jordan's suggestion that I

could hire Marcus plays on repeat in my head. "Would you tutor me in math?"

Great. All I meant to do was change the topic. I hadn't planned to actually bring up Jordan's suggestion.

Marcus stares at me as if I'd asked him if unicorns really do exist. Shocked and amused.

I step off the treadmill and turn to leave.

"How much?"

I face him, again. "How much what?"

"How much would you pay me?" His gaze doesn't roam over my body this time. He's watching my face, a dead serious glint in his eyes.

I swallow the fear that I'm making a mistake. "Forty dollars an hour. But if I get an A in math by the end of the semester, I'll give you a bonus thousand dollars."

12

MARCUS

I know I look like an idiot, staring at Amber like she's a winning lottery ticket. Is she really promising a thousand dollars if I help her get an A? And what are the odds I can do that? For all I know, she could be brain dead when it comes to math.

But brain dead or not, she's also offering to pay me hourly, and I'd rather tutor her than some dumbass jerk. Especially if I can convince her to let me show her that vectors aren't the only things hot in the horizontal and vertical position.

My junk twitches at that possibility, even as I recognize that was a lame line. "When do you want to start?"

"As soon as possible."

I've got nothing planned for the morning, and the sooner we begin, the better. "How about we meet at the Marketplace in an hour?"

She checks her watch. "That works."

"Bring your notes and book."

She nods and walks toward the locker rooms. I shake my head. Shit, what was I thinking? I need the money and Chase told me to get a tutoring gig. But did I agree to help her for the money, or was it because my cock gets tight whenever I'm near her?

Realizing it doesn't matter either way, I finish working out and have a quick shower before heading over to the Marketplace. Amber's already there when I arrive, scanning the food court, body tense.

"Relax, Kitten. You're way too tense. I'm not gonna bite." *Unless you want me to.*

She holds an edge of vulnerability that reminds me of Ryan. He used to have the same exhausted, haunted look about him. I want to ask who hurt her, but I get the feeling she won't tell me.

The protective feeling I experienced last night at the party, the one I've never felt for a girl before, stirs deep. I push it away. I don't need this.

"Would you stop calling me 'Kitten'?" she says, tone tight.

"Can't."

"Why not?"

"I have to call you something, and since you haven't told me your name, 'Kitten' will have to do."

"My name's Amber."

"Marcus."

"I know." She bites her lower lip. I don't think she even realizes how hot it is when she does that. It makes me want to gently guide her lip away from her teeth, run the tip of my tongue along it, then suck it into my mouth and see how she'll respond.

That's what I want to do, but if she runs, and something tells me she will, there goes my chance to earn some serious bucks.

We order our coffees, which Amber looks like she needs more than anything. Though from the amount of sugar and milk she pours into it, coffee clearly isn't her drink of choice.

I lead her to a table in the food court and sit. Compared to during the week, the place isn't busy. Mostly students getting together to work on group projects, and young families hanging out after using the sports facilities.

Again, Amber scans the area.

"You looking for someone?" I ask.

"No, it's just..." The fingertips of her right hand tap against her thigh. "I mean no." She sips her coffee. "By the way, thanks for helping with that guy last night." The hand with the coffee in it shakes a little when she mentions him. "I told him I wasn't interested, but he wouldn't listen."

"You know him?"

"He told me he's in my bio class. There're so many people in it, I've never noticed him before." Pain or fear, or both, flare in her eyes. Once again, she glances around.

"Don't worry about him. After last night, I doubt he's gonna touch you or talk to you again. But if he does, just let me know, okay?"

She nods, seeming uncertain what to believe. "What happened after I ran off?"

My lips curl into a smirk. "I hit him and threatened him if he comes near you again."

She smiles, the movement small. Her body relaxes a little more, though there's still an edge of wariness to her that she's had since I first noticed her at Your Designs.

"I wanted to make sure you were okay, but I couldn't find you. Where'd ya go?"

"I was there." She removes her text and binder from her backpack and opens the book to the chapter on algebraic equations and inequalities. "This is what we were covering, but I got an F on my test." She looks like she's going to puke. "I'm not sure I understood everything."

No shit.

"Do you have your test?"

"Yeah, sure." She searches through her binder and hands me the booklet. Her right hand drops to her lap, and she bounces her fingers against her thigh again.

I flip through the pages and study her answers. I can feel the grand slip away. She got a few right, but she didn't finish most of the test.

"Why do you need the class?" If she's this clueless about math, why the hell is she in the course?

"I'm taking pre-veterinary sciences. It's part of the required courses." She lets out a long breath. "So, do you think you can help me?"

No. I nod. "But it's not gonna be easy."

"I'll do whatever it takes to pass. This is important to me." She smiles, but it gets lost somewhere between her mouth and her eyes.

"Okay." I rip a page out of her binder. She cringes but doesn't say anything. "Did you know there're three kinds of people in the world?" I smirk. "Those who can count and those who can't."

This time the smile on her face is genuine and she chuckles. "And you're planning to help me with math?"

"Damn straight I am."

We spend the next hour going over what she's covered so far in class. As far as I can tell, she's not dumb. Math just isn't her thing. But I will give it to her—she works hard to figure out what I'm showing her and asks lots of good questions.

Two arms encircle my shoulders from behind, and a pair of cool lips kisses my neck. Even without Tammara saying anything, I recognize her slightly musky perfume.

"Miss me, darling?" she purrs.

Momentarily ignoring the equation I was explaining to Amber, I unhook myself from Tammara's arms. She sits next to me and rests her hand on my thigh, marking her territory.

"Math," she says, taking note of the textbook between Amber and me. "How boring." She inches her hand up my leg. "I can think of better ways to entertain you." She doesn't bother to acknowledge Amber. Everything's a game for Tammara, and this time is no exception.

I remove her hand from my lap and put it on the table. "We're busy." I don't want to be a jerk in front of Amber, but Tammara's pissing me off. This is my fault. I should have had the balls to end things with her the other morning at her apartment.

"That's okay." She glances at Amber, a sly smile edging onto her face. "I can wait. I have to study for my marketing exam."

Amber's gaze jumps from Tammara to me and back again. Her fingers return to tapping against her thigh. Mine itch to cross the space and cover her hand, stilling the movement. Tammara will see Amber's actions as a sign of weakness.

The protective urge surfaces, again. "We need to talk," I tell Tammara.

She stiffens for a brief moment before regaining her composure. The smile is on her face once more, but this time it holds a note of uncertainty. "Why don't you come over to my place after you're finished here? We can talk there." From her silky voice, it's clear what she hopes will happen, and she's making it clear to Amber, too.

Normally I wouldn't care what a girl thinks, but Amber isn't any girl. "We need to talk now." I say it more forcefully this time.

"I-I should leave." Amber reaches for her book and closes it.

"Give me a moment...unless you really have to go." I get the feeling she isn't ready to quit studying yet. I'm certainly not.

I stand. Tammara doesn't move. She's too busy glaring at Amber.

"Now, Tammara."

Without looking at me, she gives a slight nod and follows me around the corner to a quiet spot near the wall. No one pays us any attention.

She pouts. Some guys fall for it. I'm not one of them. As if sensing that, her pout vanishes. "You better not be planning to tell me that you want to remain friends." Her heated tone could melt daggers into liquid metal.

It's hard to remain friends when you weren't friends to begin with. I wisely keep that to myself. "You and I want different things, Tammara."

"Meaning you were interested in me when it was only sex. Is that what this is all about, Marcus? I want more and you're only interested in getting laid?"

Figuring it's a rhetorical question, I don't answer.

"She's not even your usual type," she says, pointing out the obvious, even though she doesn't know how right she is. My type usually doesn't need any encouragement to drop their panties.

"Keep her out of this." My voice is dangerously low, the warning unmistakable. "I'm only tutoring her."

Tammara laughs bitterly "I know you better than that. You're only tutoring her to get into her pants. That's all you care about. Screw 'em and leave 'em. That's your motto." A sliver of hurt mingles with her words, but I can't tell if it's real or not.

"At least I'm capable of caring about something," I snap.

Tammara jerks away as if I'd slapped her, and I instantly wish I could take the words back. That was pretty low, even for me.

"Fuck you, asshole." She narrows her eyes at me, then looks in the direction we came from. Before I can say anything, she storms off. Fortunately she leaves through the far exit, away from Amber.

I return to the table. Amber is busy working through a math question.

"Sorry about that," I say.

"It's okay." She smiles softly and pushes the page she was working on toward me. "I figured I would try another question while you were gone."

I lean forward and catch the sweet scent of her strawberry shampoo. I breathe her in and check her answer. "Very good, Kitten. You got it." I grin at her.

She grins back. "You're a great teacher."

I bite my tongue to keep from saying what else I'm good at teaching. I don't want to destroy this easy rapport between us.

"So what made you decide to become an engineer?" she asks.

Since I don't want to tell her about my pathetic excuse of a life, I say, "What do you get when you cross a mosquito and a mountain climber?"

She frowns slightly, either confused at my avoidance of the question or because she's trying to figure out the answer. She shrugs.

"You can't cross a vector with a scalar."

Amber groans, then laughs. "Where did you learn all these lame jokes?"

"My high school math teacher. It was the only way he could get the class to pay attention." A trick my history teacher should have tried. I might have done better in the class if he had.

At the sound of classical music coming from the floor, Amber reaches toward her backpack. The cuff of her hoodie sleeve slides up, revealing thick scars on her wrist. She tugs the cuff down and sits up, cell phone in hand. She checks it and drops it into her bag.

All I can do is stare at her injured wrist, hidden under the fabric of her hoodie. She pulls her hand farther into her sleeve, making sure I can't see even a fraction of the scars.

"It's not what you think," she says, her voice low and cracked. "I didn't try to kill myself."

How the hell could she end up with scars like that if she wasn't attempting suicide? "What happened?"

She fidgets with the cuff, eyes avoiding mine, then grabs her stuff from the table and shoves it in her bag. "I have to go." Before I can say anything, she bolts.

13

AMBER

I smile and do a happy dance while seated on my desk chair. Thanks to Marcus's tutoring session yesterday, I got another answer correct. The guy's a genius.

Someone knocks on the bedroom door. I open it.

Jordan sails into the room and flops on my bed. "I need a break from studying. You wanna hit the mall with me? Maybe see a movie?"

"Sure." She's not the only one who needs a break. I've been studying for four hours straight. My brain feels like it's ready to explode. And since I expect Brittany to reappear at any moment, snarling at me in the way only Brittany can do, I'm ready to escape.

I grab my purse, and we head downstairs to the parking lot, where Jordan's black Honda Civic sits. The warm fall wind kisses my face as we stroll across the sun-dappled asphalt.

I check the back seat to make sure it's clear, then walk around her car, ensuring the tires appear normal.

"Do you, like, do that every time you get in a car?" she asks.

"You never can play it too safe," I say, repeating a line I once read. "You never know when someone might be hiding in the back, ready to attack you, or has put a hole in your tire. Do you know how many girls are raped each year 'cause some sicko forced them to pull over because of a flat tire he caused?"

"Point taken. So, Miss Safety Officer, are we good to go?"

I turn around, scanning the area for anyone watching us. "Yep, we're good."

Jordan unlocks the doors, and we climb in.

"Is there anything you're specifically searching for at the mall?" I click my seat belt in place. "Or are we just wandering around?"

"I could use more party clothes." She starts the car. The engine purrs to life. "You know, in case we wanna go out again. I thought we could go to the dance club everyone talks about. What do you think?"

I tug down on the cuff of Trent's hoodie. "About which part?"

"Both. I thought we could go dancing this weekend."

"Sure. Why not?" I force a smile onto my face. I must have succeeded in making it appear genuine, because she grins back at me.

"And we'll look for something for you to wear. Something less, well, tomboyish."

A sinking feeling weighs inside me. What are the chances she'll want me to model them in the store for her? It's bad enough Marcus saw the scars. I can't risk Jordan seeing them and the tattoo. Marcus may have shrugged them off. I won't get so lucky with Jordan. While it might be nice to have someone to tell what I went through with Paul, other than the cops, the doctors and nurses, and the DA, I don't need to give Jordan nightmares. I have enough for the both of us.

As if pulled by an invisible force, my hand drifts to the spot where the tattoo lies, and my fingers caress the soft fabric hiding it. The tension that I didn't realize was building in my muscles fades.

"If your parents had you under such a tight rein," I say, "how come you're such a great dancer?"

"I took dance lessons for years while growing up and danced to music videos whenever my parents weren't around. Which was a lot."

The mall parking lot is busy when we arrive, but it doesn't take long for Jordan to find a spot. I guess we're not the only ones needing a break from our studies.

As we walk through the mall, Jordan homes in on a clothing store where the mannequins reveal more plastic than the clothes cover. One is wearing a black midthigh-length halter dress.

"You'd look great in that." Jordan grabs my arm and drags me into the store.

Panic shoots through me and I twist my arm free. "I can't wear that." Not unless I want to show off my scars and tattoo.

"Yes, you can. Trust me on this one, Amber."

"I can't wear that. How about..." I scan the store. "How about that one?" I point to a mannequin wearing a long-sleeved sweater dress in black, with narrow muted gold stripes running horizontally. It's almost midthigh-length, but it will look great with black tights, unlike the halter dress.

Jordan inspects it. "Won't you get hot dancing in it?"

Dancing? I'm going to have to dance, too? "It'll be fine. The fabric isn't thick." Besides, while Jordan might not be so impressed, I love it. It's not clingy, and with my black boots, it will be perfect without screaming "Look at me." And the dark color lets me remain invisible.

She inspects it again before nodding her reluctant approval. "Well, it's not quite what I had in mind, but it will look incredible on you." What she's really thinking is it'll be better than my jeans and hoodies. I can't argue with her there.

I search through the rack for my size.

"Which one do you like more?" Jordan holds up two dresses that I hope are for her, not me. One is purple and would give her parents a heart attack if they saw it.

"These are for you, right?"

She nods.

"Both of them. They're both great."

We try on the dresses. As expected, mine fits perfectly and keeps most of my scars hidden, except for the ones on my leg.

"Okay, I'm ready," Jordan says as I pull on my T-shirt.

I touch the forget-me-not tattoo. "I'm almost ready."

I slip into my hoodie and step out of the changing room. Jordan is waiting for me in the purple dress.

"Where's your dress?" she asks, even though I'm holding it so it's obvious where it is. "Aren't you going to show me what it looks like on you?"

"Sorry. I didn't realize you wanted to see it now. But yours is perfect. Turn around."

I was right. It is perfect on her. When they see her tight textured curls and slim body and golden-brown coloring, guys will be all over her. Just as long as they pay attention to *her*, I'll be fine.

She changes into the other dress, and like the first one, it looks incredible on her. The low scooping back shows off her toned body. She buys them both.

Afterward, we check out the other clothing stores. I don't buy anything else, but Jordan makes the most of no longer being under her parents' rules and no longer having to wear school uniforms. She's like a cat with catnip. Crazy happy.

She points to a store named Lingerie Rose. "Let's go there next." Without waiting for a reply, she cuts across the mall.

Inside, I find her hunting through the tables of satin bras and thong underwear. A far cry from my usual white cotton.

"I still can't believe you offered Marcus a thousand dollars to help you get an A."

I pick up a lacy black bra. "I know, but if I want to be a vet, I have to pass the class. Plus I figured he would take tutoring me more seriously if I dangled the carrot in front of him."

"I bet Brittany would be a lot nicer and would tutor you if you dangled that carrot in front of her." She snorts. "Or maybe not." She returns the purple bra and selects another one. "Plus she wouldn't be as much fun as Marcus."

"I'm not planning to have fun with him. He's just there to help me with my math. And it's a win-win situation. I do well in math, and he gets money for...for...I don't know, for his car." Isn't that what guys usually spend their money on? Cars and sports?

A bouncy pop song plays through the store speakers. Jordan sings along. Since there are no guys in the store, I join her, and we laugh and dance to the music. This is the most fun I've had in a while, and it makes me realize how much I miss dancing.

A rather stern look from a sales clerk prompts us to drop the bras back on the pile.

Still chuckling, Jordan walks to a rack of satin slips. I follow her, trying to keep a straight face and not glance at the saleswoman.

A familiar laugh breaks out behind me, and I spin around. Emma and her friends wander into the store. At the sight of me, Emma stops and a flurry of emotions cross her face, none of which I can get a firm grasp on.

"What do you think of this?" Jordan asks. I turn to her again. She's holding a short red slip with spaghetti straps.

My wrists and shoulders hurt, and my hands feel like they're floating in the air. I'm sitting, propped against a cold wall, the same temperature as the concrete floor. The cool air wraps itself around me and I shiver.

My eyes open and I gasp. I'm in what looks like a jail cell with a queen-sized bed, and I'm handcuffed to the wall behind me, in nothing but a red satin slip.

I yank at the handcuffs and try to twist my hands free. Blood trickles from the wounds on my wrists. "Let me go!" I scream.

No one comes, though I'm not sure if that's a good thing or not. Shaking beyond control, I yank at the handcuffs, again.

"Amber?" a panicked voice asks. Jordan. "What's wrong?"

I blink and I'm back in the store. Jordan stares at me, eyes wide. She's not alone. Everyone is staring at me.

Oh, God. What did I do *this* time? Sometimes I just zone out when I get a flashback. From the way everyone's staring at me, that's not what happened this time.

"What a freak," a girl next to Emma says, confirming that I did more than just zone out, but I'm too scared to ask Jordan. Something tells me I don't want to know.

Emma's face is paler than normal as she stares at me, eyes wide with confusion and pain. She takes a step toward me, hesitates, then walks to the rear of the store. Her three friends follow her.

Without meaning to, I rub one wrist as though it were still hurting. Jordan's gaze drops to it.

I jerk my hand away. "I'll meet you outside the store."

She returns the slip to the rack. "I'll come with you."

I give her a shaky smile. "I just need a moment. I'll wait for you."

Jordan nods as if she understands, but there's no missing the hurt in her eyes. She wants to know what's going on and I can't tell her. Not yet.

"I'll be fine. It's no big deal. It's just…it's just an anxiety attack. I used to get them all the time at home." It's partly true, and at least I don't have to tell her why I get them. "I'll meet you outside the store once you're finished, and we can get ice cream." This time my smile is genuine. I really do want ice cream. Paul hated the stuff.

A middle-aged woman, eyelids heavy with sparkly blue eye shadow, approaches Jordan. "Do you need help finding anything?"

"I'll see you in a few minutes." I glance at Emma again, who's busy looking through a rack of fleecy pajama bottoms, then walk out the store and into the solid wall of a person.

"Kitten," the wall says as I step away. Marcus's gaze jumps to the store's name, and his mouth slides into an amused grin. "You don't need to get sexy underwear for our tutoring sessions, but I won't say I don't appreciate it."

"Ass," I mutter, momentarily forgetting the ass helped me learn a math concept I'd been struggling with.

"Anything to make you happy, Kitten."

I somehow manage not to roll my eyes at the name. Telling him not to call me that hasn't helped. It's only encouraged him to use the name more. I narrow my eyes instead. "I thought you said you weren't stalking me."

"I'm not." He lifts a plastic bag from the bookstore and removes a book with a teenage girl and a male angel on the cover. "I was buying a birthday present for my friend's sister. And now that you mention it, how do I know you're not stalking *me*?"

From the corner of my eye, I spot a guy checking me out. Marcus brushes a strand of hair from my face. I flinch when his fingers touch my cheek, but then I see the other guy scurry away.

I think of Marcus's reputation for not getting attached, of the way he jumped between me and that guy at the party. I take a deep breath, almost positive that what I'm about to do is incredibly stupid. "What are you doing Friday night?"

14

MARCUS

"You wanna explain why we're going to Nightshade?" Chase asks as he steers his car onto the busy street. "I thought it wasn't your scene."

"It isn't."

He doesn't say anything else, his eyes on the road. Then he groans. "This isn't about Tammara, is it?"

"Why would it be about her?" But as I say it, it hits me why he asked. It's because that's where she and her friends like to hang out. How could I be such an idiot? And now I'm walking in there with Amber. "Don't worry. It's not about Tammara. It's about the girl I'm tutoring."

Chase laughs. "So the girl got to you, huh? I can't believe we're going there so you can hook up with her. Isn't that like violating some kind of tutor-student rule?"

"I'm not hooking up with her. She paid me to pretend we're dating."

Chase's head jerks around to face me, the darkened car interior hiding his expression. "You shitting me?"

"Would I do that?"

"Right now, I'm thinking the answer is yes. Since when did you become a paid escort?"

I grunt. "Look, I'm just helping her out."

A truck drives past, its headlights brightening Chase's face as he throws me a dubious expression. "How do you figure that?"

"Her friend wanted to go to the dance club, and Amber doesn't want to worry about guys hitting on her." And they will if given a chance, something I don't intend to let happen. "So, she asked me to keep 'em away."

"Like a bodyguard?"

"Yeah, like a bodyguard." Except this bodyguard is planning for a little physical action on the side. There's no way I'm going there just to hold hands. For starters, I don't hold hands.

"There's one other thing," I add.

"What's that?"

"Her friend can't know that Amber and I planned to meet up there. And she's supposed to think tonight is a one-time-only thing, so she doesn't think Amber and I are actually dating."

He laughs. "So what you're saying is you're supposed to play yourself? That shouldn't be too big a stretch of the imagination."

My cell phone pings. I pull it out of my back pocket.

Kitten: We're in. Pls hurry

15

AMBER

Where the hell is he?

When I asked Marcus to help me, I might not have been thinking things through. I was freaking out over what happened in the store. I was freaking out at what I remembered. I was freaking out over what Jordan would say once she joined me. Heck, I was even freaking out over what I would say to find out what I did—which ended up being nothing more than me screaming, "Let me go!" And when I saw the guy coming toward me and how Marcus inadvertently scared him off...

God, I hope I'm not making a mistake.

Jordan stops walking. She turns around, her gaze taking in what looks like a former warehouse. Even in the dimly lit dance club, with its multicolored spotlights zigzagging over the crowd, it's easy to see her face glowing in anticipation of her newest adventure, and yet another item to cross off her bucket list.

"Can you believe this place?" she says over the loud dance beat. Her hips sway to the erotic rhythm while her hoop earrings, thick threads of gold and silver twisted together, gleam in the light. "No wonder it's so popular."

The sound of cheering pulls my attention near the dance floor,

81

to a group of guys peeling off our clothes with their eyes. I push down the desire to cover my girlie parts with my hands, since it's not like the guys can see through the fabric of my sweater dress. And covering myself will only make things worse by drawing more unwanted attention.

Two of them break away from the group and swagger toward us while their friends watch. I groan. The guys aren't bad-looking, but I'm not interested. No matter what Jordan might believe, the last thing I want is a boyfriend.

I scan the area, searching for a way to escape before they get here, but quickly give up on that plan. I'm not leaving Jordan alone, and she's busy smiling at the guys, which means she won't want to leave just yet. She might not be on the search for a boyfriend, but she is interested in having a good time.

Just as I'm about to pretend I have to go to the bathroom, a warm breath brushes against my ear. "Here, Kitten," Marcus says behind me. "I bought you a drink." His hand glides along my hip and rests protectively on my waist. I stiffen at his touch but then remind myself why he's here and let out an uneasy breath. His scent, a combination of leather and spice, oddly enough, makes me feel safe.

I'm almost tempted to lean into him, but that would be a mistake. If I'm planning to keep Jordan from figuring out what's going on, I need to be careful. She can't know that I planned for Marcus to meet us here. All she needs to know is that this is a one-time deal and that I'm just here to have a good time.

Besides, guys like Marcus don't want girlfriends, and I'm not interested in being some guy's quick lay.

The guys heading toward us stop, consult each other, shake their heads in defeat, and return to their friends. I have to focus on the floor to keep from laughing. This will be easier than I thought.

"Thanks," I say, unsure if I meant for the drink or because Marcus successfully chased the guys away. I turn and my breath gets caught in my lungs. His messy black hair and intense hazel eyes give him the sexy vibe that's gained the attention of a few girls nearby. Peeking from under the sleeve of his gray T-shirt is a black tattoo, but the T-shirt covers too much of it for me to make out what it's supposed to be. But none of this is what caused the guys to change their minds. It's the way Marcus stands next to me and his watchful eyes that signal "Back off."

I take the drink from him and eye it nervously.

Marcus takes it from me, drinks some of it, and hands it back to me. "I can get you something else if you want," he says.

Shaking my head, I lift the glass to my lips. It burns going down, and I'm hit with a coughing fit. Rum and coke, and whoever made it for him made it extra strong.

I cough a couple of times more before the fit subsides. I glance up to find Jordan trying to communicate with her eyes, only I have no idea what she's saying.

"Marcus, this is my friend, Jordan."

Jordan breaks into her usual grin. "Hi. Amber's told me all about you."

My face heats at the implication that I have a thing for him just like every other girl. "Not that there's much to say, other than you're helping me with my math," I clarify.

Marcus's friend joins us and hands Jordan a drink similar to what Marcus gave me. Which means the guys are either older than they look, or they have fake IDs.

"Hi." He extends his hand to me and I take it. "I'm Chase. Marcus's roommate and friend, and the guy who's much smarter than him when it comes to math." Adorable dimples spring to life.

Laughing, Marcus smacks him on the shoulder. "You wish."

"Do you guys come here often?" Jordan asks, the other guys long forgotten.

"Yes," Chase says at the same moment Marcus answers, "No."

Jordan looks back and forth between them. "So, which is it?"

"We've come here a few times, but it's not our regular hangout," Marcus amends.

A new song comes on and Jordan sways to the beat while she glances longingly at the dance floor. I open my mouth to ask her if she wants to dance, but Chase beats me to it. At her "Yes," he leads her onto the floor. He's not as good a dancer as she is, but he holds his own. More so than most of the guys pretending to strut their stuff.

Jordan loops her arms around Chase's neck and grinds her hips against his. I laugh at his expression. Jordan has no idea what she's doing to him.

I'm not the only one to laugh at his reaction. Marcus chuckles, and just like that we start talking, mostly about our classes and about some of the crazy stuff we've seen around campus. Nothing personal, though. After he abruptly changed topics when I asked why he's studying electrical engineering, I got the sense he prefers to keep up a wall. But other than that, talking to him somehow isn't as intimidating as I thought it would be.

It's pretty easy, actually.

I don't know how long we've been chatting when Marcus peers over my shoulder, for a moment lost in thought. He then closes the space between us, so less than a foot separates us. His hand strokes up and down my hip, molding to my body. He lowers his lips to my ear. "If we're gonna convince everyone you're off-limits, we need to do more than just stand here and talk. Unless you want people thinking I'm your cousin."

I swallow hard. "What do you have in mind?"

"Maybe this..." He brushes his fingertips against my neck and moves my hair back, exposing my skin. His head drops and his warm lips teasingly caress my neck.

Fortunately if Jordan sees him kissing me, she won't clue into what's really going on. She'll think we're hooking up after bumping into each other here.

Or at least I hope that's what she'll think.

His tongue flicks the skin he just kissed. I jerk away.

Relax. Trent used to do that all the time and you never freaked out.

"Whoa, Kitten. I'm not going to hurt you. I'm not that asshole from the party."

"I know. It's just...it's just..." My voice fades away, drowned out by the music.

"It's just what?"

I shake my head. "It's nothing. I'm fine."

Encouraged by my response, Marcus leans in and his lips meet mine, softly, sweetly. But he's not satisfied enough with that. His lips try to pry mine open.

His mouth presses against mine, hurting me, violating me. I want to scream for him to stop. But that'll make things worse. He always punishes me when I resist.

My body tenses, my breath accelerates, and my heart scrambles to escape my chest, pounding loud and frantic. I squeeze my eyes shut for a second, fighting against the memory.

Marcus pulls away and searches my face. "It's okay, Amber. I swear I'm not going to hurt you." His fingers brush my cheek. "You're safe."

I can tell from his expression that he wants to ask who the hell hurt me. I don't want to tell him. This is my secret.

My secret. I almost laugh at the irony. The truth was on the evening news for several days after it happened. Amber Alerts were issued. My name was splashed across newspapers and the news channels. The girl who for months had been the victim of a terrifying stalker before she was kidnapped.

But once I was found and details of my kidnapping were made public, my name magically disappeared from the news reports. I became a nameless seventeen-year-old girl, a victim of horrific acts of violence. But everyone in my town knew the news reports referred to me, even if the rest of world no longer did.

People from Crossfields may know what happened, but Marcus doesn't. And I want it to stay that way.

"I'm fine," I say as an idea plays out in my head. Paul was the last man who kissed me. I've got my life back, but I need more.

Marcus is my chance for more, in a safe way. Besides, I can't think of a better candidate for the position. He's got to be a great kisser. Girls tend not to get all hot over guys with a reputation of being a bad kisser, right? And if I'm going to take back what Paul stole from me, what better place than to do it here, with Marcus? I mean, isn't that what I'm paying him for? Kind of.

"You're right," I say. "If we're gonna do this right, you need to kiss me."

Eyes narrowed, Marcus studies my face for a second, as if trying to read my mind, then his lips touch mine, again, as his arms wrap around my waist. He doesn't push me further, and I'm able to relax into him.

Gaining a little more confidence from not flashing to Paul this time, I run the tip of my tongue along Marcus's lower lip. He parts his lips and lets me tentatively explore the inside of his mouth. I focus on his spicy scent and on his strong body against mine. A body that's nothing like Paul's.

A kiss that's nothing like Paul's.

Unlike Paul's kisses, Marcus's kiss is hot, but I can tell, like me, he's just going through the motions. He's not really present in the moment. A side effect of being a man-whore, I guess.

I continue kissing him and feel something stir deep. I quickly stamp it down as I pull away. A subtle taste of victory courses through me. My experiment, a success.

"You wanna dance?" Marcus asks, arms still around my waist. Jordan and Chase are on the dance floor, laughing and dancing to the fast beat. Both are tall and can be easily seen over most people, which is just as well given that the floor's packed.

"Okay." Crowds don't bother me. It's being alone that scares me.

We squeeze our way through the mass of bodies until we reach our friends. Jordan grins and hugs me, then goes back to dancing with Chase. Marcus wraps his arms around my waist and pulls me closer. My arms instinctively go around his neck. Our bodies press together.

I don't dare glance at Jordan. I can sense she's watching me. I can also tell she's reading way too much into what's happening. Now she'll be excited for me, especially because I'm not going home with Marcus, which makes me different from most girls he knows. Especially because he's my tutor, so it's not like this is the last time I'll see him. Especially because she wants something to happen between Marcus and me, since she figures that will make my life complete.

Practically yelling to be heard over the pulsating beat, I ask, "Why do I get the feeling this isn't your kind of music?" Chase seems to fit in with the place. Marcus doesn't.

"I prefer rock music, not this dance crap."

"I don't mind it, but give me bands like Pushing Limits and Bon Jovi, and then we're talking. And I love Aerosmith, even if the band looks a hundred years old."

Marcus laughs. "So none of those guys make you want to rip your shirt off?"

"I wouldn't rip my shirt off for any musician. Doesn't matter if he's my age or sixty."

Marcus's lips move to my ear. "Well, for the record, I like those bands, too. And for the record, some guy's fucking you with his eyes." His voice sounds odd, and I wonder if there really is a guy watching me, or if he just said that to cop a feel. "You're okay, Amber," he says softly. "I won't let him touch you." His gaze locks on to mine, and I see for a brief moment a familiar pain staring back. A pain I've seen reflected in the mirror.

I don't want him to think that we're playing by his rules, but this time, as his mouth moves along my jaw, I don't flinch. And inwardly I high-five myself for not freaking out, and for once again being able to enjoy the moment a little.

But just as I think his reputation as a man-whore is overrated, he murmurs in my ear, "God, you look fuckable in that dress."

Figures.

16

MARCUS

Last night while Amber and I danced, all I wanted to do was protect her. The way she responded when I first kissed her confirmed she's been damaged, and I don't think it was the guy I hit at the party who's at fault. He never had a chance to kiss her before I nailed him in the face.

But I screwed things up. She went from being vulnerable in my arms to this stone princess now sitting next to me in the food court. I've never responded to a girl the way I did with Amber, and my reaction scared me. I've always managed to keep up my wall with most people, and I use girls purely for entertainment. That, and to prove to myself I'm a normal guy.

I'm not a complete ass where girls are concerned. I don't treat them badly, and they know where they stand with me. Sex is a one-time deal. Any more than that and girls think you want a commitment. I thought Tammara was different, that we shared an understanding. I was wrong.

When I agreed to Amber's plan, I thought it would be an easy fifty bucks. That I could walk away from last night fifty dollars closer to my goal, with no second thoughts or regrets. But then I talked to her—really talked to her—and I kissed her and listened to her talk about music. And I realized something.

Amber has gotten under my skin.

I have to escape. I can't afford to get close to anyone. I failed my brother and I'm afraid of failing Alejandro. I don't want to risk failing anyone else, too.

Amber deserves to be loved by someone who deserves her in return. That person is not me. My mother taught me that.

I didn't want to be a jerk last night. I wanted to be Amber's hero, someone who made her feel safe. But in the end, I did what I had to do, and I pissed her off.

Pushing away the emptiness worming its way in, I work through the first question of Amber's math assignment with her, explaining each step while trying to ignore her strawberry-scented hair. As if that's even possible. That scent has found its way into my dreams, and with Amber next to me, it reminds me of the most vivid ones. The ones where we both end up naked. In my bed.

Groaning inwardly at the way my cock responds to the mere thought of those dreams, I ask, "How can you tell you're in the hands of the Mathematical Mafia?"

Her warm brown eyes sparkle in amusement like they always do when she knows I'm about to tell her a math joke, even though she knows it's going to be lame. "I don't know. How do you tell?"

"They make you an offer that you can't understand."

She laughs, the sound of it as warm as her eyes. I grin at the thought of how she's the first person to laugh at my jokes, and I go back to helping her with her assignment.

By the third question, Amber's fingers start tapping her thigh rhythmically.

I touch her hand. "Why do you do that?"

Her fingers curl into a ball. "It's nothing. I used to play basketball, and my boyfriend always joked that I would dribble against my leg whenever I was nervous, or when I wanted to play but couldn't." Her cheeks redden and a faint smile crosses her face.

Irritation that she has a boyfriend gnaws at me. I shove it away. I have no right to feel that way. "Your boyfriend's name is Trent, right?" I ask, taking a wild guess.

Color vanishes from her face and for a moment I'm positive she's going to run. "How did you know?" Her voice cracks. Moisture builds in her eyes.

"I saw a picture of you with him." Shit, I hope he's not the guy who hurt her. "Since you asked me to pretend to be your boyfriend, I guess he doesn't live in Chicago, right?"

She shakes her head and the tears she was holding back break free. She turns her head away and wipes them with her fingers.

A few students walking past glance our way, and it's obvious from their expressions they think the tears are my fault. I'm the shithead boyfriend who dumped his girlfriend in the middle of the food court.

That's when I get it. Her boyfriend doesn't live in Chicago, because she doesn't have a boyfriend. Those people were right. She has been dumped, just not by me.

"Shit, I'm sorry, Amber. I didn't realize you guys had broken up."

"We didn't break up." She takes a halting breath, and her next words come out as a pained whisper. "He's dead."

Okay, not what I expected. Without thinking of the consequences, I gather her in my arms and let her cry against my shoulder. Another brick in my wall crumbles at the feel of her in my arms. I tighten my hold and kiss the top of her head. If I'm not careful, I'm going to end up permanently fucked up. But right now, there's nothing I want more than to erase her pain.

Except, I have no idea how to do that. All I'm good at is making girls scream in bed, but right now that skill's pretty useless.

Her cries eventually slow to soft hiccupping, and she sits up. "I'm sorry. I made a mess of your T-shirt."

"I don't care about that. You wanna talk about what happened to your boyfriend?" I don't want to, but I can't leave things the way they are in case she does. I have a feeling I'm the first person here she's told that her boyfriend is dead, that even Jordan doesn't know. She's been holding in her emotions for a long time, not wanting anyone to see her like this. I can relate.

"I'd rather not, thanks." She grabs a tissue from her backpack, blows her nose, and walks to the nearby garbage and tosses the dirty tissue in like it's a basketball.

And that gives me an idea. "Grab your stuff. We're going somewhere."

She glances at me for a second, confused, then packs up her books and notes, and follows me to my car.

The blue sky from earlier has clouded over and it looks like it could storm later on. But for now, it's perfect for what I want to do. I open the car door for her, but she doesn't get in. She chews her lip while eyeing the passenger seat as though it's planning to attack her.

"I promise, Kitten, I'm not going to hurt you. We don't have to go if you don't want to, but I think you'll enjoy where we're going."

"Where's that?" She peers at the sky, a slight tremor in her voice.

I interlace her fingers with mine. "It's a surprise."

Her hand starts shaking. "I don't like surprises." Her voice is so small, I get the feeling it's not me she's telling this to, but I can't tell if she's talking to herself or if, in her mind, she's telling it to someone else.

"Amber, we don't have to do this if you don't want to. I'm just taking you to my old neighborhood. If you want, you can ask Jordan to come with us." I don't want Jordan along, but if that makes Amber feel safer, I'm willing to do whatever's necessary.

Amber looks at me, really looks at me, her gaze searching for signs that I'm lying. "I'm fine. I'll come with you." Her other hand tightens around her backpack strap. If I make the wrong move, I wouldn't be surprised if she nails me in the face with the bag.

She climbs into the car but doesn't say anything else as I drive. Instead, she stares out the passenger window at the sky. I can tell she's not fully with me. Maybe she's thinking about her old boyfriend. I don't have the right to feel jealous, but I can't help it and that scares me. And what's there to feel jealous about? Her boyfriend, who I guess she loved, is dead. It's only natural she'd be thinking about him. I think about Ryan all the time, too.

I drive through the city to my old neighborhood. It's nothing like where Amber would have grown up. Here, neighbors party until sunrise and drug busts are the norm. I'm betting Amber's never been harassed by a cop and gangs don't hang out near her home.

I glance at her, gauging her reaction, but her attention is still focused on the world outside her window.

"What is this place?" she asks as I park the car in the small gravel parking lot behind the youth center.

"It's where I spent most of my time growing up. It's where I learned to play basketball."

Her head twists around, and for the first time since I mentioned her old boyfriend's name, her face lights up. "You play?"

I grin at her reaction. "It's what kept me out of trouble." Most of the time.

We enter the old brick building, and I instantly know something's wrong. At this time of day, kids are usually playing basketball or hanging out in the rec room. Instead, it's quiet.

Fear at what that could mean sucker punches me in the gut.

"Hey, Marcus," Dave says from the doorway of his office, a basketball in each hand. He tosses one at me and nods at Amber. "Miss." I've never brought a girl here before, so I can only imagine what he's thinking.

"Dave, this is Amber. She's a friend of mine from school." I turn to her. "Dave's the youth leader here. But don't let his hardcore Marine ass fool you. He's a marshmallow where the ladies are concerned." He snorts. The only lady in his life is his wife. His world, when he's not here, revolves around her. "So where is everyone?"

"There was another gang shooting the other day. Funeral's

today."

My heart stops beating for what feels like an entire minute, and I reach for Amber's hand. As if sensing what I need, she squeezes it. "Who?" And why didn't I know this?

"Tyler Whitman."

As wrong as it is, especially since Tyler was only twelve, I feel myself relax. At least it wasn't Alejandro. "I don't get it. Tyler wasn't in a gang, was he?"

Dave shakes his head, suddenly looking a lot older than his forty-five years. "No, he wasn't. He was an innocent in the wrong place at the wrong time."

"Has Alejandro been around much lately?" Or Carlos? Guilt surges through me. I haven't been around much, not like I used to. I'm too busy with school.

"Not in a few days. But I heard his mother's been getting on his case about his grades. If he doesn't pull them up soon, she won't let him join the school basketball team."

And that will kill him. "I'll talk to him."

"That'd be great, Marcus. He idolizes you. He'll listen to what you say." Dave doesn't say what he's thinking, but I can read it in his eyes. He's hoping I can talk some sense into Alejandro so that he doesn't join Carlos's gang.

"I better get back to work here." Dave smiles at Amber.

"Sounds good. We're just shooting some hoops." I squeeze her hand, letting her know this is the real reason we're here.

"Oh," she says.

I turn in time to see excitement fade to disappointment on her face.

"I don't have anything to wear."

Dave looks her over, but not in a douchebag way. "That's not a problem. I have spare gym clothes that should fit you."

Her eyes light up, confirming I did the right thing bringing her here. Confirming what I already suspected: I want to be the one to bring that smile to her face—even if it's just as a fake boyfriend.

17

AMBER

D ave leads us to a small equipment room in the back of the old building. The room is organized to military precision, contrasting with the water-stained ceiling and small cracks in the upper corner of one wall. He points to the box of jumbled clothes on a metal shelving unit against the far wall and leaves us alone to search through it.

I pull out a pair of promising-looking sweat pants that end up being way too big, even if I cinch the drawstring as tight as it will go. Marcus and I hunt through the entire box before he finds a pair of running shorts that might fit and holds them out to me.

I swallow hard. There's no way I can wear them. "Is there anything else?" I ask even though the odds of a pair of sweat pants mysteriously appearing in the box are pretty much zero.

He shakes his head. "No, this is it."

I take the offending garment and stare at it, not that staring will make a difference. It's not going to magically transform the shorts into I what need.

A voice in my head asks what difference it makes if Marcus sees my legs. Is he really going to change his mind about playing with

94

me because of the scars? Is he going to refuse to tutor me because they gross him out? I doubt it.

I hesitantly take the shorts from him and grab the T-shirt I found earlier. He's seen the scars on my wrists, so I don't have to hide them from him. He hasn't seen the forget-me-not tattoo, but I can't imagine he'll ask about it. He knows Trent's dead.

"You can change in the locker room." He points in the opposite direction from where we came in. "When you're ready, go down the hall. I'll meet you outside."

He walks me to the locker room even though he just told me where to find it. I push the door open and enter.

The place isn't very big. Just large enough for a dozen or so small lockers, a changing cubicle, a shower stall, and that's all. Even though no one's here, I carry the gym clothes into the curtained-off cubicle and close the curtain.

I shut my eyes. No one has seen the scars before today, other than the hospital staff and my mom. Even after the skin grafts healed, I didn't want anyone seeing my legs.

The thought of Marcus seeing them leaves me feeling naked and raw. I want to run. I want to hide. I want to keep him from seeing my scars, both inside and out.

But I can't do that. Because deep down I know I'm stronger than that, and it doesn't matter what Marcus thinks. It's not like there'll ever be a "him and me." At least not beyond our tutoring arrangement.

I change out of my clothes, pull on the shorts and T-shirt, and go outside through the exit Marcus told me to use. He's not hard to find, and it looks like I'm not the only one who changed out of street clothes. He's wearing long basketball shorts and a Chicago Bulls jersey.

And he's not alone. He's playing two-on-one with two dark-haired boys who could be fourteen or fifteen.

"Who was the nineteen ninety-four All-Star MVP?" the taller boy shouts.

Without missing a beat, Marcus answers, "Scottie Pippen," and takes a three-point shot. The ball makes a perfect arc in the air and swooshes through the net. The boys groan. Marcus turns toward the building and catches sight of me.

I want to run back inside and change into my clothes, but the opportunity vanishes as Marcus approaches, and all I can do is turn to stone. The two boys pivot to see where he's going.

Marcus's gaze is locked on my face. He doesn't see my scarred leg. I'm not so lucky with the boys. The shorter one asks, "What happened to your leg?" But he doesn't say it with disgust in his voice, more like curiosity and awe.

His friend shoves him in the arm. "*¡Meirda!* Didn't your *mamá* teach you any manners?"

Marcus's gaze drops to my leg, and he frowns as if he's trying to figure out how I ended up with several hand-sized patches of scar tissue on my right thigh and calf. The scars are smooth, but the color doesn't match the rest of my leg. They're paler, making me resemble a patched quilt. But the burns would have been worse without all the skin grafts.

"It's okay," I say to the boys. "I was trapped in a burning building, and the ceiling caved in on me."

"Cool." The short boy's tone is matter-of-fact.

"How did you get out?" the taller one inquires.

I fight against the memory. I don't want to go there. "I just did. That's all." The words are shaky, but it doesn't seem as though either of them notice. I turn to Marcus and stare at his chest instead of his face. "So, are we playing ball, or what?"

"Playing ball," the boys chorus.

"Okay," Marcus says. "By the way, Amber, this is Alejandro"—he points to the taller boy—"and Juan."

Juan looks me over, visibly impressed by what he sees. I have to work hard to keep from rolling my eyes. They glance at me, then Marcus. Juan says something to Alejandro in Spanish and they high-five. They've written me off and figure I'll mess up Marcus's perfect game.

Grinning on the inside, I take my place. Alejandro passes the ball to Juan. Marcus blocks the pass, dribbles past Alejandro, but instead of taking the shot, he passes it to me. I line it up and purposely miss. The boys whoop and holler and high-five again.

"Maybe you should let Marcus give you some pointers," Alejandro says. "He's an awesome coach."

I pretend to think about it. "Can you show me how to do a lay-up properly? I was never good at those."

"Okay." Marcus holds out his hands, ready to receive the pass, and Juan sends the ball to him. Marcus bounces it twice and explains the steps to a perfect lay-up before showing me how to do it full speed.

All I can do is admire his technique and the way his body effortlessly executes the move. I nod and ask him to show me again. Not that he needs to. I love watching his muscles and limbs flex and contract in the beautifully orchestrated move.

Marcus performs another perfect lay-up and hands me the ball. "You think you got it?"

"I think so." I bounce the ball twice and slowly perform the move, as if mentally talking myself through it. The lay-up is perfect like his. "Wow, you really are a great coach. Can I try again?"

"Sure, go ahead."

Alejandro passes me the ball from where it rolled near the fence. But instead of setting up at the line where Marcus showed me how to do the move, I dribble the ball into position on the other side of the hoop and perform another perfect lay-up, this time at full speed.

The boys' mouths flop open and I grin. "Oops! Did I forget to mention I was voted MVP during my junior year of high school?" I ask with feigned innocence.

Marcus laughs loudly. The boys appear notably impressed.

"I'm playing with Amber," Juan says, which surprises me. It's not like Marcus is a slouch on the court.

"Which referee made the controversial foul call against the Bulls in game five of the playoffs during the nineteen-ninety-three to ninety-four season?" Alejandro asks.

Juan's face is blank. Marcus looks thoughtful for a moment. "Hue Hollins." He passes Alejandro the ball.

Alejandro bounces it. "Correct." Without warning, he dribbles it four steps and passes it to Marcus. I intercept it and send it to Juan. He catches it and goes for the jump shot. The ball bounces off the hoop and lands in Marcus's hands.

For the next thirty minutes, we play a hard game of two-on-two. Alejandro is a stronger player than Juan, who's still pretty good. It's easy to see that Alejandro has the potential to go far in the game— if he makes the necessary grades.

"What three players from the same team were on the All-Defensive First Team?" Marcus asks. "Their team was the only one in history to achieve this."

I know the answer but let Alejandro reply. This is part of the game for them, and it's fun watching them test each other's knowledge. The game is similar to one Emma, Trent, and I used to play when we were younger. I get the feeling these guys, especially Alejandro, mean a lot to Marcus...and it's sweet. Just like it's sweet that Marcus tells me those lame math jokes just to make me laugh while he helps me with my homework.

"Jordan, Pippen, and Rodman." Alejandro replies without hesitation.

Juan grins. "Too bad that wasn't on your math test, Alejandro. Then your *mamá* wouldn't have grounded you."

Alejandro throws him a dark look. Juan chuckles and attempts a basket. The ball bounces off the backboard and ricochets in the opposite direction to where we're standing. Alejandro cracks up while Juan jogs over to retrieve it.

"Yo bro," Marcus says. "You need help with your math?"

Alejandro starts to shake his head but changes his mind and nods.

"If you want, I can come over after work tomorrow and help you."

Alejandro nods, eyes averted. I can relate to how he feels. I never thought I'd need a tutor; I mean, other than Trent. But our tutoring sessions were more about us making out than his helping me with math, which he did anyway. He knew if I didn't do well on my tests, I'd be grounded and there would be no make-out sessions.

"He's a great math tutor," I tell Alejandro as Juan returns with the ball. And I mean it. "He's been helping me."

"I could help you with your math." Juan's tone is suggestive, and this time I don't contain the urge to roll my eyes.

"So how come you don't play for UIC?" Marcus asks, changing the subject.

I take the ball from Juan and bounce it near a crack in the concrete, watching the ball instead of Marcus. It still hurts that I'm unable to pursue my dream of playing for a woman's collegiate team. That, and being a vet were my lifelong goals. But Paul took one of them away and has put the other in jeopardy.

"I couldn't play during my senior year 'cause I was recovering from the burns." And I couldn't face my former teammates. Trent was the star player for the boys' team. The player who could have taken them to the playoffs last year. He never had the chance.

I blink back the tears. "How come you aren't playing with the men's team?" Marcus is good enough that he could if he wanted to.

I bounce-pass him the ball. He catches it and turns it in his hands, studying it, the corners of his mouth twisted down. "I had to work, so I couldn't play varsity."

I sense there's more to it, but I don't have a chance to ask. Lightning lights up the sky and the crackle of air molecules sets me on edge.

I stand by the car and stare at my flat tire. "Hurry up, Michael," I mutter to myself. Headlights approach, then pull off to the side of the road. The car parks behind mine. It's too dark to make out the driver. I just know it isn't Michael.

The driver's door opens, and someone steps out. I can't see who it is with the headlights glaring in my face.

Lightning streaks across the sky and I startle at the crackle of electricity. I hate storms. My father walked out on us during a storm. Trent died during a storm. My throat closes in on itself at that memory, still fresh, like his grave.

"Hi, Amber," a familiar voice says. I can't place it, but something about it sets off alarms.

18

MARCUS

One minute, I'm talking to Amber. The next, she's curled up on the ground, arms around her knees, muttering to herself and crying. It's like she's not even here. Her mind is somewhere else.

I crouch next to her. "Amber?"

"What's wrong with her?" Juan asks.

I touch her arm. She flinches but other than that, it's like she doesn't even know I'm here. *Shit.* "Kitten, tell me what's wrong." I don't know how to help her or what to do. She seems so lost and helpless.

"Go get Dave," I tell the guys.

They don't hesitate. They both run inside, leaving me alone with Amber.

Another flash of lightning brightens the sky and thunder rumbles, loud and deep, not long after. Amber screams and buries her head in her arms.

I reach out to touch her but snatch my hand back. I rub the nape of my neck instead. What the hell is wrong with her? I want to hold her, comfort her, but after how she reacted last time, I'm not sure that's a good idea.

The youth center door opens. Dave spots us and rushes over, blanket in hand. He drops next to us and examines Amber without touching her. "What happened?"

"I don't know. She was talking to me; then she collapsed to the ground and started doing this. I don't even know what she's talking about."

Dave is silent at first, nodding as if answering his own question. The one he never voiced out loud. "Was there anythin' else that happened before she collapsed? A loud noise perhaps?"

"There was thunder and lightning."

Dave scoots closer. "Amber, I want to help you. Is that okay?"

She doesn't respond.

"I'm not going to hurt you," he explains in a slow, calming voice.

Without warning, the sky opens up and pea-sized ice pellets pound us with their stinging touch. I can't tell if Amber even notices. She doesn't flinch when the hail hammers her skin.

"We have to get her inside," Dave yells over the noise. Her T-shirt, shorts, hair are plastered to her skin, and she shivers uncontrollably. Dave wraps the blanket around her shoulders, shielding her, then scoops her in his arms and carries her to the building, her head on his shoulders. The entire time, he tells her that she's safe, no one is going to hurt her, and that I'm here. I'm not sure if the last one matters to her, but I have a feeling the first two are important. Between what happened with the guy at the party and her wanting me to fake being her boyfriend at Nightshade, I sense it's been a while since she's felt safe.

And more than anything, that makes me want to be the one to help her feel safe again.

A pinched feeling in my gut reminds me that I don't have a strong track record when it comes to keeping the people I love safe. So far, I've failed every time. Me trying to keep Amber safe is nothing but a joke. The kind with a disastrous outcome.

Once inside, Dave carries her to the common area and settles her on a tired-looking couch. He motions with his hand for me to sit next to her, and an overwhelming desire awakens inside me to cradle her against my body and make her feel safe, or at least attempt to shelter her from her demons.

Even with the blanket, she's shivering. I sit next to her, and praying I won't upset her again with my touch, pull her against me. She stiffens at first, but just when I think she's going to pull away, she relaxes and cuddles closer. I kiss her on the head and hold her tighter.

I've never held a girl like this until now. Never wanted to. I've only wanted one thing from them, and that's all I've ever given of myself.

Dave crouches in front of her. "Amber, do you remember what happened?"

She shakes her head and glances around the room as if she doesn't remember how she got here. I almost expect her to pull away from me now that she's aware I'm holding her, but she doesn't. More than anything, she seems too exhausted to move more.

"Have you ever been diagnosed with post-traumatic stress disorder?"

"No," she says, voice weak.

"How do you get it?" I've heard of it before, but that's about it.

"What?" Dave asks. "The diagnosis or the disorder?" He pulls a plastic chair closer and sits. His folded arms rest on his knees.

"The disorder."

"It's the result of being traumatized. So a car accident, combat, being attacked. Any of those can cause it."

Being in a burning building. Amber's scarred leg peers from the opening in the blanket. A scar that could have been a lot worse.

Her boyfriend's dead. Was he in that building, too? That would be enough to traumatize anyone.

"Not everyone who is in a traumatic situation experiences PTSD," Dave explains, "and it's hard to predict who will suffer from it. Some people can experience a horrendous situation and be fine, and someone might witness something on a smaller scale and end up with it."

"Why did you ask if she's been diagnosed with it?"

Amber remains silent. I check to see if she's awake. Her eyelids are drooping. We should leave so I can drive her back to her dorm, but I'm not ready yet. I want to learn more about what she might have.

Dave studies Amber for a long moment and lets out a slow breath. "A few of my friends have been struggling with it since the Gulf War. The way Amber was acting outside reminds me of them." He looks at her again, taking in the dark circles under her closed eyes. Or maybe it's just me who notices them. "How well does she sleep?"

"I don't know, but I know she gets nightmares." I just don't know how frequently.

"She's in college, right?"

I nod.

"How's she doing in her classes?" Obviously Dave thinks Amber and I are closer than is the case. I don't know any of these answers, and that leaves me feeling strangely empty.

"She was failing her math class. That's how I know her. I'm tutoring her."

"What about her other classes?"

I shrug. We've never talked about how she's doing in her other classes. We haven't talked about a lot of things. Before today, what a girl did or didn't do outside the bedroom hasn't been of interest to me. Amber is the first girl I've talked to in which the conversation goes beyond trying to seduce her into my bed. But even so, we've kept away from more personal topics.

"I don't know about her other classes. She's smart. I do know that." But now that Dave has brought it up, I plan to ask her, once she's awake.

"I'm no expert on PTSD, but I do believe she needs to talk to someone about it. If she does have it, it'll continue eating her up inside until it destroys her." The way he says it makes me wonder if the condition has destroyed someone he cares about.

An unexpected *boom* of thunder shakes the building. Amber snuggles closer and mumbles, "Bad things happen in storms."

I gently nudge her shoulder. I feel bad about waking her so we can go, but I don't have a choice. "Kitten, it's time I get you back to the dorm." She doesn't stir, and I'm not sure how I'll get her into her dorm if she's half-passed-out when we get there.

I thank Dave for his help, and after promising to keep him updated on her condition, I carry her to my car and settled her on the passenger seat. Dave hands me her clothes and I drive to my apartment.

Amber wakes up on the way, but when I ask if she wants me to drive her to her dorm or if she wants to come to my place, she mutters "Your place." Her head lolls to the side on the headrest. I'm beginning to think she hasn't slept for at least a week, given how exhausted she seems.

At my building, I carry her into the elevator and make it to my apartment without bumping into anyone. I'd hate to have to explain the sleeping girl in my arms. The girl who looks like she could be drugged.

Chase's sneakers aren't in their usual spot when I enter the apartment. I head for my bedroom and lay Amber on my bed. She stirs, then falls back asleep.

I study her for a moment, the tattoo on her arm. It's not the kind of thing I'd expect to see on her body. She doesn't seem the type to get inked. Especially not with the names of her past boyfriends. But there they are—Trent's name, along with the name of another guy.

I trace my finger over the tattoo, as if the simple act will bring me answers. All I come up with is a blank. And a girl in my bed who remains a mystery to me. A girl I want to learn more about. A girl I don't want to run from.

A definite first.

AMBER

"**A**m-ber," a singsong voice calls out, echoing around the concrete room. I hold Smoky closer; his warm body against my chilled one is the only thing keeping me alive. The moment I give up, he dies. I love him too much to let that happen, though I'm not sure how much longer I can hold on. My body hurts. My mind hurts. My spirit hurts. I want to let numbness consume me, but the last time I tried that, Paul tortured me a hundred times worse than before.

I barely survived.

"Am-ber." The voice is louder now. I want to block it out, but I can only do that if I put Smoky down, and I don't dare. "Am-ber, I want to make love to you again."

My body starts shaking and it has nothing to do with the cold room. My gaze falls to the bruises from the last time he "made love" and the shaking becomes a violent tremor. Smoky lets out a soft meow and tears cloud my vision, turning him into a blurry gray furball.

"Am-ber." I blink, clearing my vision. I'm back in the room with a thousand mirrors, except this time the mirrors aren't the only things here. In the center of the room is a table covered in various torture devices— straight from the Spanish Inquisition. Just one glance at them and the memories of the last time he "made love" claw their way in.

I scream.

SOMEONE SHAKES ME AND THE NIGHTMARE FADES. "AMBER." UNLIKE the voice in my dreams, this one's filled with concern, not cruelty. "It's okay, Kitten," Marcus whispers. "You're safe."

I open my eyes. Marcus is leaning over me, fully clothed, on the queen-sized bed. The only light comes from the streetlight leaking through the blinds. Like in my dream, I begin shaking uncontrollably.

"I'm not gonna hurt you, Kitten." His words are soft but not soothing enough to erase the nightmare and the memories of the torture now flooding in. "Are you cold?"

I nod, barely holding in a sob as some of the more vivid memories haunt me.

Marcus brushes a strand of hair behind my ear; then his thumb skims from my temple down along the side of my face. His eyes never leave mine. "Do you trust me?"

I nod again, even though I'm not sure if I do. But it doesn't matter. He can't do any worse to me than what has already been done.

Marcus lifts the covers and slides under them to join me. I hadn't realized he had been lying on top of them. He scoots over to me.

His heat wraps around my body and his arm shifts to rest across my stomach. I roll onto my side, so my back is against his hard chest and stomach, and sink into his warmth.

Outside his window, the storm is blowing full force, but for once I feel safe.

I vaguely remember Marcus bringing me here and helping me into a T-shirt and pair of sweat pants because the clothes I was wearing had been cold and wet. I also vaguely remember him looking unsure where to put his hands when he helped me change, a concept I'm positive isn't normally so foreign to him. At that point, though, I was too tired to care if he saw me in my bra and underwear. I just wanted to sleep. Still do. I close my eyes and fall asleep with Marcus protecting me.

TRENT NUZZLES MY NECK, HIS LIPS SOFT AGAINST MY SKIN. HIS familiar spicy scent wraps around me and I let out a satisfied sigh.

With my eyes still shut, I turn my head and find his lips. It doesn't take much convincing for him to open up to me, to let me taste him, to want him. He welcomes me in, and my tongue explores his. Dancing. Touching. Stroking.

Feeling.

Trent's calloused fingers slide under my T-shirt and trace their way up, up, up to my breasts. His thumb brushes a nipple and I whimper in his mouth. Desire builds between my legs, begging for the release I know Trent can give me. I shift and press against the thickening length in his jeans. We haven't gone all the way yet, but we've played this game many times.

The hand on my breast moves and drifts to the waistband of my pants. Wetness pools between my legs and dampens my underwear.

Still kissing me, Trent slides his fingers under the waistband of my underwear and continues until he finds the throbbing ache between my legs. As his finger swirls over it, I arch my back, turning my head slightly and breaking our kiss.

"Oh, God. Trent!" I moan.

The finger stills for a fraction of a second, then pulls away. The light flicks on, and it's only then that I realize I was dreaming.

Except, I'm not.

Marcus is staring at me, like he can't believe I'm lying next to him. That makes two of us.

"Fuck!" He scrambles off the bed and shoves his fingers through his hair. "Fuck. Fuck. Fuck." He looks at me one more time and storms out of the room, flinging the door shut behind him. A few seconds later, the shower turns on and water hammers the bathtub.

I pull my knees to my chest and drop my head forward, resting my forehead on my folded arms. The realization of what just happened hits hard, and a sob bubbles up in my chest. I wanted that dream, the one with Trent, to be real. I can't believe I let myself think he was alive.

Tears escape. I do nothing to hold them back.

The bathroom door eventually clicks open, and the soft tread of feet against the carpet approaches. It stops outside the bedroom. I wait for Marcus to return to the room and explain what happened. Comfort me like he did after the flashback. But he doesn't. Instead, I'm met with silence for a minute before the apartment door opens and slams shut.

And I'm left here alone, abandoned.

Too exhausted and shocked and broken to do anything, I crumple onto the bed and cry.

———

SUNLIGHT STREAMS THROUGH THE BLINDS WHEN I FINALLY OPEN MY eyes. Last night's storm is a distant memory, but what happened between Marcus and me isn't.

Without turning to look, I can tell that Marcus never returned to bed. It feels like an invisible hand reaches in and squeezes my heart tight in its grip, even though I don't have the right to feel that way. It's not like we're dating. At least not for real.

And I shouldn't be surprised that he left last night and didn't return. He's a guy. A guy with a reputation of sleeping around. A lot. He didn't get what he wanted from me, so he went somewhere else to get it.

The hand reaches in my chest again and fists once more around my heart. Anger knocks it away. Anger at Marcus for pulling that stunt last night. Anger at myself for not realizing what was going on. Anger at my body for responding that way, for betraying Trent.

Though I can't be too pissed off at my body. Until last night, I never thought it would react that way again after what I went through last spring.

Sighing heavily, I peer at the alarm clock on a pile of books next to the bed. My eyes widen. *Crap.* It's already 8:10 a.m. I still have to get back to my dorm without anyone noticing—especially Jordan—and shower and change before chemistry. In less than an hour. And I have no idea where I am. All I remember is that Marcus drove us to an apartment off campus.

Embarrassment flares through me at the memory of him witnessing my flashback. Now he thinks I'm some crazy girl who can't keep herself together. And maybe he's right.

I spot my jeans, T-shirt, and hoodie draped over the back of Marcus's desk chair and put them on. The bed, desk, and chair are the only furniture in the room. He doesn't even have a bookshelf, other than a single shelf attached to the wall above his bed, with a dozen or so Matchbox cars lined up on it. His textbooks are on his desk and piled in small groupings on the floor. His white walls are empty of photos, posters, or any other artwork. The only picture in his room is the small, framed photo on his desk with him and a man who must be his older brother or another relative.

I open the door and slip out of the room. I find the bathroom and splash cold water on my face. My eyes are red from crying. Nothing I can do about that.

I leave the bathroom, grab my sneakers, and escape out the front door.

I'm tying my shoelaces when a surprised male voice says, "Hi?"

I look up to find Chase gaping at me. My face heats a hundred degrees. Geez, how could I have forgotten Chase and Marcus are roommates? And now Chase thinks I'm just another girl Marcus had sex with. The thought angers me, but it's too late to worry about that now.

"Where's Marcus?" Chase cocks his head to the side, like I'm an alien life-form he can't wait to dismantle to see how I'm assembled.

I make a move for the elevator. "I don't know. He left last night and didn't return." I try to keep the hurt out of my voice. Hurt for what he did, just when I was starting to trust him. Hurt for the way he reacted.

Get a grip, Amber. Marcus owes you nothing. It's a business relationship. Nothing more.

"If you give me a sec," Chase says, "I'll give you a ride."

I'm about to say no, since being in his car after he thinks I had sex with Marcus doesn't exactly appeal to me, but unless I call a cab, I really don't have another way to get back to campus. Not if I want to do so in time for my first class. "Okay."

He disappears into his apartment and returns a moment later with his backpack. "All right, let's go."

"I didn't have sex with him," I blurt, once we're in the car, driving.

Chase smiles at me, but I can't tell if he believes me.

He drops me off at my dorm and I hurry upstairs. I'm approaching my room when Jordan steps out of hers.

"Hey, where were you yesterday? I came by your room several times, but you weren't there."

I don't want to tell her about Marcus, and I definitely don't want to tell her about what happened at the youth center, so I do what I'm getting good at. I lie. "I was in the library studying for our chem exam." My stomach hurts that I can't even be completely honest with my friend, and at the kind of person Paul has turned me into. Trent used to joke he could always tell when I lied, because I was so bad at it. Good thing he can't see me now.

Jordan frowns. "I thought that wasn't till next week."

"It isn't. I wanted to get a jump on it." And it was the first class that popped in my head, mostly because we'll be late for it if I don't hurry.

She releases a heavy puff of air. "Thank God. You ready? You look like you need to hit The Coffee Shack before class. Just how late were you studying last night?"

"I need a quick shower first," I say, not bothering to come up with another lie. "I won't be long." I don't wait for a response. I unlock my room and grab my shower supplies and clean clothes.

Fifteen minutes later my damp hair's pulled in a ponytail, and Jordan and I speed walk to The Student Center to get caffeine.

We're standing in The Coffee Shack line when music starts playing from my phone. Dreading it's my mom, and I'll have to talk to her with everyone listening—something I'd rather not do—I pull my phone from my bag and brace myself for her voice. Why does she always have to phone me in the morning, like I'm part of her to-do list? Interview murdering clients. Check. Cross-examine innocent victim and make it appear as though the crime was her fault. Check. Phone daughter.

Only it's not Mom who called. It's a number I don't recognize. I ignore it.

20

MARCUS

A gust of wind sends red and gold leaves scattering in all directions as students rush to their next class. Up ahead, Kitten's familiar ponytail swings with each jerky movement of her head, as she keeps checking over her shoulder. Even from here, I can see she's tense. If she were an elastic band, she'd snap.

A twisting in my gut stops me short, knowing that it's my fault. I practically assaulted her last night, not realizing who she was. I'd woken up restless and horny beyond belief. It was dark and I was still half-asleep. I thought she was just some random girl I'd gone home with. It wasn't until she moaned Trent's name that I put everything together.

Including that she still cares about him, and I'm nothing more than a business arrangement. Just like we agreed.

Amber either hasn't spotted me or she's avoiding me. I wouldn't be surprised if it's option B. Since she and I are headed in the same direction, I continue to watch her. It's like she expects the bogeyman to jump out at her at any moment. Dave said PTSD could be the result of being attacked. If it's true, that could explain her strange behavior, which goes beyond my asshole mistake.

I send Chase a text that I have to pick up a library book and will meet him in a few.

I'm almost at the library when a familiar, tall blond steps in front of me. I can't place her, which means I've slept with her. Which means she'll expect me to remember her and ask her out.

She wouldn't be the first.

"Hi, Marcus." Blondie smiles with a feigned shyness and runs her hand up the sleeve of my leather jacket. "Sorry 'bout the other night."

"That's okay," I say, having no idea what she's talking about. Which other night?

"I must have had food poisoning."

Oh. Now I remember her. The girl with Amber's picture in her room. Though if she were to quiz me on her name, I'd get an F. I remember her brother's name, but hers is a mystery.

Good thing she doesn't know that.

"I thought maybe we could go for coffee." She lightly squeezes my biceps.

A few weeks ago, I would have jumped at the chance if it meant getting to screw her. But now the idea is a million miles from appealing. That's not to say she isn't hot. She's scorching hot. But she's not Amber.

"Sorry, I'm busy."

"Maybe later." She smiles again, tilting her head to the side. "I'll make it worth your time."

I glance away and catch Amber walking down a different path than the one she was on a few minutes ago. What the heck is she up to? It's like she's wandering aimlessly around campus, yet there's purpose to her movements. She knows exactly where she's going.

"I wouldn't waste your time with her," Blondie whispers, voice cracked like dry timber.

"Why not?"

"Because Amber's boyfriends have a habit of getting murdered." Pain flickers briefly in her eyes and she looks toward Amber.

"That shouldn't be a problem for Marcus, then," Tammara says, startling me. I didn't see her approach. "Amber isn't Marcus's girlfriend. I am."

Even if I *had* said something, neither girl would have heard me. Both are glaring at each other. Shit, I could probably walk to the library before they realize I'm missing.

I take a step back, ready to test that theory.

Even though Blondie is several inches taller than Tammara, Tammara stares her down. Blondie's gaze flicks to me one last time, and she hurries off in the direction I was headed. The library.

Tammara touches my arm in the same spot. She's re-marking her territory, and the thought of that turns my stomach. I'm not hers. Never have been.

I snatch my arm away.

"I'm free for a few hours. Want to go somewhere"—her mouth moves into a slow, sensual smile—"to do what we do best?"

"We're not dating, Tammara," I say, not answering her question. My mind's still spinning over her comment earlier to Blondie—that she's my girlfriend. Apparently my message wasn't clear enough when I told her where things stood between us.

The smile vanishes from her face, but she doesn't seem shocked by my words. Nor does she seem resigned by them.

"I'm sorry, Tammara, but we both want different things." She's more interested in being in the spotlight, and I'm not. I turn on my heels and head in the direction Amber went. With Blondie skulking around the library, that's the last place I want to be.

I keep to the path where I last spotted Kitten. The stream of students making their way to their next class has dried up, so it's easier for me to find her. Except she doesn't want to be found. She's already disappeared.

Knowing Chase is waiting for me, I head for The Student Center. I'm almost there when a little girl, no older than maybe two, runs across the path on her chubby legs. She trips and lands on her hands and knees. Instinct takes over and I rush to her. But before I can get to her, she stands, grins, and toddles into the arms of a woman I hadn't noticed.

A hand lands on my shoulder from behind. "I'm starving," Chase announces.

"What do you know about post-traumatic stress disorder?" I ask as the mother kisses the girl's palms.

Chase shoots me a look. "Yo, dude. I'm an engineering major, not a psych major."

I shrug, having no real answer.

"Why do you wanna know?"

I shrug, again. I don't want to share what I know about Amber, yet. I know if I did, I would never hear the end of it. As it is, he drove her to school this morning, and he knows nothing happened between us—at least not intentionally—which is making him curious about what she is to me. I can see it in his eyes. "No reason."

He doesn't say anything, but I can tell he's not buying it. We've been best friends since second grade. He knows me too well. But he also knows that if I don't want to talk about something, I won't until I'm good and ready.

As we walk into The Student Center, Chase is talking about some of his lame-ass professors, but I don't hear much of what he's saying. My mind keeps replaying Blondie's words: "Amber's boyfriends have a habit of getting murdered."

21

AMBER

I walk at a near jog across campus, taking a different route than Friday. The cool wind whips around me as I check over both shoulders.

Jordan and I always meet for lunch at The Student Center, and even though I have the same class just before then on Mondays, Wednesdays, and Fridays, I never take the same route twice in the same week. Each time I duck out the building from a different exit, which is kind of ridiculous when I think about it. It doesn't matter if I go a different route when I end up at the same location every time. If someone wants to stalk me, they just have to wait for me there.

It doesn't take long to find Jordan after I buy chicken noodle soup and a Diet Coke from my favorite deli, even though I'm not very hungry. The not-very-hungry part is nothing new and has nothing to do with what happened between Marcus and me last night. But I did promise Grandma I would eat more than I have been, even if I don't really want to.

Jordan checks her phone, a frown on her face. She rarely frowns, especially when she's checking her phone. Usually she's grinning and busy responding to her boyfriend.

117

I sit across from her at the table. The loud chatter and laughter and arguments filling the space press in on us.

"Is something wrong?" I ask.

She shrugs. "I don't know. Garrett hasn't called since Friday."

"But he's still texting you, right?" They text each other several hundred times a day. Or at least it seems that way.

She shakes her head.

"Have you called him?"

She nods, eyes damp. "Several times, but I only get his voice mail. What if something bad happened to him?"

I'm not sure what to say. I'm not sure I *can* say anything around the dry lump in my throat at the memory her words dredge up.

"Amber," Michael says, voice thick. He sits next to me on my bed. "Mr. Kincaid called."

My body turns to glass, stiff yet easily broken. Michael never refers to Trent and Emma's dad as Mr. Kincaid. It's always Trent's dad or Emma's dad, depending on the situation.

"There's been an accident."

The wind outside my window howls. An unexpected chill grips me.

"Who?"

Michael looks out the window for an agonizing second. When he turns back to me, his face is pale and he can barely get the words out. "I'm sorry, Amber. Trent's dead."

I blink away the tears so I don't alarm Jordan. "Can you call his parents?"

"But what do I say? If he's fine but he hasn't talked to them either, they're going to freak."

She has a point. "Try phoning him one more time," I say, at a loss.

I wait while she phones Garrett, silently praying he's okay. That there's a good reason for his silence. But it quickly becomes obvious he's still not answering, and she has to leave him a message. Again.

She hangs up, her expression even more miserable than before.

"What if he's moved on, and is avoiding talking to me as a way of saying it's over?"

"Would he do that?"

"I didn't think so, but maybe I'm wrong." She wipes away a tear.

"Have you tried emailing him?"

She shakes her head. "We usually just text or talk on the phone."

"Maybe his phone's broken," I say, grasping for anything to give her hope. I hate seeing this Jordan. The Jordan whose heart is ripping in two.

While she sends Garrett another text, I remove my phone from my backpack and check Marcus's message. I haven't had a chance to respond to it yet, and I'm not sure what to say. All he wrote was:

I'm really sorry, Amber.

I start to type a reply but delete it.

I'm still not sure what to make of what happened last night, both at the youth center and then at his place.

"You know what I want to do?" Jordan sets her phone on the table. I'm too afraid to ask. Who knows what else she has on her bucket list? For all I know, skydiving is next. "Go clubbing again."

I almost sigh with relief that it isn't skydiving. Next to that, dancing doesn't seem so bad, as long as Marcus is fine with assuming the role of my boyfriend again...despite what happened last night.

The seat next to me pulls away from the table. Marcus sits while Chase joins Jordan on the other side.

"Amber and I are going to Nightshade on Saturday," Jordan says, glancing between them. "You two wanna come with us?"

I cringe. Cringe because if Marcus says no, I'm screwed. Cringe because of the memory of last night in his room, when he almost tried to screw me. Cringe because everything is so messed up, all because I made friends with the wrong person last fall.

Chase smiles at her. "I'm in." They turn to Marcus, who nods.

His face is free of emotion, other than a slight twitch of his jaw as his gaze fixes intently on me.

My hand taps my thigh. Bounce. Bounce. Bounce. Marcus reaches under the table and interlaces his fingers with mine.

"I'm sorry I fucked up last night." His voice is soft against my ear. No one else can hear. "I was half-asleep and didn't realize it was you. Otherwise, I never would have done what I did."

Jordan and Chase watch us with growing interest, like we're a new animal exhibit at the zoo. Between Marcus moving his hand to my lap and whispering in my ear, they've failed to notice the odd tension between us.

Ignoring them, Marcus straightens and nods at the container in front of me "So what's for lunch?"

"Chicken noodle soup."

"You have to try their minestrone soup." Jordan takes a bite out of her sandwich and checks her phone again.

"No, thanks. I love chicken noodle soup. It's like an addiction." Grandma used to make it whenever I was sick, though hers was a lot better than this stuff.

"Marcus makes great chicken noodle soup," Chase says.

Marcus gives him a funny look and removes his hand from mine. "I guess if you like chicken noodle soup from a package, then yeah, I make great soup."

Chase chuckles. "Dude, compared to the other things you've tried cooking, I'd say your chicken noodle soup rocks."

"I bet Amber makes great chicken noodle soup," Jordan says, as if Marcus and I are now involved in a great soup cook-off, and she and Chase are our individual cheering squads.

"When's your math test?" Marcus asks me, and I can almost feel the whiplash in my neck from the abrupt change in topic. But considering where the other conversation is headed, I'm not complaining.

I check my watch. My heart rate jumps several notches, racing me to class. I grab my backpack and stand. "I've gotta go. I'll see you later," I tell no one in particular.

Marcus unfolds from his chair. "I'll come with you and give you some last-minute pointers. See you guys later."

"Good luck," Jordan calls out as I walk away. I guess she means good luck with the test and not good luck with Marcus, given she has no idea what happened between us.

True to his word, Marcus gives me a quick review session after he asks how I'm doing in my other courses and I tell him fine. At least I'm still sitting at an A in them.

We arrive with a few minutes to spare, and he pulls me aside. "I'm really sorry about last night, Amber. And I'll understand if you don't want me to tutor you anymore and if you don't want to"—he swallows hard, sending his Adam's apple rocketing up and crashing down—"be around me anymore." Gone is the usual cocky attitude. I've never seen Marcus so uncertain, so vulnerable.

"You honestly had no idea it was me?" I ask quietly as a guy from my class walks past.

"I swear to God. I thought you were...you were..."

"One of your one-night stands?"

He flinches, then nods.

"It's okay. You made a mistake. We both did." He wasn't the only one involved in what happened. I might have *thought* I dreamed of making out with Trent, but it wasn't him I was kissing. It was Marcus. And it wasn't Trent's scent I had noticed. It had been Marcus's. I should have realized that last night.

"You gonna be okay? For the test?"

I nod. He leans in and gently presses his lips against my jaw.

I think about pointing out that we aren't at a club and there's no need for him to kiss me here, but a warmth spreads from the spot and travels throughout my lower limbs. It's been a long time since my body has reacted this way—other than when I was dreaming of getting hot and steamy with Trent last night—and I'm not sure how I feel about it, or how I feel about Marcus blurring the lines of our arrangement. When we played ball, he treated me like a buddy. In bed, I was almost another name on his long list of one-night stands. But now I don't know what he wants, just that he's offering me comfort and I'm somehow accepting it.

His lips move away from my skin. "Just remember to breathe."

Easy for him to say. All I can think about is the tingly sensation easing its way through my body, a repeat of last night.

The last thing I can think about is math.

AMBER

Two days later, my stomach does several backflips as I make my way to my math instructor at the front of the class. With shaky hands, I take the test paper from him but avoid checking the grade.

Once I'm in my seat, I place the test on my desk, facedown, and stare at it for several excruciating seconds. The instructor continues calling out names over the murmur of voices comparing test scores and answers.

Just remember to breathe. I do what Marcus told me to do Monday before I took the test. I take a long slow breath and flip it over. On top of the page, scrawled in red ink, is the mark I never thought I'd come close to achieving in this class: Ninety-three percent.

I did it. I can't believe I did. Though I wouldn't have come close to that if it hadn't been for Marcus.

I send him a text.

Me: 93 on math test!!!

Next, I send Jordan a message.

Me: Want to see movie tonight? Got A on
math test. Need to celebrate.

By the time class finishes an hour later, it feels like I've been sitting here for sixty hours instead of sixty minutes. My grade might have picked up, but my love for the subject hasn't. I pack up my stuff and check my phone. Nothing from Marcus. Jordan says she wants to see *Hearts on Fire*. A romantic comedy. But even knowing that, the combination of words makes it hard to breathe and sends me off-balance.

I weave my way through the crowded hallway. I don't bother using a different exit from the one I used Monday. I need some air. And I need it now.

Once outside, the chilly wind swirling around me, I walk over to a tree in the middle of the grass. Dry leaves crunch underfoot, and I lean against the thick trunk. While I watch the world walk past and regain my equilibrium, I try not to think about Trent or Michael or Paul or the fire.

The guy from my bio class who attacked me at the party walks toward me, looks in my direction, pales, and turns abruptly on the spot. He can't get away from me fast enough. I've seen him a few times in class since that night, but he's made a conscious effort to avoid me.

I text Jordan.

Me: Sounds good.

Right now, a romantic comedy does sound like a good distraction, despite the stupid title.

"Congratulations," a low, sexy voice says in my ear. A shriek tumbles from my mouth.

I whirl around, and the breath I was fighting to get back after class catches in my throat at the sight of Marcus.

"Guess I'm not such a bad tutor after all?" His tone is smug, and I laugh.

"No, I guess not." Still overjoyed at my grade, I give him a quick kiss on the cheek. Since the incident the other day after the flashback at the youth center, the tension between us has faded. It was a mistake. It won't happen again.

He pulls me close so our bodies almost touch. "You're gonna have to do better than that Saturday night, if you're planning to convince guys you're not my cousin."

I laugh again and poke his rock-hard chest with my finger. "That was a thank-you kiss. Remember, I'm paying you to chase guys off, not to get into my pants. If I want to kiss you, I'll do it because I want to, and not because you're using this fake-boyfriend thing to get the same thing from me that you get from all your other girls."

He stares at me for a long moment. "I'll try and remember that."

I almost melt into a puddle at the sound of his rough voice. Like every girl. Not good. Not good at all.

His intense gaze focuses on my eyes and then my lips. His head moves toward mine and he waits. I meet him partway, and he brushes my lips with his, making no demands, letting me know he respects my boundaries. He leans downs and presses his mouth on the sensitive spot below my ear.

The warm, tingling sensation from the other day is back. It spreads through my legs, turning them into cooked spaghetti. I moan softly.

No one can hear me. No one except Marcus. His lips, still against my neck, spread into a grin, and I silently curse my body's reaction.

I try telling my body that it's getting things wrong, that he and I have a business relationship, nothing more. Sure, he seems to enjoy teasing me, but how much of what he's doing is part of our arrangement, and how much is genuine?

An image of Tammara joins the debate in my head and brings it to a crashing end.

I pull away from his arms, even though my body screams for me to stay put. Well, pull away as far as I can with his arms still around me, which isn't far.

"Chase and I are gonna check out a local band tonight. Along for the Ride. They're like a cross between Aerosmith and Pushing Limits. You wanna come? I thought we could celebrate your A."

"Jordan and I have plans to see *Hearts on Fire*," I say, working to keep the disappointment out of my voice. I used to love seeing live bands with my friends, and this one sounds like my kind of music.

"How 'bout Chase and I join you guys? Then you and Jordan can see the band with us. They won't be on till later anyway."

"You do realize the movie's a chick flick, right?" The only guys I could imagine wanting to see it willingly are those hoping to get laid.

He chuckles. "I'm sure Chase and I can handle it."

"Just so we've got it straight, this isn't a date."

"Just so we've got this straight," he replies, "I don't date."

A small part of me pouts at that news. The rest of me is relieved. "Good, we're on the same page."

Marcus leaves after telling me he and Chase will meet us at the dorm. Even though it's not a date, he figured he would drive us to the movie and the bar where the band is playing. I argued against it but in the end I let him win.

I text Jordan to tell her about the change of plans, and that we can cancel on the guys if she wants. I make it clear we're going as friends and it's not a date. Last thing I need is for her to think I'm setting her up with Chase, even though she has a boyfriend.

As I walk back to the dorm, after stopping off at the library, Jordan texts me again.

Jordan: Sounds great

To my surprise, Marcus and Chase are already waiting outside my residence building when I arrive, standing at the bottom of the steps to the main entrance. Chase gives me a goofy grin.

"I just need to change," I tell the guys. "Jordan should be here in a minute."

"There she is," Chase says, glancing over my shoulder.

I turn to see my friend approach with what appears to be a bouquet of flowers wrapped in striped paper.

"You're not gonna believe this." The words rush from her mouth like a speeding train. "Garrett finally called. He's been sick with the flu and forgot to charge his phone. That's why he wasn't responding to my texts and calls." She rips the tape away from the paper and removes a dozen red roses from the wrapping.

I OPEN MY EYES AND TRY TO SHAKE OFF THE EXHAUSTION SMOTHERING ME.

"Am-ber. I have a surprise for you." The voice is soothing, but I know he's trying to lull me into believing everything will be all right. That I'm safe. He always does that before the torture begins.

I close my eyes, desperate for the exhaustion to knock me out again. Anything is better than what he has planned.

A small meow next to me on the bed is a splash of cold water in the face. If I don't do what I'm told, Smoky'll be hurt. It's all a game to Paul. A sadistic game.

The sweet smell of roses taunts me. I must be dreaming. This prison doesn't smell like roses. It usually smells like death waiting eagerly for its turn.

I turn my head toward the smell and crack open my eyelids. The bed is covered with hundreds of red rose petals. It's like a sea of blood.

"Am-ber. It's time."

23

MARCUS

It's like last time. Amber's standing in front of me one moment, gone the next. All that remains is her body. But unlike last time, she doesn't curl into a ball. She stands in a trance, staring at the roses like they're a five-headed monster, all blood drained from her face.

"Amber," Jordan says, gaping at her friend. "What's wrong?"

Amber doesn't answer. She just keeps staring at those goddamn roses.

"Jordan," I say, a little too sharply. She turns to me, her brown color lightening a shade, either because of what's happening to Amber or because of me. I have no idea which. "You need to get those roses away from her. Put them in your room."

She frowns. "B-but I can't leave her. She's my friend."

"I know, but something about those roses is scaring her."

The confusion on her face deepens. "I don't get it."

I don't have time for this. "Jordan," I snap, "just take them upstairs and come right back."

She looks at Chase, who nods even though he's as clueless about what's going on as she is. I will her to do what I said—and now. I need to deal with Amber, but I'm not sure if that's possible as long as she's lost in the roses.

"Okay, I'll be right back." Jordan sprints up the steps and disappears through the main doors.

I return my attention to Amber. "Kitten, it's okay. You're safe." I start to reach out to hold her, but then freeze. What if I make things worse by touching her? *Fuck.* "It's me, Marcus. Can you come back to me? Everything's going to be okay."

She sways unsteadily on her feet. Before I can reach her, she stumbles, smacking her head on the metal railing. I ease her to the ground.

Blood gushes from above her right eye. "You're going to be all right, Kitten." I remove my jacket and slide it under her head, then whip off my T-shirt and press it against the cut. She nods, but I'm not sure if she understands what's going on. Her eyes are a little out of focus.

Chase crouches next to us. "What the hell happened?" His gaze is locked on Amber, but the question's directed at me.

"I'm not sure. Dave Williams thinks she has post-traumatic stress disorder."

I can tell Chase wants to ask more questions but is saving them for later.

"Please don't tell Jordan," Amber whispers. "She doesn't know. I don't want anyone to know."

I have a feeling it's not the PTSD she wants kept secret. It's what led to it that she doesn't want anyone to know. And it goes beyond being trapped in a burning building.

My stomach churns as I think about my brother and the secrets he was forced to keep. That we were both forced to keep.

"It's okay," I say. "Chase and I won't tell anyone if that's what you want."

She gives a small nod and grimaces. Then she smiles. "I must have hit my head harder than I realized. You're half-naked."

I laugh. Until she said it, I'd forgotten about that. I hadn't even noticed the chill October air nipping at my skin. "Like what you see?"

"Apparently I'm not the only one." Her eyes move meaningfully to the side. I turn to see what she's talking about.

Four or five girls are giggling and watching me like I'm a Calvin Klein model in nothing but my boxers. Normally that wouldn't bother me. Normally I'd make the most of the situation and get laid. This time irritation gnaws at me. Amber's hurt, and they don't give a damn.

I turn to Amber and let her last words push away the irritation. At least she likes what she sees. For some reason, her opinion is the only one that matters.

I lift my T-shirt from her wound. It's still bleeding. "You need stitches. Can you stand or should I carry you?"

She smiles softly. "I think I can stand."

She presses her hand on my T-shirt, keeping it in place, and with her free arm, pushes herself up so she's sitting. I slip my arm around her and help her stand. She leans into me, surrounding me with her strawberry scent. I envelop her in my arms while Chase watches, an amused smile on his face, my leather jacket in his hand.

Chase has waited a long time to see me act like this around a girl, which is why he's finding the situation so humorous.

"Oh, God!" Jordan gasps and rushes down the stairs. "Are you hurt?" Unlike the other girls, she doesn't seem to notice I'm half-naked. She's only concerned about her friend. My appreciation for her climbs several notches.

Jordan starts rummaging through her purse. "I've got some Band-Aids in here somewhere."

"It won't be enough," Chase explains. "We need to take her to the hospital. She needs stitches and she could have a concussion."

"Can you drive?" I ask him.

He nods. "I'll meet you out back." He tosses me my jacket after grabbing my keys from the pocket, and he runs toward the parking lot to get my car, leaving Jordan with me and Amber. Though from the glances he's been throwing Jordan, I doubt he'd have complained if she'd joined him. Too bad she has a boyfriend.

A sudden urge to hit her boyfriend, or whoever sent her the roses, slams into me. If it hadn't been for him and his damn roses, Kitten wouldn't be hurt. And I wouldn't be standing here with her pressed against me. Trusting me when I don't deserve her trust. So maybe I should send *him* roses to thank him, instead.

"What happened?" Jordan asks as I slip on my jacket. The girls who were staring at me sigh and walk off.

"I tripped," Amber tells her.

"No, before that."

Eyes wide, Amber looks at me for answers. I'm not sure she even knows what happened. "It was just one of my anxiety attacks."

Her body starts shaking in my arms. She might not remember what just happened, but she does remember a terrifying memory with roses. I tighten my hold on her, and not for the first time, wish I could do more. I did some research the other day on PTSD and found a book that I'm reading. But I'm still a long way from under-standing how to help her, especially since I don't know what happened to her to begin with.

We don't have to wait long for Chase to drive up. I help Amber into the back seat and join her, forcing Jordan to sit up front. Amber closes her eyes and leans her head over, the side window her pillow. Dark half-moons shadow under her eyes, appearing even darker against her pale skin. She's exhausted. *Shit*. How much sleep *has* she been getting lately?

She doesn't seem too comfortable sitting like that. I tap her thigh. She opens her eyes and I gesture at my lap. She hesitates for a heartbeat, then lies down, using my legs as her new pillow. Natu-rally, my junk gets the situation all wrong and jerks to life. *Crap*. I try to remember the look of horror on Amber's face when she real-ized I was the one touching her the other night instead of her dead boyfriend.

But that's not the face I see in my head. It's her reaction to my kiss and my touch, it's her sexy moans, that find their way in.

I bite my lip hard, willing my junk to get the message and stop reacting this way around Amber. It's a huge mistake. Girls like her aren't interested in guys like me. Girls like her deserve so much more than what I can give, beyond a great time in bed—and several other places.

A few minutes later, her breathing is slow and even. My heart twists painfully at how fragile she appears; yet at the same time, she seems oddly at peace.

At the hospital, we sit in the crowded waiting room for Amber's name to be called. She asks Jordan about her boyfriend while Chase and I discuss our robotic engineering project. Around us the injured, the sick, the family members waiting for news of a loved one become a kaleidoscope of emotion.

It feels like forever before Amber goes back to the exam room, with Jordan by her side. Long enough for Jordan and Chase to grab some pizza for us from the cafeteria, as well as chicken noodle soup for Amber and me. Though from the mischievous look on Amber's face, I'm guessing the soup was her idea.

"So, you wanna tell me what's going on with Amber?" Chase asks the moment she disappears through the double doors.

"Like I said, Dave thinks she has post-traumatic stress disorder. Something happened to her, but she won't tell me what."

"No, I don't mean that. If Amber had been any other girl, you'd have let someone else, most likely Jordan, deal with it. We wouldn't be here. The Marcus I know doesn't care about girls, other than for sex." He chuckles. "It's about time you stop treating girls like crap. My sister would be proud."

"I thought you hated Tammara."

"Tammara isn't a girl. She's a vampire out for blood."

I roll my eyes. I've never understood why those two don't like each other. Not that I've bothered to ask.

"I know what you've been doing," Chase says, apparently on a roll.

"What?" I ask, having no idea what he's talking about.

"Just because your mom's a bitch who doesn't know what love is, doesn't mean all girls are like that. Other than Tammara. She's only capable of loving herself."

I frown. "When did you become such a girl?"

"When I got sick of you beating yourself up over something that isn't your fault."

24

AMBER

"How did you injure yourself?" the physician asks while stitching the cut in my forehead. The nurse asked me the same question, so I don't know why he has to, too. Didn't she write it down?

I will him to move faster so I can get out of here. Even though I'm fully dressed, I feel exposed. It wouldn't be so bad if I had tripped like I told the nurse.

"I tripped. All the years of ballet I took as a kid didn't exactly leave me graceful." *Shut up, Amber. Now he's gonna think you're lying.* Which I am, but he doesn't need to know that.

"Do you have a boyfriend?" he inquires casually, which sets off warning bells. It'd be one thing if he were much younger, but he must be a least fifty-five. He's not asking because he wants to ask me out.

"No," I say at the same time Jordan answers, "Yes." The physician glances between us, not sure who to believe.

"Is there something I don't know?" I ask Jordan, who's sitting on a plastic chair next to the examining table.

"You and Marcus? Isn't that what tonight's supposed to be about?"

134

"It's not a date. He wanted to help celebrate my math grade, and he and Chase already had plans to see the band perform." I guess I wasn't clear enough in my text when I told her it wasn't a date. That, or she chose to ignore that part.

The physician looks expectantly at Jordan, waiting for her next volley. She doesn't say anything, but her disappointment is unmistakable. She really thought Marcus and I were going on a date. So what did that make her and Chase? Our chaperones?

"So, there's no boyfriend?" the physician asks.

"That's right," I say.

"Did someone hit you?"

Huh? "No. Like I told the nurse, I felt dizzy and tripped." *Don't say anything, don't say anything, don't say anything,* I silently plead to Jordan.

He glances at Jordan for confirmation.

"I was in my room." Her gaze remains steady on me. "She was already hurt by the time I arrived. But a bunch of witnesses saw what happened."

Bunch? The only thing those girls witnessed was Marcus taking his shirt off. Godzilla could have stomped across campus, and they wouldn't have noticed anything beyond a half-naked Marcus. Not that I can blame them. A slight smile tugs at my lips at the memory of him shirtless.

"Any idea why you were dizzy?"

What is this? Twenty Questions? "No idea, but I'm fine now."

He's silent for another minute or two as he continues stitching my wound. "All right. I'm finished. You'll have a small scar, but nothing too bad." He checks my chart. "Your blood pressure was normal. Do you often get dizzy or faint?"

"No. Usually I'm fine." If you don't count the flashbacks.

He goes over the signs of concussion, which Jordan listens to intently. She then promises wholeheartedly to keep an eye on me over the next few days.

Marcus and Chase are sitting on the hard plastic chairs in the waiting room when Jordan and I emerge from the treatment area. I can't believe they're still here, that they didn't bail to do something more exciting. I can't believe Marcus is watching me as if nothing else exists. And most of all, I can't believe I ruined everyone's plans for tonight.

It's too late to catch the movie, but it's not too late to watch the band perform. "You guys ready to head over to the bar to see the band?" It's the least I can do considering everyone blew their evening sitting around the hospital waiting for me.

All three gape at me as if I've just walked into a glass door. Though from the way my head is aching, that pretty much describes how I feel.

Jordan recovers first. "You can't go anywhere. You're injured, plus Marcus's T-shirt's covered in blood."

"I'm sure the girls at the bar won't mind if he goes shirtless." I know I wouldn't.

Chase laughs.

Marcus leans down and murmurs in my ear, "There's only one girl I would consider going shirtless for." His tone is flirtatious, but his eyes are watchful, as if he's monitoring my reaction. Much like the physician did.

My face heats up. Marcus chuckles.

"Are you positive you want to go?" Jordan asks the question, but I can tell she really wants to see the band, too. Going to bars and watching live bands probably doesn't make it to her parents' list of acceptable activities, along with partying, dancing, and everything else we've done so far.

"Our place is on the way," Marcus says. "I can change first. Are you sure about this?"

I smile. "Positive."

At the guys' apartment, Jordan and I stay in the car with Chase while Marcus goes inside to change. He returns a few minutes later and we drive to the bar, which isn't far away.

The parking lot is busy when we arrive, and at least twenty

people are standing in a line at the door. Instead of joining the end of the line, Marcus walks us directly to the main entrance.

The bouncer, a man who looks like he could play professional football, greets Marcus and Chase with a man hug and waves us in.

Inside, the place is dimly lit and reminds me more of a pub than a nightclub. The dark wood floor, tables, and chairs, along with the dark-green walls, give the place a warm, welcoming feeling. The aroma of french fries and hamburgers might have something to do with that, too.

We make our way to a table large enough for the four of us on the far side of the room, close to the bar. It doesn't take long for our waitress to show up, though from the way she consumes Marcus with her eyes, it's obvious the rest of us don't exist. The girl is in her early twenties, with a skirt that barely covers her butt. Her top isn't much different. Or rather, her tight vest that leaves her pierced navel and ample cleavage exposed.

"Hi, Marcus," she purrs. It doesn't take a genius to figure out they've slept together. It also doesn't take a genius to figure out she's eager for an encore.

I glance away and catch Chase watching the exchange, a smirk on his face. Maybe it wasn't such a good idea to come here after all. I wanted to see the band, not some waitress hitting on Marcus.

Turning around so I don't have to witness their reunion, I pretend to check out the crowd in front of the stage. Pretty much all the girls there are dressed like the waitress. And like the waitress, they've perfected the art of applying their makeup to give them the smoldering looks guys fall for. A skill I've never quite managed to achieve. I wind up resembling a raccoon.

I turn to Jordan, careful not to turn in Marcus's direction. I'm sure by now the waitress is on his lap, tongue down his throat, reminding him what he's missing. Jordan and Chase are busy talking, their heads close together.

Needing to keep preoccupied so I don't stare at Marcus, I head for the women's bathroom.

As I push the door open, a man says, "Look, babe, you need to loosen up."

I don't get to find out why the girl he's talking to needs to loosen up. At either the sound of the door, or because he senses they're no longer alone, the man jerks around. He's tall with hair so short he could almost be bald. A choice no doubt used to heighten his intimidation factor, along with his tattooed arms and studded belt. But that's not what leaves me gaping. Brittany's standing next to him, her back pressed against the sink.

I almost don't recognize her. With the same smoldering eyes as the groupies near the stage, she's wearing a black sleeveless dress that's only slightly longer than the waitress's skirt, and black boots that reach to midthigh. She's seriously hot. And makes me appear downright dowdy in my jeans and long-sleeved T-shirt.

Like she always does when she sees me, Brittany glares at me, though I'm not sure why she's looking at me that way. I'm not the one harassing her.

The guy doesn't say anything. He gives me a withering glance and storms out, leaving Brittany and me alone.

"Are you okay?" I ask.

Her gaze darts to my forehead and the gauze covering the stitches. "Let me guess." Bitterness drips from her words. "You walked into a wall." She doesn't wait for a response. She's out the door before I can even formulate one.

After I finish up in the bathroom, I stride down the dimly lit hallway. A couple of guys are standing to the side, talking. I walk past.

"Hey, beautiful." A hand grabs my arm. "Can we buy you a drink?"

I turn to find the guy smiling at me. It's the kind of smile that gets him what he wants, and he knows it. I shudder and back up into something solid.

"That's okay," Marcus says from behind me. He places his hands on my hips. "I've got her a drink. But thanks anyway." His words may have been polite, but his tone is the opposite. There's no missing the underlying warning.

The guy steps away, hands raised. "Sorry, dude." He leaves.

Marcus interlaces his fingers with mine and leads me to the table. As we walk through the thickening crowd, I scan it for signs of Brittany. I don't see her, but the creep who harassed her is standing with a group of men, drinking and laughing.

At our table, Marcus's hands guide my hips onto his lap. His arms move around my waist and slide me back against his chest. I stiffen for a moment but remind myself it's okay. That this feels... okay. Marcus is doing his job like I hired him to do. Nothing nefarious about that.

The waitress who was all over him a few minutes ago places our drinks in front of us. Unlike before, slight creases line her brow at the sight of me. On Marcus's lap.

"I got you a Diet Coke," Marcus says. "Is that all right?"

I laugh. "What, no rum?" Turns out the reason he got the drinks last time, even though he's underage, was because the male bartender had a thing for him and didn't card him. It also explains why the drink was so strong. The guy hadn't realized it was for me.

I reach for my drink and catch Jordan watching me, grinning. At first I can't figure out what she's grinning about, then it hits me. I'm on Marcus's lap and she's reading too much into it. She doesn't realize he's doing this to save me from guys who are interested in me when the feeling isn't mutual. Which pretty much describes everyone here.

Once we return to the dorm, I'll tell her the truth about the plan. I owe her at least that much.

Marcus and I don't get to talk beyond that. The dim house lights grow darker, and the stage lights burn bright. A few blue spotlights start roaming over the crowd.

The rock band comes on and they're loud. More than loud. But they have to amp up to be heard over the screaming girls in front of the stage.

The first notes of a ballad settle in the room and the girls in the front scream louder than before, if that's even possible. The lead singer closes his eyes and sings as he sways to the music.

The song at first sounds like it's about a guy being in love with a girl, but as I listen to the lyrics, the meaning behind the words change.

You're my fire girl,
My forever and ever girl,
I'll die for you, girl, if you do the same for me.

The song has nothing to do with Paul and me. But every time the singer mentions fire, burning, heat, and death, I'm in that prison, again, waiting to die. The room suddenly feels overly hot and I'm fighting for air.

Unable to take any more, I jump up from Marcus's lap, grab my jacket off the seat next to us, and push my way through the crowd to the main doors and past the bouncer. I have no idea where I'm going. I just know I have to get out of here before I have another flashback. The nightmares are bad enough. I don't want to flash back to the fire.

The cold air dampens my fears, but it's not enough. I run down the street, past a German deli and a store selling antiques, and round the corner. I pause long enough to get my bearings, then run again, breathing heavy. And for the first time in a while, I feel free —and I don't want to stop running.

I duck onto a side street and end up in a neighborhood with older single-level houses stuck between several low-rise apartment buildings. Some of the houses are well maintained, with gardens that would make my grandma proud. Others have kids' toys scattered on the front lawn. Most have lights shining through the curtains of at least one room facing the street.

I stop to turn back. A hand grabs my arm.

I scream and try to pull away.

25

MARCUS

One minute Amber's on my lap, listening to the music. The next, she's pushing past people, her jacket in hand. The bathroom isn't in the direction she escaped, and she isn't getting a drink. Not with her jacket. Something spooked her.

Jordan and Chase are busy watching the stage. Without telling them where I'm going, I shove away from the table and make my way to the main doors. I don't have time to explain. I might already be too late.

Outside, I check the sidewalk. *Fuck.* Which way? I ask Sean, the bouncer, and he points where he remembers seeing her run. Shit, I hope he's right.

I chase after her and catch sight of her running along the sidewalk on the other side of the road. She disappears down a side street.

I follow, unsure if I should call out her name or not. I have no idea why she's running. Calling her name might make things worse.

She's fast, especially since she's wearing sneakers, but I easily catch up with her. As I approach, she pauses. I expect her to turn around at the sound of my boots pounding against the concrete and my labored breath. But she doesn't. She seems lost in her own world.

I grab her arm, which probably isn't the brightest idea, considering the circumstances. She screams and yanks it from my grip.

"Kitten, it's me," I pant.

Her arm muscles relax and she turns around, a faint smile on her face. "I'm sorry. I didn't mean for you to chase after me. I just needed to get out of there for a bit."

She doesn't elaborate and I don't ask her to. Not yet.

I hold out my hand. "C'mon. There's somewhere I want to take you."

"Where?"

"You'll see."

On the way to my car, I text Chase, telling him I'm taking Amber to her dorm. She and I need to talk. We're both keeping secrets. As long as we do that, Amber's not going to get better. She won't beat the PTSD. She'll always be running. She'll always be torn apart by her nightmares. She'll always be scared.

As long as we're not honest with each other, there will always be that invisible barrier keeping what's growing between us—that undeniable connection—from becoming something more, something stronger.

And I realize I do want that something stronger. With Amber.

I park on a small hill overlooking a cemetery and we walk to the lone picnic table. The ground around the table is nothing but a patch of dirt, long since dead and forgotten. In its place are cigarette butts, abandoned Band-Aids and discarded pieces of trash and torn newspaper, scattered on the ground or caught in the small brushes around the area.

Surprisingly, no one's here. Not that I'm complaining. I was hoping we'd be alone. But I know from past experience this is a popular make-out spot with the local high school crowd. And although I'm not averse to the idea of making out with Amber, that's not why we're here.

I sit on the table and pat the spot between my legs. She glances at it for a second, uncertain, then joins me. I envelop her in my arms, breathing in her sweet strawberry scent I love so much. I was never a big fan of strawberries until now.

We don't say anything at first, both trapped in our own thoughts. Eventually, I remove a Matchbox car from my jacket pocket and fidget with it for a moment, before pointing at the cemetery. "My brother's down there." I hug her closer, gaining the strength from her I need to keep talking. "That's why I'm tutoring you. He died a hero, but my mom and stepfather refuse to buy him a gravestone. He deserves better."

Amber strokes my hand with her thumb, gaze fixed ahead. "How did he die?" Her voice holds a slight tremble.

"He was shot."

Amber's head drops forward, her thumb still caressing my hand. Even though she remains quiet, there's a noticeable change in her I can't quite explain.

"My stepfather abused Ryan and me for as long as I can remember." I close my eyes. I'm about to tell her things that not many people know. Things I've never told any of the girls I've been with, including Tammara. But if I want Amber to open up, I'll have to cut a vein and release some blood. It's the only way I can get her to tell me what's going on with her. It's the only way I can help her.

If I can help her.

"Ryan took most of the abuse," I tell her. "I was sixteen when we left home. My mom and stepfather didn't care. They were just happy to get rid of us. But I made the mistake of going back there a few months ago to talk to my mom. She wasn't there, but Frank was. Ryan showed up and found Frank threatening me with a gun." I open my eyes, wanting to focus on Amber and not on the image in my head.

"What happened?" Her voice is so small I can barely hear it.

"Ryan aimed his gun at Frank and when Frank didn't move, my brother shot him. I'm not completely sure why he did that. Maybe the years of abuse pushed him over the edge. He wasn't planning to kill Frank, not that Frank didn't deserve it. Ryan shot him in the leg. Frank shot Ryan in the chest and killed him." I squeeze her a little tighter, to keep myself together. The last thing I want to do is fall apart now. That won't help either of us.

Amber doesn't stiffen or flinch at my touch. The thought of that lightens the weight in my heart a bit. And it makes me want to be with this girl in a way that I never thought would be possible. I want more from her than I have any other girl. I want more than just a one-night stand.

"So, your stepfather's in jail?"

"No. Ryan's death was ruled self-defense, and Frank got off scot-free."

Amber shifts off the table and stands in front of me, eyes shiny. "B-but didn't you tell the police what happened and about the abuse? Surely they wouldn't have let him off after all of that."

I avert my eyes, unable to look at her for the next part. I can't tell her everything. It's not my truth to tell. "Ryan wanted me to keep quiet about what happened. He didn't want anyone to learn the truth. He never did, even when we were kids."

"Why not?"

"He didn't trust the system when we were kids. Neither of us did. We knew a kid in foster care. He got bounced around from one abusive home to the next. Once we were in the system, we'd be separated. The abuse was bad, but at least we had each other." I can feel the corners of my mouth move into a slight smile. Despite the bitter memories, there are some good ones, too. With my brother. "You would have liked Ryan. He really did make the best chicken noodle soup around—at least from a package."

Amber laughs, the sound of it feels like silk across the skin. She cradles my cheek, her fingers cold against my face. "What about your mom? Didn't she try to stop your stepfather from hurting you?"

"It usually happened when she wasn't around." Not that it would have made a difference. She wouldn't have done anything to stop him. She wouldn't have cared. "The world doesn't give a shit what happens to victims, especially kids. It only cares about the people who count."

I glance back at the cemetery. "What happened to Ryan and me is the reason I coach basketball at the youth center. I wanna help kids who don't know where to turn or who to trust. And I wanna help the kids turn their lives around, like my high school math teacher helped me."

Amber appears as though she wants to say something. Instead, she kisses my cheek, and the look in her eyes, the one that says she thinks I'm the sweetest guy around, makes me feel weak. In a good way.

She touches the car in my hand. "This was his, wasn't it?"

I nod and smile at how perceptive she is. "Ryan used to save up all the spare change he found and buy us Matchbox cars. He'd wait until he had enough money and buy one for him and one for me."

"Those are the ones you have in your room?"

"Yes. When we lived at home, we hid them in a box under the bed. We took them with us when we left, but it wasn't until Ryan died that I put them on the bookshelf." I owed it to him.

Amber takes the car out of my hand and inspects it. I can almost feel the sadness filling her, and I have a feeling it has nothing to do with Ryan or me.

I want to say it's her turn. I've shared my secrets with her. Now it's time she tells me who hurt her. I want to say that, but I let the silence blanket us instead.

Amber sits back down next to me, and her body starts to shake. She peers toward the cemetery and her voice cracks when she says, "My brother was murdered, too."

26

AMBER

Marcus gathers me in his arms and kisses me on the temple, his hint to keep going. He's here for me.

Something inside me cracks. And the secrets I've held back for so long, the secrets Jordan doesn't know exist, beg to be told. I've kept them quiet all this time because no one can comprehend how I feel, but listening to Marcus makes me realize that if there's anyone who could understand what I've been through, it's him.

I look at the cemetery. My body shakes at the memories rushing to the surface.

A brief wind rustles the leaves on the ground and a bird squawks from a nearby tree. Not far from us, a small dark shadow stalks low on the ground. A cat, visible in the light of the half-moon. A sign.

"It's a long story." I don't even know where to begin.

His arm hugs me tighter, giving me the strength I need to continue. I can tell he won't judge me for my mistakes. We're both broken. We're both searching for someone who can understand.

"I'm not going anywhere," he says. Even though I know what he means, that I've got all the time in the world to tell my story, I hear

146

something else in those few simple words. He's not going anywhere, no matter what I tell him.

"A year ago, my life seemed…" I was going to say perfect, but that's far from true, what with my father leaving us when I was young, and my mom then struggling with depression and alcoholism for a while. "Everything was good. My GPA was great. My coach told me if my senior year on the team was anything like the previous years, I was bound to be recruited by Chicago, my dream university. And I had an amazing boyfriend. Trent had been my best friend forever, and my boyfriend since our sophomore year." My eyes water at the memory of Trent, whose life was cut short because of my mistakes.

"During the summer before my senior year, I started volunteering at the local animal shelter. It was my dream position. I've wanted to be a vet since I was three. Volunteering at the shelter would look good on my college applications. Mom wanted me to intern at her law firm, but I wasn't interested." My throat closes up as a voice in my head reminds me how different things would have been if I had taken the internship instead. Trent and Michael would be alive, Emma wouldn't be hurting, and Mom wouldn't be so distant.

"I met a guy while working at the shelter. He was twenty-four, but I was only interested in him as a friend. I didn't realize at the time he was twisting everything around in his head. What I considered to be friendly chats, he considered my declarations of undying love. He never said anything about this. He acted like we were just friends. He knew I had a boyfriend." A boyfriend who'd visited me a number of times while I worked, and who'd kissed me passionately in front of Paul.

I pause. Marcus doesn't say anything, but he's waiting for me to continue.

"Things were going well until the fall, when I started receiving strange messages. They were never signed."

"What kind of messages?" Marcus asks.

"Mostly quotes and poems. They weren't about love, at first. They seemed random more than anything. But then the messages became threatening and sexual in nature. My mom reported it to the cops, but there was nothing they could do. There was no way to track down who was sending them, and since he hadn't done anything to physically hurt me, their hands were tied." My heart is pounding so loud at the memories, I'd be surprised if Marcus doesn't hear it hammering against my ribs, trying to escape.

"For several months, I received love letters and hate letters and letters threatening my life. I had trouble sleeping. I was afraid I'd never wake up again, because the stalker would break into my house and kill me in my sleep. When I did finally fall asleep, I wouldn't stay asleep for long because of the nightmares.

"Then it suddenly stopped. I didn't receive any more letters, and the cops figured the stalker had moved away." My voice catches, knowing I've skipped an important event in my nightmare, but for now I focus on what happened to my brother.

"Then one night I was driving home from practice when I got a flat. It was stormy and I didn't know what to do. I called my brother, and he said he'd be right there. He was supposed to be away at college, but he'd come home that weekend, 'cause he had something important to discuss with Mom. Something to do with me, but he didn't tell me what." Guilt at what I unwittingly cost my brother squeezes my heart so hard, I can barely get any oxygen into my lungs. If Michael hadn't come home, he'd still be alive.

"I was waiting for my brother when *he* showed up. I didn't recognize the car, but I recognized the driver. It was Paul, my friend from the animal shelter." I pause, not wanting to relive the next part but at the same time knowing I need to.

I glance at Marcus. It's like he's stopped breathing, already having a good idea what happened next. To Michael. His hand around my waist tightens into a fist, clutching the fabric of my jacket.

"Paul offered to help me, but Michael showed up." A tear drips down my cheek followed by another. "Even then, I didn't realize Paul was the stalker. Michael started to change my tire." A small sob escapes at the memory of what happened next. "Michael didn't even see it coming. Paul shot him three times. In the back."

I press my hands against my eyes, trying to drive out the image, and take a shaky breath, doing my best not to break down into inconsolable sobs. "I didn't know Michael was dead at first. I begged Paul to let me call for help. I'd do anything he wanted, but we had to help my brother first. He knocked me unconscious with the gun and left Michael bleeding. He wasn't found till the next day." He spent the night alone, on the side of the road, with no one realizing he was missing or dead. "My mom was working late to defend a serial bank robber. She stayed at the office all night and didn't know Michael was dead and I had been kidnapped."

I wrap my arms around myself, trying to keep the chill out. With each word I utter, each memory I share, an icy numbness works its way in.

Marcus kisses me again, reminding me I'm safe. It helps a little, but not enough. "Where were you?"

"At Paul's house. Except, he had a prison in the basement. I don't know why he had it, but it was there and I couldn't escape. There were no windows, and the door was impossible to break down." I tried before Paul gave me Smoky. Then I stopped trying.

Marcus brushes his finger lightly against my scarred wrist, his hand shaking. "Did he do this?"

I nod. "While I was unconscious, he handcuffed me to a metal ring embedded in the concrete wall above my head. He kept me like that for several days, till he figured out another way to pacify me. By then, my wrists were a mess from me frantically trying to pull free."

"How long were you his prisoner?"

"Almost three weeks."

Marcus inhales sharply. "You were with that asshole for three fucking weeks! No wonder you have nightmares, and no wonder you freaked out, thinking I was stalking you."

"No one knew where I was or who had kidnapped me. No one suspected Paul." I hate how it sounds like I'm defending the cops. I'm not. They let me down. By the time the firefighter found me, the damage both inside and out was done, leaving me with scars that will never go away.

Marcus drags his hand through his hair. "Shit. How did you escape?"

"Paul planned to kill us both in a murder-suicide. He set the building on fire. Someone driving past saw the flames and called it in. If it hadn't been for that man, I would have died."

"Did the creep die?"

I shake my head. "He's in a psych ward."

"That's it?" Marcus says almost yelling, his body tense. "He should be in jail!"

"It's a prison psych ward. But there's a chance he could get off. The case hasn't gone to trial yet."

Marcus is thoughtful for a moment, though there's no missing the anger still wrapped in his muscles. "The flashback you had today. Was it because of the roses?"

I nod. "I didn't know they would affect me. I guess, until today, I had avoided red roses. They reminded me of one of the times Paul drugged me. While I was passed out, he covered the bed with red rose petals. He thought he was being romantic. It was before... before..." I can't say the rest.

Marcus hooks his fingers on my chin and turns my face to his, forcing me to look at him. "Did he hurt—did he rape you?"

I expect to see disgust in his eyes but it's not there. Tenderness is the only emotion staring back at me.

"Yes." My voice wavers at the word.

Marcus brushes my cheek with his thumb. "Is that why you stiffened when I tried to kiss you at Nightshade? Was he the last guy who kissed you?"

I avert my head and nod.

"Look at me, Kitten." His tone is a gentle caress.

I sigh and my eyes flick up to his warm hazel ones. A cascade of emotions—hope, desire, fear—sweeps through me at their intensity.

"I'm not that asshole, Amber. I'll never hurt you."

I smile, the movement a slight flicker at the corners of my lips. "I know." And I do. "It's been a long time since I've felt safe. It's hard to feel normal when you never feel safe, not even in your dreams....All I want is to forget what happened and feel normal again."

"That's all I've ever wanted. To feel normal."

That's when I get it. All those girls he sleeps with. "You use sex to numb the pain, don't you?" I keep my voice soft, free of accusation.

Marcus drops his hand from my face. His gaze drifts back to the cemetery. "I started having sex when I was fourteen with a girl two years older than me. I meant nothing to her even though I really liked her. But when I had sex with her, it was the only time I felt anything." Something in his voice makes me think he hasn't told me everything, but I don't push it. I've also kept details from him that I'm not ready to admit yet.

"What happened to her?"

He shrugs. "Our relationship only lasted the summer, but I quickly discovered that plenty of girls wanted to have sex with me. I was fine with that." He looks at me. "I was fine with that till I met you. You're the only girl who makes me feel something."

"Me? I haven't had sex with you."

Pain flickers on his face for a brief second. I can tell he's thinking of the night he almost tried to take things that far. "No, but just holding you makes me feel alive. This makes me feel alive." He lowers his lips to mine and lightly kisses my mouth.

His smell, a combination of safety and spice, wraps me in a comforting cocoon. He makes *me* feel alive.

My lips part, and I feel brave enough to run the tip of my tongue along his lower lip. He moans softly, echoing how I feel.

His tongue dances with mine as we deepen the kiss. Exploring. Conquering. Becoming one. My fingers slide along his arm, his shoulder, his neck, and wrap around the silky strands of his hair. I can't get enough of him, and I want this feeling to never end.

His hand traces a path up my back, teasing me, driving me to want more. It settles on the nape of my neck, keeping me close as our kisses intensify. If it weren't for the table we're sitting on, my knees would have buckled and I'd have collapsed to the ground.

All too soon, Marcus pulls away and rests his forehead against mine as we fight to regain our breath.

"What do you say?" he asks, voice low and rough. "You wanna try normal? With me? With none of that fake-boyfriend crap?"

27

AMBER

I wait for Marcus in my car, outside his apartment building. It's midmorning, and the crisp blue sky promises another beautiful day. That should make up for where I have to go.

Marcus exits the building, looking as gorgeous as usual, with his messy black hair, jeans, and leather jacket. My heart skips happily along at the sight of him.

He climbs into the passenger side and lightly presses his lips against mine. So far, I'm enjoying trying to do normal, with him.

Last night, we spent a long time kissing, working on feeling whole. He wanted to spend today with me, but I already had plans to stop by my house, then visit Grandma.

"If you want company, let me know," he'd said after I told him last night where I was going today. After telling me he wanted to try being normal, just him and me.

I'd gaped at him. "You wanna meet my mom?" Marcus doesn't come off as the parent-meeting type.

"Not really. But I do wanna spend the day with you. So I can do this." He'd lowered his mouth to mine and teased my lips with his tongue. It took only a moment before I gave in and welcomed him inside. He didn't drop me off at my dorm until one in the morning.

If only I could go back to what we were doing last night. But since we don't have enough time, I move away from Marcus, smiling, and shift the car out of Park.

"Never thought of you as the type to get a tattoo," he says, a smile in his voice, as I drive away from the building. Usually I'm wearing Trent's hoodie, or a long-sleeved T-shirt, but it didn't seem right to wear it now that I'm with Marcus. That's not to say I've gotten rid of the hoodie. I can't. It's a part of me.

"I'm full of surprises." I glance at the small blue flowers and cursive writing. I don't even want to think about what Mom's reaction will be when she sees it. That's if she even notices it. She stopped noticing a lot about me after Michael died. I was nothing more than a painful reminder of how his life ended.

"So how many tattoos do you have?" I ask. All I've seen is the one on his arm, peeking out from under the sleeve of his T-shirt.

"Just the one."

At the red light, I push up the soft fabric to reveal the entire design. "It's a bird."

"Falcon," Marcus corrects. "I got it after Ryan died. The falcon represents the protector. Ryan did what he could to protect me from our stepfather." His voice holds a note of sadness but also pride. The same way I feel about my brother.

"I got mine to honor my brother's memory, too. His and Trent's. I don't want to ever forget them or what they meant to me." I can feel Marcus's gaze on my tattoo, and I brace myself for the question I know is coming.

"Can I ask you how Trent died?"

I nod and will myself to make it through the story, will the tears away. "We had a fight one night, 'cause I hadn't envisioned our life together like he had. My father left our family when I was six, without ever contacting us again. As much as I trusted Trent not to hurt me like that, I was living day-to-day, afraid to plan too far in advance when it came to a future with him. He thought that meant

I didn't love him. He was hurt and he was angry. He drove away to blow off some steam.

"At first, the police thought the accident was exactly that—an accident. But it wasn't. Paul knew how much I loved Trent. When he kidnapped me, he kept telling me how he had tampered with Trent's brakes and forced him off the road. Paul believed Trent was the one obstacle standing between his and my happiness."

Marcus mutters "Shit" under his breath. "So that's what his sister meant when she told me your boyfriends have a habit of being murdered."

I whip around to face him. Good thing the light's still red. "You know Emma?"

"Not really. She's talked to me a few times, but that's it."

The light turns green, and I push down on the accelerator, wishing he hadn't brought her up. But since we're being honest with each other, I decide to keep nothing from him. "She used to be my best friend. Until Trent died."

"Used to be? What happened?"

"I couldn't talk to her after I found out it was my fault Trent was murdered. I wanted to so badly, but I knew how much she was hurting. Trent meant the world to her. I knew she deserved better than having me as a friend. I was nothing more than a constant reminder of how much she lost because of me."

Marcus frowns. "You didn't kill him. That psychopath did."

"Yes, but if it wasn't for me, he wouldn't have had the need to kill Trent."

"You can't blame yourself, Amber. It wasn't your fault."

I shift in my seat. "How come you only have one tattoo?"

He doesn't answer at first, but I can sense him watching me. " 'Cause I only believe in getting tats that mean something."

I glance over in time to see his frown fade into a one-sided grin.

"Any other tattoos you wanna tell me about?" he asks.

I smile. "Nope. This is it."

In Crossfields, I drive toward the cemetery. Before I head home, I want to visit Trent and Michael first. Marcus has been quiet since we entered the town, since I announced where I want to go. I'm not sure how he feels about me visiting Trent's grave, but that doesn't matter. It's important to me.

I look over to see if Marcus is okay. We spent most of the trip talking and learning more about each other, now that our walls are down. Those little details that neither of us were previously interested in revealing, those details that made us feel more vulnerable, come out as we joke and laugh, and talk about our brothers. It's like the floodgates have opened, now that we've shared our tragedies with each other. We discovered that we both love chocolate ice cream, hate it when people talk during movies, and don't drink much alcohol because family members have struggled with it. And we both love the Chicago Bulls, but that's a given.

Marcus's hands are clenched in his lap. "You need to stop punishing yourself for what happened." His tone is filled with an unexpected tightness. "I've watched you in the gym. Fuck, Amber. You've got to stop doing that to yourself."

I frown. "What exactly am I doing?" And where the hell did this suddenly come from?

"You know what the fuck you're doing."

"No, I don't. Maybe you'd care to enlighten me."

"You're not working out to get fitter or to train for a sport. You're punishing yourself."

I take my eyes off the road long enough to quickly glance at him again. "No, I'm not. Working out hard helps me forget." It's hard to remember when you're gasping for air.

"That's not true," he snaps. "It's obvious you're punishing yourself, and I want you to stop."

"Excuse me. You don't get to tell me what I can do. I got enough of that from Paul, thank you very much." I flip my indicator on and steer into the cemetery parking lot.

Even without looking, I can tell Marcus is glaring at me. "I'm not that asshole, Amber. Don't make me out as if I am."

"That's right, Marcus. Telling me what I can and can't do doesn't make you an asshole at all." I park the car, and not giving him a chance to say anything, storm off toward Trent's final resting spot.

With each step I take, it feels like claws are slashing away at my insides. What the hell just happened back there? Marcus has never acted like this before now. At least not to me.

I find Trent's grave and sit on the damp grass next to it. A bouquet of fresh flowers in a ceramic vase sits against the impressive black marble gravestone. I don't say anything at first. I just try not to break down in tears, for Trent, and for whatever just happened with Marcus.

In my head, a voice taunts me, telling me that maybe, just maybe, Marcus is right. I have been punishing myself for what happened by pushing myself too hard at the gym. But it's so hard not to. I've been doing it for so long. I wouldn't know how to stop.

It takes me a few minutes, but I eventually start talking to Trent, like I used to do when we were growing up. With me lying on my back, pretending we're in his yard, staring up at the stars. Except it's daytime. There are no stars.

I tell him everything about school, about my friends, about my classes. The only things I don't mention are Emma and Marcus. One is too painful to talk about. Though I'm sure if Trent were alive, he would tell me to get over myself and talk to Emma. The other one just doesn't seem right to discuss with my former boyfriend, even if he is no longer with me.

I'm not sure how long I've been here when I finally push myself up. Marcus is sitting on the ground several yards away. He's not looking at me. He's staring at the ground, lost in thought. I can't tell what he's thinking. It could be anything. Our argument. His brother. Life.

I tell Trent that I love him and that I miss him, and that I always will. Then I walk over to join Marcus. "Have you been here long?" My voice sounds worn, tired. Wary.

He shrugs. "Long enough." He unfolds himself from the ground. The uncertain vulnerability from the other day has returned, covering him like a heavy winter coat during summer. He looks away, his gaze going to a nearby gravestone. "I'm not used to having a girlfriend. I'm not used to caring about someone the way I care about you, Kitten. I'm scared of losing you, and it's making me fucking crazy."

I nod, unable to find the right words to tell him that I'm scared of losing him, too. I might not be new to having a boyfriend, but I'm new to feeling this way. And it terrifies me.

Marcus looks back at me. "I wish I could tell you I won't fuck up again, but I can't. I still have no idea what I'm doing. I only know how to make girls happy in bed. I don't know how to do this." He points between us.

"I need to visit my brother before we leave," is all I'm capable of saying. I know I should say something more, but I can't. Not yet.

I do, though, thread my fingers with his and lead him over to where Michael is located. As hard as it was to visit Trent, it's even harder visiting Michael. I didn't see Trent die. I did see Michael's life stolen from him. Tears well up in my throat, threatening to choke away my own life.

As if sensing my turmoil, Marcus pulls me to him and holds me, his arms strong and sure around me. He doesn't say anything. This can't be any easier for him. Michael might not be his brother, but the situation is the same for both of us. We both witnessed our brothers being murdered. Their lives were cut short because of us.

I shift in his arms and kiss him gently on the mouth. "Thank you. Thank you for being here with me. And I promise I'll do better." I don't elaborate on what I'm promising. But it's implied in my words. It goes beyond what I'm doing in the gym.

"Me, too." Marcus kisses me back, the kiss slow and filled with hope and a deep-rooted understanding between us.

It's noon by the time we arrive at my house. I drive up to the metal entrance gate, which is rarely closed. Tall skinny trees skirt the perimeter, separating the property from the road and the neighbors.

I continue along the driveway and park in front of the large Tudor-style house. Emma used to say it looked like a home straight out of a fairy tale. If that's true, my fairy godmother needs to review her job description. She failed me when it came to my happily ever after, something I no longer believe exists. At least not for me.

I can't tell if Mom's home. Usually she's at the office, even on a Saturday, more so since Michael's death.

"You wanna come inside with me or stay in the car?" I unclick my seat belt.

Marcus's mouth slides into a mischievous grin. "And miss the chance to check out your room?"

"You do realize my mom might be home?"

"Don't worry, Kitten. Moms love me." There's no missing the sarcasm. He's thinking about his mom. Just the thought of the life he endured before he started college makes me want to take away his pain.

I cup his cheek with my hand. My gaze drops to his lips. I'm tempted to turn the car around and go back to his apartment, to spend the rest of the day with him there.

Instead, I give him a quick kiss, wanting to get away from here as soon as possible. The memories of Michael and Trent sit heavy in the air, ready to suffocate me. As it is, when we drove here, I took the longer route so I could avoid the place where I had the flat tire. I haven't been there since that night. I don't ever want to go there again.

Marcus and I walk up the path to the house, holding hands. Even though it's fall, and the flowers have long since died, the garden still looks great. A bounty of autumn colors.

"My mom can't even keep a houseplant alive," Marcus says, checking out the meticulous garden. A leaf wouldn't dare be out of place here.

"My mom can't either. The housekeeper and gardener take care of ours."

"You have a housekeeper and gardener?"

I unlock the door and disarm the alarm. The house is silent. Mom's not home. If she were, the stereo or TV would be on.

The familiar zesty smell of lemons greets me. The housekeeper must have been here this morning. The house always smells this way on cleaning day. It's one of the things I miss most. The dorm bathroom never smells like this.

Marcus's gaze sweeps over the grand foyer and the polished floor, which resemble a black-and-white chessboard. When we were kids, Trent, Michael, Emma, and I used to love pretending we were chess pieces.

"My room's upstairs." I point to the spiral stairs in case it's not obvious enough where we need to go. Marcus follows me, his hands resting on my hips.

As we walk up the stairs, his fingers slip under my T-shirt and brush against my stomach. A familiar warmth ignites in my lower body, and I have to focus on each step or else risk stumbling. By the time we make it to my room, I almost forget why I'm here.

"Nice," Marcus says, taking everything in: the basketball trophies from when I was a kid; pictures of me, Trent, and Emma; my black-and-fuchsia bedding that I've had since I was twelve. Trent and I spent many hours curled up on it together, talking when we were younger. Making out when we were a couple. Naturally, Mom knew none of this. She would never have approved of Trent being on my bed.

I turn away from my memories and search through my closet for clothes I haven't worn in a while. The clothes I turned my back on after my life changed, and I decided hiding in jeans and over-sized hoodies was a better idea. If I want to be normal again, it only makes sense that I wear the clothes I used to love. At least the ones I still feel comfortable wearing.

I remove my favorite sweater dresses and skirts, long-sleeved tops, tights, boots, and shoes. A small part of me wants to include my sexier tops, too. The rest of me squelches the idea. That part of me's dead. I don't want people to see my scars. Even Marcus hasn't seen them all.

"What's this?"

I glance over my shoulder to see what he's talking about. In his hands are scraps of light-pink satin. "My prom gown," I whisper.

Deep lines form in Marcus's forehead. "What happened to it?"

"I cut it up prom night. I was supposed to go with Trent. Then he died. I couldn't go. I couldn't face my classmates and pretend everything was all right and that nothing had changed."

Marcus rests his hand on my shoulder and turns me around to face him. I tilt my chin up, hinting at what I need. Remembering the past makes me feel numb. I don't want to feel numb. I want to feel alive.

He lowers his mouth to mine and I let him in, knowing I need his touch more than anything. Knowing this moment, like every moment before it, and every moment after, will help me heal, bit by slow bit.

Our tongues play together, tasting, teasing, chasing away my pain as Marcus walks me in reverse until the bed hits the backs of my thighs.

I sit on the edge of the bed, Marcus's lips still attached to mine. Vertebra by vertebra I lie back, Marcus's body partly covers me. Not once do our mouths break contact, the kisses becoming more intense, more hungry.

My hands thread into his soft hair. I've been kissed plenty of times in the past, but never has it been this hot or made me feel this alive. Trent's kisses were great. But Marcus's kisses go beyond great, to body-melting amazing.

One of Marcus's hands traces down my thigh to behind my

knee. He slides my leg up so it wraps around his hips. His erection presses on the seam of my jeans, taunting the throbbing ache that's rapidly building. A moan slips from my lips, pleading for so much more.

Marcus's mouth moves from mine. "Tell me when to stop. Okay?"

I nod. Right now I don't want him to stop. I just want to focus on him, on us. This is normal. This is what I want.

Marcus's fingers edge along the bottom of my T-shirt and across my exposed skin. They inch their way up my stomach, my ribs, to my breast. I tense at his touch.

"Do you want me to stop?" he asks, voice husky, yet there's a tenderness in his words that I hold on tight to as his spicy scent wraps around me, reminding me I'm safe. Marcus is my safe.

All remaining tension evaporates as molten lava fills every cell, and I melt into the bed, not wanting this feeling to end. "I'm fine," I murmur.

His hand cups my breast, still covered by my bra, and his thumb strokes across the nipple. His intense gaze never leaves mine. I swear I'm going to combust just from the way he's looking at me.

His body rocks against my jeans. The throbbing ache between my legs grows more intense, sending me higher and higher. I'm almost going insane with wanting him. Wanting him more than I ever thought would be possible.

The shattering of glass from downstairs jerks me out of the moment and sends me careening back to earth.

28

MARCUS

My entire body tenses. "Your mom?" I ask, keeping my voice low.

"I don't know," Amber whispers and scrambles off the bed. "It could be the housekeeper."

Shit. Did someone break in while I was seeing how far Amber trusts me? While I was determining where the invisible boundary had been placed after she was raped? I clench my teeth. Anyone could have walked in on us. Including Amber's mom.

"Did you reset the alarm?" I ask.

"I don't remember." Her lips are swollen from my kisses, and it takes everything I have not to press her into the wall and kiss her again. She doesn't realize how tempting she is.

"It's probably just my mom." She drops her arms to her sides, as if each weighs a thousand pounds, and a sudden sadness seeps from her pores. "I'll be right back." She starts walking toward the door.

I grab her arm. "You're not going by yourself. What if it isn't your mom?"

"I have to get Michael's suitcase. I'm just going to his room. It's next to mine."

I let her go and watch her slip into the next room. If anyone comes up the stairs, they'll have to get past me to get to Amber.

I lean against the doorjamb, arms crossed, keeping an eye on the stairs. She returns a few minutes later with a large suitcase, which she fills with her clothes and shoes. I take it from her, and we walk down the stairs, cautious not to make a sound.

A woman's voice floats up from somewhere at the back of the house.

"It's my mom," Amber says, still whispering. At the bottom of the staircase, she indicates for me to stay put and walks in the direction the voice came from.

I stay in place for a few seconds, so she thinks I'm going to listen to her, then stride after her.

Even though I move quietly, she must have either heard me or realized I wasn't planning to stay where she left me. She glances over her shoulder and rolls her eyes, then pushes the door open and steps inside the room.

I follow her into the kitchen. It's bigger than the house I grew up in, and is filled with stainless steel appliances, all shiny and new. At the kitchen island, a woman with the same dark-blond hair as Amber pours whiskey into a glass. From the way her hand's shaking, it's obvious this isn't her first or second drink of the morning. I recognize the look all too well from Frank.

"When did you start drinking again?" Amber doesn't sound upset, just defeated.

"I don't have a problem, if that's what you're insinuating," the woman says.

"You're upset about what happened to Michael. I get it. But drinking isn't going to bring him back."

"You think I don't know that?" the woman snaps. She takes a step toward Amber, narrowly missing a shard of glass with her stiletto shoe. Whereas I would have held my ground if it were my mom, unless she had a gun aimed at me, Amber retreats a step. "I have to get to work." With the glass still in her hand, her mom walks unsteadily past, knocking into Amber on her way out.

"Mom..." Amber slumps against the kitchen counter.

Unable to bear seeing her in such pain, I pull her to me and hold her securely in my arms.

She rests her head on my shoulder. "I don't know what to do. I don't know how to help her." Sighing, she bends down and picks up the shards of glass.

Remembering doing the same on more than one occasion with Ryan, I help clean up the mess. She doesn't speak the entire time. She doesn't need this. I can tell she blames herself for what happened like she does for everything else.

"It's not your fault, Amber. She's an adult. If she's drinking, it's her choice. You had nothing to do with that."

Amber doesn't appear too convinced.

Once we're finished, we drive to her grandmother's house. The place is much smaller than Amber's home. A lot friendlier, too. It doesn't look like it stepped out of an issue of some fancy-ass house-decorating magazine. Unless high class now includes a village of gnomes sitting on the lawn and in the flower beds.

Amber parks her car in the driveway and smiles. It doesn't take much to realize she has happy memories here. She's lucky. I've never met my grandparents. I'm not even sure they're alive.

Once we're out of the car, she takes my hand, and we walk along the cobblestone path to the house. The garden isn't meticulous like at her home, but I can tell it's cared for by someone who isn't paid to do it.

"My grandma loves to garden," Amber says, and for a second I wonder if I said my thoughts out loud. Pride beams on her face.

She opens the front door. My palms grow clammy, but she doesn't seem to notice or care. She just keeps smiling like she's finally home.

"Smoky. Grandma. I'm here." She steps into the house, and I follow.

The place isn't much bigger than my mom's home, but instead of cheap-looking furniture from garage sales, the furniture is made of real wood, painted in white, yellows, and blues. Everything about the place makes me think of sunshine and spring. I just hope her grandmother is as welcoming as her furniture.

A chubby gray cat limps around the corner and rubs against Amber's legs, purring.

"There's my baby." Grinning, Amber scoops up the cat. She cuddles it in her arms and nestles her face in its fur. A streak of jealousy shoots through me. Right now, I'd do anything to be that goddamn cat.

I've always thought cats were aloof, believing they're better than humans. But this cat is nothing like that. You'd think it worships Amber the way it responds to her.

"He misses you." A woman, who I can only guess to be Amber's grandmother, joins us, warmth radiating from her face. Until she sees the stitches above Amber's eyebrow. Amber has bangs that sweep to one side, but she didn't bother to sweep them to the side with the cut.

"What on earth happened?" The woman's cutting gaze jumps from Amber to me, lingers on me before jumping back to Amber.

"It's nothing. I had a flashback and hit my head."

Amber's grandmother frowns. "You're still having them?"

"It's the first one I've had in a while. It was no big deal," Amber hastily adds.

"What about the nightmares?"

"Not anymore."

"Is that so? And you're still going to therapy?"

Amber nods. I bet even the cat can tell she's lying.

Her grandmother, who looks nothing like I expected in jeans, a Rolling Stones T-shirt, and white chin-length hair, returns her attention to me. "Hi, I'm Kathryn. You must be Marcus."

"Yes, ma'am."

The earlier warmth returns to her face, and she smiles. "Why don't we all go into the living room? I have a feeling Amber and Smoky want to catch up. Would you two like some lemonade?"

We both say yes, and I follow Amber while Smoky butts his head against her chin.

"He sure likes you," I say.

"He's the only reason I survived Paul." At what is no doubt a confused expression on my face, she continues, "With Trent dead and after I watched Michael shot to death"—she squeezes Smoky, but the cat doesn't seem to mind—"I lost all will to live when Paul kidnapped me. He punished me, but it didn't change anything. I wanted to die." Her voice cracks at the last word and she sits on the couch.

I sit next to her, wishing more than anything I could hold her close and take away her pain. The only thing stopping me is the cat. It's eyeing me as though it'd be willing to scratch my eyes out to protect Amber. And I can't say I blame it. I'd do the same.

"Because I worked with Paul at the animal shelter, he knew my kryptonite. He brought me Smoky, who was just a defenseless kitten, and punished him in front of me. I was already dying inside, but seeing him abuse Smoky was the worst form of punishment he'd come up with yet." The tortured expression on her face warns me I only know a fraction of what she endured. I want to ask her, but not now, not with her grandmother in the recliner, watching us.

"I did what Paul wanted without complaint after that and did everything I could to keep both me and Smoky alive. I knew once I died, Paul would kill him."

My opinion of the cat skyrockets. I reach out and scratch it behind the ears. It leans into my hand and for now we have a truce, a shared understanding that Amber means everything to both of us. Neither of us is willing to hurt her. Only, Smoky has an advantage over me. He saved her.

"The DA called yesterday," Kathryn tells her. "They had the competency hearing last week and Paul Carlson was found fit to stand trial. The court case is scheduled for the beginning of next year."

Amber's gaze drops to Smoky. Biting her lip, she gives a small nod. She appears more fragile than usual. I put my hand on her leg.

"It's going to be okay, sweetheart," Kathryn says. "You're strong. Like a lotus flower. What happened to you made you stronger."

"But everyone's going to hear everything that happened to me." Amber's voice is frantic. She avoids glancing at me or her grandmother, further confirming what I suspect: she's been holding things back from me, and maybe even her grandmother. "I know how defense lawyers work. They'll try to destroy me."

"Your mother will help you prepare."

"Every time Mom looks at me, she just gets worse. When she looks at me, she remembers Michael is gone and that it's my fault." Unshed tears strain her voice.

Kathryn closes her eyes, but not before I see the pain in them. It's gone when she reopens them a second later. "That's not true." She doesn't sound too convinced herself.

"Did you know she's drinking again?"

Kathryn nods.

"And that she's dealing with depression again?"

Her grandmother's head drops forward and she nods again. "I've tried to get her to see someone, but you know how she is."

Amber scoots off the couch with Smoky still in her arms. "I need to go to the bathroom."

I have a feeling she doesn't. She wants to be alone. I stare at her retreating back as she walks away, trying to figure out what I'm supposed to do.

When I look at Kathryn, she's eyeing me in the same way Smoky had before our truce.

"Amber's been through a lot, and the last thing she needs is another guy hurting her. If you're going to be that guy, Marcus, it's best you end things with her now."

29

AMBER

In the bathroom, I slide to the floor, my hands full of Smoky and my cell phone.

"Oh, God," I say to Smoky. "What am I going to do? Mom and Emma will be there. In the courtroom." Listening to things I want neither of them to hear.

Maybe Mom has the right idea about drinking. Right now, I need something stronger than the lemonade Grandma gave Marcus and me.

I text Jordan.

> Me: R we still on for Nightshade tonight?

She replies less than a minute later.

> Jordan: Yes! Will you be back in time?

> Me: Yes. Leaving soon.

I don't move right away. I continue stroking Smoky. If only I could bring him with me. We're both broken. We need each other.

After a few minutes, someone knocks at the door. "Kitten, you okay?"

169

The concern in Marcus's voice tears me apart and leaves me dying deep in the ground. How will he feel about me once he knows the truth?

"I'm coming. Give me a second." I put Smoky down. He meows and paws my lap like he used to when we were scared. "It's gonna be okay," I tell him. "We're safe now. Paul can't hurt us anymore."

I stand and dry the tears from my face with a tissue. My T-shirt's covered in gray fur, but I don't care. I scoop him up again and unlock the door.

"We should go now," I tell Marcus. "Jordan and I still plan to go to Nightshade tonight."

"All right."

There's something off about him. I recognize that look and inwardly groan. "Whatever Grandma said, just ignore it. Okay? She's overly protective. She used to interrogate Trent all the time." Though he turned it into a game. They both did.

Marcus scratches Smoky behind the ear. The furball purrs a little louder.

"Smoky likes you, and he's not easy to please," I say. Maybe he senses Marcus is damaged, too.

After saying bye to Smoky, I tell Grandma that Marcus and I have to leave.

"Has your mom seen your tattoo yet?" she asks.

I shake my head. During my run-in with Mom, I'd been careful to hide it behind my back. The situation had been bad enough as it was, what with her drinking again. I didn't want to make things worse.

Grandma takes hold of my forearm and examines the design. "Well, for the record, I like it." She gives me a hug, and then she hugs Marcus and whispers something in his ear. He pales.

"I'll meet you at the car," I tell him, and wait for him to walk down the path before I shut the door. I turn to Grandma. "Leave him alone. I like him."

"I don't want to see you hurt, sweetie. You've been through enough."

"I know, but he's safe. Neither of us is looking for love."

A frown creases her brow. "What's wrong with love?"

"It's hard to lose someone you love if you don't love anyone."

She turns as pale as Marcus did a few minutes ago, eyes glistening. She throws her arms around me and hugs me hard. "Oh, Amber. Don't let what that sick bastard did to you change who you are. You do that, and he wins. There's nothing wrong with loving someone. Just make sure the person's worthy of your heart when you're ready to give it to him."

"Okay," I say, even though I don't mean it, and pull away. "Just give Marcus a chance. Smoky likes him, and you know how he is about most people."

Grandma chuckles. "I'll give you that."

I hug her once more and join Marcus outside. At the sight of him still looking a little shaken, I wrap my arms around his neck. "Ignore her. I like you and that's all that's important." To prove it, I slide my hand up the back of his head and guide it down to mine. I don't care who sees us or what they think. I just care about erasing what she said from his memory.

I kiss him long and hard, my tongue exploring his mouth, my entire body coming alive. The ache between my legs from earlier returns, pleading for Marcus to take me to the heights we reached in my room. I pull away, knowing I'll have to tell him the truth, but not now. Not here.

I give him a quick kiss on the lips. "We should go." I walk around the car, checking the tires and the rear seat. Once I'm satisfied, I unlock the doors and climb in. If Marcus thinks my behavior's a little odd, he doesn't say anything.

"How come Smoky lives with your grandmother?" Marcus asks after we drive for a few minutes in silence.

"My mom didn't want him anywhere near her. I think she blamed him for what happened even though he had nothing to do with it. He was as much a victim as I was. But because Paul bought him, Mom believes Smoky is just as evil." I shake my head at that. She has no problem defending criminals, yet she can't accept my furry best friend. "When I was rescued, I was clutching him and refused to let him go. I was afraid they would put him down because he was badly injured. They had to sedate me before they could get him away from me. My grandma offered to take him in." At the therapist's suggestion.

"How come you stopped going to therapy?" *And why did you lie to your grandmother?* Is the unspoken question I sense he wants to add.

"I just did, that's all. I didn't find it all that helpful." *Only the weak ask for help, Amber.*

I can tell Marcus wants to press the issue, but I can also tell he's reluctant to do so, knowing I can turn the table on him. I wasn't the one who used sex as a way to dull the pain. That was all him.

I drop Marcus off at his place and return to my dorm, contemplating what to wear tonight. It will be hot at Nightshade, so I want to wear a skirt and tank top, but that isn't possible. Instead, I change into a black fitted top that scoops down in front without showing any cleavage. With my low-rise jeans on, a thin strip of belly peeks out, but not in a way that screams "Hey, look at me!"

The club is packed by the time Jordan and I arrive with the guys. Once we're in, we make our way to the bar through the press of sweaty bodies.

"What do you want?" Marcus asks.

I want something stronger than Diet Coke, but none of us are old enough to order it, and it doesn't appear as though the bartender who was crushing on Marcus last time is working tonight. I don't want to get drunk, not like Mom can get, but I need to dull the edginess that's been growing since Grandma mentioned the court case.

"I wanna dance." I grab Marcus's hand and lead him onto the crowded floor. I manage to find some space. Not that I need much when all I want is to press my body against Marcus and forget about everything else.

I wrap my arms around his neck and sway my body in time to the fast-paced beat. Marcus's hands rest on my hips. We focus on each other. As far as everyone else is concerned, they don't exist.

I'm half-aware of Jordan dancing with Chase. They're close together, but not as close as Chase looks like he wants to be. The way she's moving, her back to him, his hands on her waist, it's all very sensual.

Wanting the same and more, I pivot and press my back to Marcus's chest and grind my body against him as I move to the music.

"You're killing me, Kitten," Marcus growls in my ear. His voice is so sexy, so full of want, an electrifying warmth spreads through my body. I want him. God, how I want him.

A slow song comes on. I turn around and loop my arms around his neck again. Focused on his smoldering hazel eyes, I sway my hips in a seductive dance. The edginess fades, though I don't know if it'll ever truly go away.

I press my lips to his, and he immediately welcomes me in.

We kiss for the entire song, and even for part of the next one, until someone bumps into me, almost knocking me over. That's when we realize the music is no longer a slow song, and head for the bar.

I have no idea how we've lasted this long without a drink. We must have been dancing nonstop for hours. Or at least it feels that way. As we wait to order our drinks, Jordan and Chase join us.

"I don't know about you," Chase says. "But I'm ready to go home and have a real drink."

Considering Marcus and Chase are from a tough neighborhood, I'm surprised they don't have fake IDs. Before I can point that out, a girl carrying a black plastic bucket filled with an assortment of roses approaches.

I turned away to let her know I'm not interested, but she moves in front of me and pulls out a red rose. "A guy wanted me to give this to you. He said you'd know who it's from."

In a daze, I take it from her and stare at her, all words stuck in my throat.

Marcus places his hand on my lower back, steadying me. "What guy?" he snaps.

The girl takes a nervous step back. "I-I don't know."

The harshness in Marcus's voice softens. "Sorry. What did he look like?"

She shrugs. "I don't remember. Do you know how many guys I've talked to tonight?" Given that she's wearing a little black dress that reveals more than it covers, my guess is quite a few.

I scan the area but see no one who seems familiar, or anyone watching for my reaction. It's possible she confused me with someone else, and another girl was supposed to get the rose.

Marcus takes it from my hand and drops it in the bucket. "She's with me."

A smile spreads on her face. "Then maybe you'd like to buy her one."

"She's allergic to them," he deadpans.

I wipe my hands against my jeans. It's not like the rose was from Paul, but I still feel like I have to wipe my hands clean of it. Clean of him. "I need a drink. A strong one."

30

AMBER

I know I'm being ridiculous. Paul had nothing to do with the rose. But I was already hovering near the edge after my run-in with Mom. The rose just pushed me a little closer.

Luckily, Jordan is as eager as the rest of us to go back to the guys' apartment. Once there, she and I make ourselves comfortable on the worn navy couch.

"What's your poison, ladies?" Chase asks.

"Do you have tequila?" Jordan says. "I've always wanted to try body shots."

I laugh. "You do realize what a body shot is, right?"

She starts to nod, then shakes her head.

The guys laugh.

Jordan's gaze jumps to each of us as she tries to figure out why we're laughing.

"Wanna demonstrate, Kitten?" Marcus's lips move into a seductive half smile as his eyes lock on my mouth. I can almost imagine his X-rated thoughts, and they're destroying my self-control, which has pretty much melted away.

"Okay." The word comes out more like a breath than a real word. I've never done a body shot, but Emma used to do them at parties. I know what to expect, which is more than I can say for Jordan.

Chase walks to the tiny kitchen and returns with his hands full, carrying the salt, lime wedges, a couple of shooter glasses, and a bottle of tequila. He places them on the kitchen table, which separates the kitchen from the living room.

Marcus turns on the stereo to a rock station. The music's loud enough to be heard but not loud enough to annoy the neighbors.

Emma did the body shots at parties while lying on a kitchen table, but Marcus suggests standing instead since the table is too small for any of us to lie on.

He takes my hand and runs his tongue slowly along the side of it, teasing me. I almost moan at the erotic sensation of his tongue against my skin. He sprinkles salt on the spot he licked and places the lime in my mouth, fruit side facing him.

Chase hands him the shooter glass filled with tequila.

Marcus lifts my hand to his mouth and traces his tongue across the salt. This time I do moan at the feel of his warm tongue on my now ultrasensitive skin.

He curls his lips around the glass and shoots back the liquid. Eyes blazing, he removes the glass and lowers his mouth to mine, encircling the lime with his lips.

My legs melt under me, barely keeping me upright. Marcus slides his arms around my waist and pulls me close, as if sensing I'm about to become a puddle of hot liquid. He moves his head away, taking the lime with him.

Jordan stands there, mouth open, face flushed, looking like she's ready to fan herself at the steaminess between Marcus and me. Chase is grinning. I have no idea where his thoughts are, but he's obviously amused by either Marcus and me, or Jordan's reaction.

"That's the PG version," I tell her.

"Though the R-rated one's fun too," Chase points out.

Marcus's lime-and-tequila breath, mingling with his usual

intoxicating scent, caresses my cheek. "You're next," he murmurs in my ear. I swallow the moan begging to break free, again. Maybe tonight's exactly what I need.

I run my tongue over his hand, my attention focused on him. I'm vaguely aware of Jordan and Chase shooting back tequila, but without the partner dance Marcus and I are wrapped up in.

I shower a small amount of salt on his hand, take the glass from Chase, then lick, shoot, and kiss my way to happiness. The tequila burns on its way down, but it's worth it. Smiling, I remove the lime wedge from my mouth.

"We should do a toast." Jordan raises her glass. "To fun."

"To not having to get up early tomorrow," Chase says.

"To winning," Marcus adds.

To forgetting, I want to say but go with "To friends" instead.

We tap our glasses together before tossing back the fiery liquid. A slow smile spreads on Jordan's face.

Marcus watches me closely, and for some reason this makes me think of my mom. Although I can't imagine her having tequila shots with friends, did her drinking begin the same way, with her struggling to find a way to dull the pain?

That thought lasts only until the next round, then the only thing occupying my brain is a welcome buzz. At Chase's insistence, we have two more rounds and Jordan starts giggling. A lot.

"Okay, that's enough," Marcus says. "We don't wanna get you two drunk."

Jordan bursts out laughing. "Too late." She grabs my hand. "Time to go home."

Marcus locks his arms around my waist. "Sorry. She's staying with me tonight."

I am?

He drags me back so I'm leaning against his chest. "I'm keeping an eye on you." His words contain more meaning than Jordan and Chase could possibly understand.

Jordan pouts. "So, I'm going home on my own?"

"You can stay in my bed." One corner of Chase's mouth slides up, making him look even more adorable than usual. He raises two fingers. "Scout's honor. I won't try anything."

"Was he a scout?" I whisper to Marcus.

He laughs. "No. But if he says he won't try anything, he won't. She's perfectly safe with him." He leans down and says in a low voice so only I hear him, "And you're perfectly safe with me." At his words, I sink farther into him.

We say goodnight to Jordan and Chase and head to Marcus's room.

Once we're on his bed, still fully clothed, Marcus leans over and rains soft kisses on my lips, jaw, neck. I run my fingertips under the edge of his T-shirt and marvel at the contrast of hard ab muscles and soft skin. Hard and soft. A true reflection of the real Marcus, not the jerk he first came off as.

Craving to feel all of him, I flatten my hands against his stomach, absorbing the heat, and feeling each ridge of his muscles with my fingertips. With my hands still on his skin, I slowly slide them up, taking his T-shirt with me.

Marcus sits up and rips the distracting piece of clothing off over his head, leaving me with a smile on my lips as I take in his gorgeousness, inside and out.

31

MARCUS

Amber's drunk. Hell, I'm drunk, too. Drunk and screwed. I want to rock her world, but I don't want this to be our first time together. Not after everything she's been through. Not after she's been raped. Not after I've used sex as a way to dull the pain.

I want our first time together to be special for both of us. For it to mean something more than a drunken roll between the covers.

At least that's my plan until Amber places her hands on my stomach. My head says go slow. My junk says to hell with that.

I sit up, yank off my T-shirt, and toss it on the floor. I glance down at Amber and my breath steals away. She looks goddamn irresistible. Too irresistible.

She bites her lip in that adorable way of hers, which she does whenever she's unsure, oblivious to the effect it has on me. It leaves me craving her soft, passion-filled lips against mine.

I position my hands on either side of her and slowly lower myself. Her hands move to my chest, and she pushes me back up before shifting her body so that she's sitting. Her gaze remains locked on mine.

For several rapid heartbeats, we stay frozen this way. Then she hooks her hands under the hem of her top and inches the fabric up, revealing her firm stomach and a pink bra that seems as innocent as she does.

I run the tip of my tongue along my lip in nervous anticipation. In the moonlight shining through my window, she's perfect. She's more than I ever deserved.

And still don't deserve.

"You're beautiful," I breathe. Everything about her is beautiful. Her face. Her passion. Her inner strength. I tremble at the thought of how I could lose all of this, once she learns my secrets.

Her gaze averted, Amber chews her lip again. This time I get the feeling she's not just uncertain about us and about what we're on the verge of doing. Before she looked away, there was no missing the pain in her eyes.

I touch her cheek, wanting to destroy whatever's hurting her, hoping it has nothing to do with me.

I run my thumb against her lip, releasing her teeth's hold on it, and kiss her mouth. I linger there for a moment, enjoying her sweet taste, enjoying the sweet smell of strawberries. Her lips part, and I hungrily plunge my tongue in her mouth.

My hand tangles in her hair, slides down her back, and skims over a thick raised scar. And then a second one and a third. My hand freezes; my heart careens into my stomach. I jerk away from her lips. "What the hell?"

Amber's pained expression returns. Tears leak from her eyes. She pushes herself off the bed and moves away. Before she can get too far, I grab her arm.

"I'm sorry," I whisper, wishing more than anything I could reverse time and react differently. "I didn't mean to be an ass. I-I wasn't expecting it." I swallow. "Show me."

She doesn't, and I silently curse my stupidity.

"Please, Kitten."

She stares at her jeans for what feels like several minutes. Eventually she nods and turns her back to me. Large, thick scars crisscross over her skin. It looks like the sick fuck whipped her several dozen times. God, how is she even alive?

Tears prick my eyes. It takes every ounce of will not to snatch up my textbooks and hurl them against the wall, one by one. I blink away the tears and tenderly kiss her skin, my lips brushing a scar that will always be part of her. Like my scars will always be part of me.

I wrap my arms around her, the drunk feeling suddenly washed away. I've never felt so sober until this moment.

Amber leans back into me and I lower us onto the bed. Not wanting her to get cold, and wanting to form a protective cocoon around us, I pull the bedding over us and snuggle her closer. She shivers in my arms, and I know without a doubt she'll have nightmares tonight. I'm just glad she won't have to deal with them alone.

"I have no idea how you survived that," I say. "I'm not even sure I could have survived it." And it's true.

She's silent for a moment but I can tell she's not asleep. Her breathing's uneven and slightly fast. "I almost didn't. He started whipping me because I refused to eat or talk to him. Then he wouldn't stop because I kept crying out in pain. Eventually I stopped screaming 'cause there was nothing left in me. Even when he left me bleeding on the bed, I couldn't cry. Not out loud. I could only curl up with Smoky and focus on him, and not let myself completely die, even though a large part of me already had. Smoky helped me through the toughest pain by giving me someone to love and hold on to."

I owe that damn cat a...well, I owe Smoky whatever makes cats happy.

Something inside me stirs. Hope, maybe. Amber loves her cat, who is no less broken than she and I are. Would it be possible for her to love me, too, as broken as I am?

I kiss her shoulder. A few minutes later her breathing has evened out, the effects of the tequila having lulled her to sleep.

I close my eyes and let the world fade away.

I HEAR KITTEN CALLING ME, BUT I CAN'T SEE HER. I'M IN THE LIVING room of a house I've never been to before, with oversized pictures on the wall. Each one is of Amber. It's obvious the owner of the photos has been stalking her. None of the pictures are of her posing for the camera. They all show her frozen in action. There's even one of a guy with short, spiky blond hair and a navy varsity jacket. I can't see his face because they're making out, but I recognize the hair and jacket from the picture Emma has in her room. It's Trent. Jealousy knots inside my stomach even though it shouldn't. He's dead.

I'm not the only one who's jealous. A red cross has been painted over Trent's face, and he has splashes of paint on his varsity jacket. A few drops are on Amber, too. By accident or by design, I don't know.

"Marcus. Help me!" Amber screams.

It feels like someone has injected ice water into my veins. I struggle to catch my breath. When I finally do, the acrid taste of smoke fills me with dread.

Amber screams again, but I can't tell where the sound came from. I turn around, hunting for any indication of which way to go. But it's useless. Five hallways lead away from the room, all identical. What kind of crazy place is this?

"Marcus. Help me!"

This time I know where to go. I sprint down a hallway. The sound of her voice grows louder, the smell of smoke stronger. Where the hell's it coming from?

The hallway is long and never ending. I keep running, ignoring the burning pain in my legs from pushing myself hard.

Then I see it. A door at the end of the tunnel with smoke curling from under it.

"Marcus. Help me!"

"Marcus, you've gotta get us the fuck out of here," Ryan says from the other side of the door. "We don't have much time."

Ignoring everything they taught us in school about fire safety, I grab the door handle and turn it. It doesn't budge. What the hell am I thinking? If it was that easy for them to get out, wouldn't Amber and Ryan have already tried?

I scan the area for a key or a heavy object so I can break down the door but come up empty. Smoke continues pouring from under the door. Uncontrollable coughing from the other side tears at me, and I run my fingers around the doorframe. Fuck, where's the goddamn key?

All I feel is the cold empty wall.

Someone hammers their fist on the door. "Please help us!" Amber barely gets the words out. She's coughing hard.

"Fuck." Ryan.

Amber screams. A loud crash from their side of the door drowns out her voice.

I JERK AWAKE. MY BODY'S COVERED IN SWEAT AND MY HEART SLAMS into my ribs, again and again and again. It takes me a minute to reorient myself. I'm in my bed and Amber's asleep, snuggled against me. That's all I need to know.

I cuddle her closer, trying to push away the gnawing fear but I can't. In the end, I'm going to fail her like I failed Ryan.

32

———

AMBER

O ver the next couple of days, Marcus and I quickly fall into a routine of boyfriend and girlfriend. We don't see each other much at school, other than when we get together in the mornings to work out. I usually go over to his apartment after dinner, when he's not working or coaching, and snuggle up with him while he helps me with my math. I might have gotten an A on the last test, but I'm not fooling myself into believing it was all me. Marcus had everything to do with it.

Marcus leans in as I work on my math question, his minty breath brushing my ear. "How many mathematical logicians does it take to replace a lightbulb?" His voice is low and husky and sends all kinds of chills over me.

I laugh and turn to him. "How is it only you can make lame math jokes sound sexy?" Not giving him a chance to reply, I press my lips against his for a soft, lingering kiss. I pull away slightly, my mouth a hair width from his. "So, how many mathematical logicians does it take?"

"None," he murmurs. "They can't do it, but they can prove that it can be done."

I laugh, again, like I always do with his math jokes. I can't help it. The reaction on his face makes it worth it, even if the jokes are pretty bad. He enjoys telling them as much as I love hearing them.

I push my assignment across the small space between us at the kitchen table. "Is this right?"

He takes it from me and mentally works through the equation. "Almost. You need to add these values first, then square them."

I slump back in the chair. Its green color doesn't match the others at the table. None of them match, but the guys don't seem to care.

"I'm never gonna get this," I groan.

He kisses my temple. "Yes, you will. You're just tired. You had another nightmare last night, didn't you?"

I let out a heavy sigh. I don't even have to sleep here for him to know I'm still struggling. I must look really bad. "Am I that predictable?"

The only night this week I haven't had a nightmare was when I slept over on Saturday. Maybe that had to do with the tequila shots. But I'm not my mom. Alcohol won't solve my sleep issues, and I've seen how dangerous it is when you constantly use it to numb the pain. When Dad left us, Mom turned to the heavy stuff. She was brilliant at hiding what she was doing. For a few months. Until it started affecting her work, and her partners told her she needed to get straightened out or she'd lose her job. She did and had been sober for the past twelve years.

Until now.

"Kitten?"

I peer up at Marcus. He's watching me, eyebrows drawn together. "Yes?" I say, hoping he didn't notice I zoned out while he was explaining the equation.

"You okay?"

"I'm just worried about my mom. I still haven't gotten hold of her." I've been phoning her and leaving messages since Saturday. So far, she hasn't returned my calls.

"I wish I knew how to help. Your mom's at least made an

attempt in the past to stay sober. My stepdad never has." He shrugs but it's hard to miss what he doesn't say out loud. That I'm lucky. The worst I have is a mother who's off the wagon and who's dealing with depression. She didn't abuse me the last time she turned to alcohol.

I push myself off my seat and sit on Marcus's lap, my legs straddling his hips. Marcus doesn't like talking about his parents, but I can see how much his situation kills him even if he won't admit it. It's responsible for the slight wall still between us. The wall I haven't tried to bring down, because I need it as much as he does. I can't risk what we have, our feelings for each other, becoming more serious.

Marcus watches me, amusement, lust, curiosity burning in his eyes. I run my fingers through his hair, enjoying the silky feel of it against my skin. He turns his face up to look at me, and my lips plummet to his, our math homework momentarily forgotten.

Part of me wants to take his hand and lead him into his bedroom. The throbbing ache between my legs, which seems to come to life whenever I'm near him, presses into his hardness and it's driving me wild. But the part of me that doesn't reside in the throbbing area warns me I'm not ready to go that far, as much as I want to believe I am, and Marcus isn't pushing for it, either. Ever since he found out how badly I was tortured, he's given me a little extra space.

I just worry how much space he'd give me if he knew the truth.

Marcus grins against my lips. "We're never going to get any homework done at this rate."

Grinning back, I pull away. "Sorry, I needed the distraction." I start to climb off his lap but his hands on my hips keep me in place.

"Tell you what. How 'bout we finish our math assignments; then we'll go to the youth center and play ball. Deal?"

"Deal." I give him a quick peck on the lips and crawl off his lap. The promise of playing is all the incentive I need.

Once we finish our homework, Marcus drives me to my dorm so

I can pick up my gym clothes. I gather my mail from the mailroom. With the exception of one envelope, which is addressed to my dorm room, the rest was forwarded from home. Mom didn't even put it all in one envelope and send it. She had her assistant cross out the old address and write in my current one.

On our way to my room, we pass two giggling freshmen girls who stop to ogle Marcus. He pays no attention, which warms me on the inside. Not that I wasn't already warm after our hot make-out session at his apartment before we did some serious math homework.

We duck into my room, and I toss the unopened mail on my desk. Brittany's not here, much to my delight. I'm not sure how she'll react to Marcus, and I don't need the usual glare she reserves for me to accidentally turn him into an ice sculpture.

I remove my track pants and T-shirt from my drawers, as well as my sweat shirt. "Wait here," I tell him.

He hooks his fingers in the belt loops of my jeans. "Where you going?"

"To get changed."

"You can get changed here." A devilish grin tugs at his mouth. "I promise I won't look."

Once upon a time, I would have said no because of my scars, but since he's already seen them, that doesn't matter anymore. Now it has to do with modesty. I'm not used to guys seeing me half-naked. Guys who aren't Paul. Or Trent.

"I have to go to the bathroom," I lamely explain.

I'm washing my hands when the two freshmen girls enter the bathroom.

"That guy you're with. Isn't that Emma Kincaid's boyfriend?" one of them asks, as if everyone should know who Emma is.

I shake my head. "No, he's my boyfriend." Except instead of saying it like it's the truth, it comes out more like a question.

The other girl giggles. "I could have sworn they're together. I saw him leave her dorm room a few weeks ago. It was late at night so she would have had to sneak him in. She couldn't stop talking about him the next day."

Emma and Marcus? She never said anything about that to me, but it would explain how he knew about Trent. He must have seen a picture of Trent and me while he was in Emma's room.

My stomach twists.

Emma. Marcus. Together.

Having sex.

33

MARCUS

mber returns a few minutes later, but she's changed. And I don't mean her clothes.

She's quiet, and I have a feeling she's withdrawn to a place that has nothing to do with me. Or everything to do with me. I can't tell which.

"You okay?" I ask, wanting back what we had before she left for the bathroom.

"I'm fine. Let's go." She doesn't wait for me to respond. I'm not sure what I'd say even if she did give me a chance.

I walk with her down the stairs. We're side by side, but it feels like the distance between us is stretching. Unsure what to do, I let my mind drift to the conversation with Dave this afternoon. I'd taken the call in my room, while Amber was working on her math, so as not to disturb her.

He had talked to Alejandro's mother this morning. She was worried about her son, but Alejandro wouldn't tell her what was going on with him. So she called Dave to see if he had any ideas.

That's the real reason I want to go to the youth center. I need to talk to Alejandro and see what's up. I have a feeling there's something more going on than his poor math mark. And if he's not

189

there, I'm prepared to scour the neighborhood until I find him. Starting with where Carlos and his dickheads hang out.

I hadn't planned to bring Amber, not when it could be dangerous. But she seemed so distracted while doing her homework, what with everything going on with her mom. Before I could dwell on the risks involved, the words slipped from my mouth, and I asked her if she wanted to join me.

So now I have to worry about what's going on with Alejandro *and* Amber, and both situations leave me feeling like I'm walking across a wire suspended over a crevasse.

"Did something happen in the bathroom?" I press.

She swallows hard but keeps looking at the steps. I reach out and squeeze her hand. She doesn't pull away, which is good, but she doesn't squeeze back, either. "You can tell me. No matter what it is."

She worries her lip. "How do you know Emma?"

I startle at the name. I've mentioned Emma before but never explained how I know her. I was focused on Trent at the time, and Amber never questioned me about her ex-best friend. And let's face it, the reason I know Emma isn't a conversation I want to have with Amber, especially now.

But I have a bad feeling she already knows. Or at least knows some twisted version of the truth. *Fuck.*

"It's not what you think," I grumble even though I've already been tried and found guilty.

"And what's that?"

Since I want to avoid having this conversation in the stairwell, I say, "I'll tell you everything, but not here." I want to smile and reassure her that everything is okay, but it's hard to make your face muscles obey when the girl you care a lot for isn't sure she trusts you.

I clench my fist, ready to slam it into the wall, but decide for once to show a little restraint. I do, though, slam the door open when we get to the bottom of the stairs. The loud bang causes

Amber to flinch, making me feel like a bigger piece of shit for letting my anger get to me.

Once we're outside the building, I lead her to where I parked my car in the nearby parking lot. I want to hold her, but it's better if she sees my face while we talk. Then she's more likely to trust me.

"I met her at a party a few weeks ago," I say once we're inside the vehicle. A few students walk past the front of it, oblivious to the tension inside. "I didn't know who she was at the time, and it was before I started tutoring you." I pause, watching for Amber's reaction. She nods but gives no indication of what she's thinking. "She flirted with me, and I ended up going to her dorm. Yes, I was planning to have sex with her." A mix of emotions crosses Amber's face but none I can get a grip on. "We didn't in the end. I saw a picture of you, Trent, and Emma, and all I could think about was you." And him. "I left after that. I swear I never had sex with her." Never mind that she was puking in her trash can at the time. Amber doesn't need to know that.

"I believe you," she says, voice soft.

Those three words have more impact on me than I could have ever envisioned. After everything she's been through, I can't imagine it's easy for her to trust anyone. Not just because of the psychopath who kidnapped and tortured her. Too many people she's cared about have let her down.

"I swear I haven't had sex with anyone since the first time I saw you at the gym, when you glared at me."

Her eyebrows draw together into a puzzled line. "But what about that night when you confused me for a one-night stand? You left and didn't come back."

Inwardly I groan. Is that what she thought all this time? That I'd spent the night screwing another girl? "I was pissed at myself for what I almost did. I drove to the lake and didn't return until later that morning. I haven't wanted to be with another girl. Just you." It feels weird saying that, but it's true. Even when I went back to Emma's room, deep down I didn't want to do anything. No one other than Amber has had this kind of hold on me, which is both exhilarating and scary.

"I'm sorry I acted the way I did," she says. "But I've hurt Emma enough. I don't want to hurt her even more if there was once something between you."

"There wasn't. I swear." I want to pull her onto my lap and kiss her senseless, but the damn steering wheel's in the way. I settle for a small kiss on her lips, mine barely brushing against hers. A promise of things to come.

We drive to the youth center. On the way, I explain that I need to find Alejandro first. I don't explain why, and Amber doesn't press for an explanation. She nods, understanding this is important to me.

I thread my fingers with hers. "As soon as I've talked to him, we'll play ball."

We stop at the youth center and check in with Dave. He still hasn't heard from Alejandro, and none of the guys he hangs out with have seen him since yesterday at school. I wait while Dave calls Alejandro's mom.

They talk for a minute or two before Dave hangs up. "She says he's not there. Do you have any idea where he might be?"

"I'm not sure, but I might have an idea." I look at Amber. "Stay here with Dave."

"I'm coming with you," she says firmly.

"It could be dangerous. I don't want you getting hurt."

She levels her gaze at me. "I've survived a lot worse, Marcus."

I want to say that dealing with a lovesick stalker and the leader of a gang aren't the same, but then I remember the scars on her back and that she survived being raped. She's tough. A lot tougher than most people. Which means she's going to be stubborn about this.

I give a curt nod. Hopefully she'll at least stay in the car while I talk to Carlos.

It doesn't take long to track him down. He and his merry band of losers are hanging around a couple of benches in the courtyard behind my old high school. Why make it tough for your customers to find you if you can hang out after hours on school property? It's not like anyone patrols the area during the day, even on the weekend. The cops tend to only come out at night.

The five men laugh and pretend to be laid-back, unconcerned. There's not a single laid-back bone in their bodies. Every part of them is fully wound up, ready for trouble.

I park the car in the empty parking lot, where I can keep an eye on Amber. "I know you've survived hell, but I need you to stay in the car. For my sake. If things get bad, you need to call nine-one-one. These guys have guns and mean business."

She grips my arm. "Then maybe the police need to do this, not you."

"I wish it were that simple. But it's not. And it's something I have to do. For Alejandro and his family."

Amber opens her mouth. I still the argument on her lips with my finger. "You need to trust me. This is the only way I can help him."

Her mouth shuts. I can tell she doesn't agree with my plan, but she knows nothing she says will change my mind.

I give her a quick kiss on her lips, just in case this is the last time I'll be able to do that.

Silently praying nothing goes wrong, but at the same time relieved I'm not here alone, I climb out of the car. While my parents might not give a damn about me, it's nice someone cares enough to watch my back.

Someone I don't deserve.

As I approach Carlos and his losers, I scan the area for additional threats and for Alejandro. The air feels heavy, tense. Several crows search the ground for discarded waste, attracted to the stench of trouble.

At the sight of me, the men move closer to Carlos and take up a protective stance, hands on hips. Even though I can't see any weapons, I know they're carrying heat. They never leave home without it.

" 'Sup?" Carlos nods at me, a smirk on his ugly face.

"I'm looking for Alejandro," I say stiffly.

Carlos gestures to his oversized apes. "As you can see, he's not here."

"You know where he is?"

The smirk widens. He steps closer. It takes every ounce of will not to step back and give him the satisfaction.

"And why do you think I'd tell you?"

I can't tell from his expression whether he knows or is just shitting me. I don't bother answering. Instead, I glare down at him. Not that my additional three inches to his six-foot frame does much to intimidate. He might have his men do his dirty work, but that doesn't mean he's let his body go to shit. He's as lethal as any of them.

His gaze darts to my car, and the smirk transforms into a leer upon seeing Amber. "I see you brought your latest lay. Tell you what. I'll tell you what you want to know, and I get to show her how a real man fucks."

I make the mistake of clenching my hands into fists.

Carlos laughs. "So, it's like that, is it?" He fires off a stream of Spanish. His men laugh and the biggest ape—bald, with winter-white skin and a faded English or Aussie accent—makes a move toward the car.

I grab at him, but my hand doesn't have a chance to make contact before the guy next to me slams his fist into my gut. I double over from the impact. Shit, what's that guy's hand made of —iron?

Knowing I'm outnumbered and don't stand a chance in hell of surviving this, I straighten, ready to swing at whoever's closer. My fist rams into the smaller ape's face. I don't have time to enjoy the satisfaction. A strong hand lands on my shoulder and whips me around. My eye gets in the way of someone's fist. The impact is so great I stumble backward.

A foot shoots out in a martial arts move, and kicks me in the ribs, knocking the breath out of me. An overwhelming pain keeps my breath from returning, and I collapse to my knees.

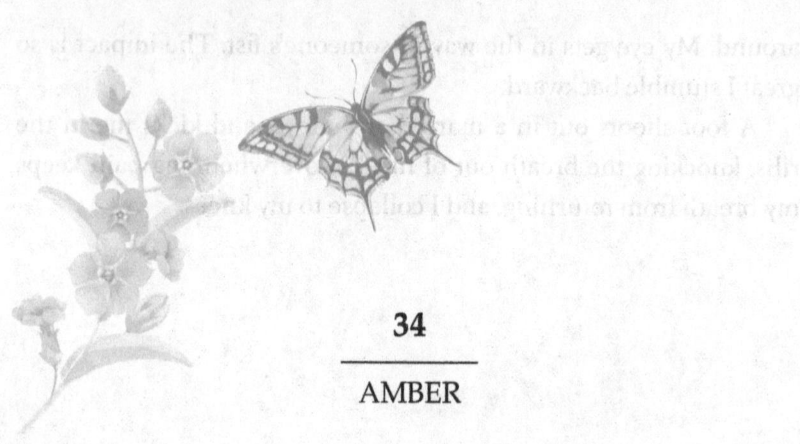

34

AMBER

I watch, frozen in horror, as Marcus is attacked. One of the guys kicks him in the ribs. Marcus doesn't so much as flinch, but then drops to his knees, unable to take any more abuse. I can't believe he lasted as long as he did.

Another man pulls out a gun and aims it at him. *Oh, God. They're going to kill him.* The thought knocks me out of my frozen stupor, and I snatch my cell phone from my pocket, berating myself for not having it out sooner. I manage to punch "9," but my hands shake so much, I hit "2" instead of "1."

I hear a shout and look up. Marcus is lying on the ground, unmoving. The thugs are casually walking away, as if they haven't just beaten up a guy, but are simply leaving after a friendly conversation.

As soon as they disappear around the corner, I scramble from the car and race over to Marcus. I kneel next to him and blink away the tears at the sight of his messed-up face. His eye is rapidly swelling, and he has a small cut on his cheek.

I place my hand on his arm. "Marcus?" He's breathing, but his breaths are shallow and it's obvious from his grimace that he's in a lot of pain.

His closed eyelids flutter for a moment before his beautiful hazel eyes gaze up at me. "I think I've died and gone to heaven." He somehow manages a cocky grin. I roll my eyes but can't stop the small smile tugging at the corners of my mouth.

"Can you get to the car, or should I call for an ambulance?"

Holding his ribs with one hand, Marcus slowly pushes himself up. My heart clenches in a tight knot at how much pain the movement must have caused him, even though none of it shows on his face.

I help him to his feet, afraid to let him go in case he collapses again. He groans, then bites his lips to keep from betraying how much pain he's really in. I wouldn't be surprised if he inwardly shuts down, so I don't know how bad things are. I did that all the time with Paul.

"Car," he whispers. "Need to go to...youth center."

"No, you need to go to the hospital, Marcus. You might have a broken rib."

"Youth center...then hospital."

I want to scream at his stubbornness. "You can go to the youth center afterward. I promise I'll drive you there after the hospital."

"I'm not going there till I've talked to Dave. I'll take an uber if I have to."

"Fine," I huff. "But I'm driving."

He doesn't argue, though I can tell he's not thrilled with the idea. I'm not a bad driver, so it must be a male ego thing.

I get him into his car, and he gives me directions to the youth center. Once there, I help him into the building. Light spills from the crack under Dave's office door.

"Dave!" I call out. "We need help."

He appears a few seconds later from his office; it takes him only a second more to figure out Marcus is in even worse shape than he looks. He waves for me to bring Marcus into the office and shuts the door behind us.

The room isn't large, but there's enough space for a couch,

along with a desk and a bookshelf. Sandwiched between the desk and bookshelf is a file cabinet with a first-aid kit on top.

"He might have a broken rib," I say. "But he insisted I bring him here first."

"I hate hospitals," Marcus mutters.

Dave grabs a couple of cushions scattered on the couch and props them against the armrest, while I retrieve the first-aid kit in case he needs it.

"Lie down," he instructs.

It seems as though Marcus is going to say no, but then he changes his mind and sags into the cushions. While Dave scoots the hem of Marcus's long-sleeved T-shirt up, I take hold of Marcus's hand. His long fingers wrap around mine and he squeezes. I can tell he wants to squeeze harder against the pain but doesn't want to cause *me* pain.

A bruise is already forming over his ribs where the man's foot made contact. Luckily the skin isn't broken. Other than that, I can't tell how bad the injury is. But I can tell this isn't the first bad injury he's suffered from. Faded jagged scars dot his chest and shoulders. Nothing like mine, but I can tell they were once bad enough to need stitches, only he was never taken to the hospital to be treated.

"You want to tell me what happened?" Dave asks Marcus.

"Not really."

Dave looks at me, eyebrow raised in question. Not knowing what to say, I shrug. If Marcus doesn't want to tell him the truth, I'm not going against his wishes. There might be a good reason he doesn't want to tell Dave what happened. Or he's just being an idiot and is letting pride stand in his way.

"I think I know what's going on with Alejandro," Marcus says. "He's been recruited by Carlos's gang. Or is in the process of being recruited."

"Shit," Dave mutters under his breath. "Well, either way, you need to get your ribs checked out. You do realize, of course, the cops are gonna ask questions."

"I'll tell them I walked into a wall."

My heart clenches for the second time at the realization Marcus has probably used that line before, and a mountain of other ones when his stepfather abused him.

"Can you drive him?" Dave asks me. I nod.

He helps me with Marcus. As we walk along the path, Alejandro pulls up on a bike. His mouth flops open as he takes in Marcus's appearance. "*¡Mierda!* What happened?"

Marcus narrows his eyes. "You wanna tell me where you got the bike from?"

"Didn't steal it, if that's what you're wonderin'."

"Then it shouldn't be too hard to tell me where you got it from."

Alejandro glares at him, mouth pressed shut.

"Fuck. Are you screwing around...with Carlos and his gang?"

Alejandro lets loose a stream of Spanish, then races off on his bike. Several people jump out of the way and yell curses after him as he continues past parked cars and rundown small businesses.

"Shit," Marcus mutters, shaking his head, eyes never leaving Alejandro until the boy's too far away to be seen. And even then he keeps staring down the street as if expecting Alejandro to return at any second.

"C'mon." With my arm still around his waist, I nudge Marcus toward the car. He doesn't move at first, but he eventually gives in and climbs into the passenger seat.

Once he's in, I fasten his seat belt. The strap cuts across the bruised area, pressing into it, and a faint groan falls from Marcus's lips. I give them a light kiss, to let him know everything will be all right. Before I can pull away, his hand drifts to the back of my head and he kisses me harder.

"Please don't leave me tonight," he murmurs against my mouth.

35

AMBER

The empty white walls of Marcus's bedroom glow softly in the early morning sunlight. Marcus's arm is draped over my waist. It's the only thing covering my waist. At some point during the night, the covers were kicked off, forming a puddle of fabric around my hips.

I glance at the alarm clock on his stack of textbooks. Even though I already suspected it wasn't super early, I gasp at the glowing red 8:02 a.m. I'm going to miss my first class, and maybe even my second one. I don't want to wake Marcus up. He had a rough night. First, with being beaten up by the gang, followed by an excruciatingly long wait in the ER, and to top it off, he woke several times during the night with nightmares. Nightmares he refused to talk about.

If anyone needs more sleep, it's him.

Careful not to wake him or accidentally hurt his injured rib, I wiggle from under the covers and search the floor for my long-sleeved T-shirt. I'm already wearing my jeans but had agreed to remove my top at Marcus's insistence. He wanted to feel *me* next to him, not my clothes, when he finally fell asleep.

I find the T-shirt and slip it on. Chase's bedroom door opens as I step into the hallway. I quietly close the door behind me and raise my finger to my lips. His mouth slides into a knowing smile.

"Late night, huh?" he whispers. His grin vanishes when he sees my serious expression. "What's wrong?"

I nod for him to move to the kitchen and proceed to tell him in a low voice what happened. I can only hope that Marcus won't have a problem with his best friend finding out the truth.

"You're the only other person who knows what happened," I say. "He refused to tell Dave or the cops."

"Is he okay?"

"His ribs are bruised. He has a black eye and will be sore for a while, but he should be okay."

Chase offers to drive me to school, and I wait for him to shower while I watch the news. Other than a possible gang shooting, there's nothing of interest. If the karma gods are shining down on Marcus, the person who was shot was one of the men who attacked him.

"You ready?" Chase asks, coming out of the bathroom. Part of me had hoped Marcus would wake up before I left, so I could check on him. The painkillers must have really knocked him out.

"I bet I'm not the first girl Marcus has slept with who you've had to drive to school. Not that I was, you know, doing more than... sleeping with him." My face grows hotter with each idiotic word.

Chase chuckles. "I've never had to do that. You know why?"

Because they're not stupid enough to get stranded here without a car? Deciding not to point out the obvious, I shrug instead.

"You're the only girl he's brought home." Chase opens the apartment door.

"Really? Not even Tammara?"

"Thank God, not even her. You being here, Amber, is a huge step for him." We walk down the hallway. "I've known him since kindergarten, and you're the first girl, other than my sister, he's allowed to get close to him. It's about damn time. Marcus has had one fucked-up life, and I can tell there're things he's kept from me. But he's changed since he met you. Changed for the better."

I have no idea how to respond. I'm still stunned by Chase's earlier revelation: I'm the first girl Marcus has brought to his apartment.

Chase drops me off at my dorm and I race upstairs to get ready. Thanks to him, I'm not going to miss any classes.

Brittany's in our room when I return from the bathroom, my ponytail damp on the ends. She does her best to pretend I'm not here as she gathers her books. Not that pretending changes the fact that I still have nightmares and wake up several times a week, crying out. I even had one last night. Luckily, Marcus was drugged up with painkillers, so he slept through it.

Since I have a few minutes before I'm due to meet up with Jordan, so we can walk to class together, I pick up the unopened mail from my desk.

A new envelope sits on top of the pile. It's identical to the one not forwarded to me by Mom's assistant. Both are plain white envelopes with no return address. I select one and drop the rest on my desk, then tear open the envelope and read the typed letter.

A flower cannot blossom without sunshine, and man cannot live without love. Max Muller

My mouth dries up like a pond in a drought. This can't be happening. There's no way Paul can know where to find me. I don't use any social networking sites. And I'm studying at a different university from the one I told Paul I wanted to attend.

But even as I try to convince myself of that, the evidence is staring right at me.

He's found me.

I snatch up the matching envelope and rip it open. This time there are two separate pieces of paper. I read the first one.

For it was not into my ear you whispered, but into my heart. It was not my lips you kissed, but my soul. Judy Garland

My stomach threatens to heave at the memory of Paul's cold, hard lips against mine. I toss the offending piece of paper down and read the next one.

Man dies of cold, not of darkness. Miguel do Unamuno

I gasp, my body turning cold like the message. Just before Paul killed Trent, his love quotes changed to ones about man and death.

I sit on my bed, hard, staring at the messages in my trembling hand. "D-do you know where this other letter came from?" I don't even glance at Brittany, unable to tear my gaze away from the last quote.

"Some weird guy dropped it off," she mutters. "He said something about it being delivered to his mailbox by accident. Are you okay?" Her last words hold a trace of concern.

I peer up at her. All hints of concern have been transformed into curiosity. "What guy?"

She shrugs. "I don't know his name."

"What did he look like?"

"I don't really remember. It's not like I hang out with the losers around here."

"Please try to remember. It's important."

"I don't know. He was tall and skinny and wears glasses. And he might have curly blond hair."

"Is he good-looking?" Her description matches at least five guys living here. And those are just the guys I remember.

"He's okay, I guess. Not exactly my type." I'm not sure what her type is, so that doesn't help much, though I hope it isn't guys like the jerk who was harassing her the other night.

"Does he live on our floor?"

She shrugs, again. "Dunno. Maybe."

I want to scream. Can she be any more unhelpful? I can't even tell if she's doing it on purpose to get back at me or if she genuinely doesn't remember.

Since there's nothing I can do until I talk to every guy in this building who fits that description, I collect my backpack from the floor. Then pause.

"That guy in the bathroom the other night..." I leave it at that, unsure what I really want to ask her.

She opens her desk drawer and riffles through it. "It was no big deal. Jack can be a jerk sometimes, especially when he's been drinking."

"So, he's a friend?"

"Boyfriend." She continues searching through her drawer.

I want to tell her she deserves better, but she won't give a damn what I think.

I spend the morning in a daze. Memories of when Paul stalked me pound in my head. How could he even know where to find me? Isn't that privileged information? And even if it isn't, very few people know I'm here.

But then, this is Paul we're talking about. Stalking is what he excels at.

Except, how's he doing this? He's still in the psych ward. Mom or Grandma would have told me if he were free. Considering he's up for two murders, kidnapping, torture, rape, and a host of other charges, I've been told I'll never have to worry about him again. Once convicted, he'll be locked away for a very long time.

I'm eventually able to breathe again, after spending what feels like several hours holding my breath. I'm safe. Paul can't hurt me, and he can't hurt Marcus. The only person capable of hurting Marcus is Carlos.

By lunch, I haven't heard from Marcus, and my worries take a new direction. I try phoning his cell after my text goes unanswered. We were supposed to get together tonight to study, but that plan was made before he was beaten.

After my final class of the day, I pick up my mail, which consists of a single envelope. The same style of white envelope without a return address that I opened this morning. I'm tempted to throw it away unread, but that won't change anything. Paul's sending me a message and he wants me to figure it out, because whatever it is matters in his warped mind. And none of this is going to change, even if I want to live in denial.

With shaky legs, I walk up the stairs, my hand gripping the railing. It's the only thing keeping me from collapsing on the stairs and tumbling down the steps.

Brittany isn't in our room, which is just as well. No one can know about this.

I rip open the envelope and remove four pieces of paper. Like the others, each page contains a typed quote.

Everything is clearer when you're in love. John Lennon

I read the next ones in the order he put them in the envelope.

From the deepest desires often come the deadliest hate. Socrates

Friendship is a single soul dwelling in two bodies. Aristotle

Death's in the good-bye. Anne Sexton

It's not just the quote that's important, as Paul explained after he kidnapped me. The order of the messages is relevant, too. Paul has left the interpretation up to me, but it doesn't take long to figure out what he's saying. With the exception of the friendship quote, the idea behind the messages is similar to the ones I received just before Trent's death. Only this time Paul has a friend helping him. I'm positive that's what "Friendship is a single soul dwelling in two bodies" means.

His friend has been stalking me. Even with all my precautions, I'm still a target, and worse yet, so is Marcus. That's what Paul's trying to tell me. As long as I'm dating Marcus, he's not safe.

Choking back a scream, I stare at the letters and envelope. The thing I love the most about him—that he would do anything for the people he cares about—will get Marcus killed if he knows the truth.

Because I can't risk him trying to talk me out of what I have to do, I take the coward's way out. I text him, my heart ripping into tiny pieces.

Me: This isn't going to work out between us.
We want different things. Sorry.

36

MARCUS

I drop onto the grass next to Ryan's grave. The dead grass partially obscures his small grave marker, making it easy to miss that someone's buried here.

"I fucked things up big-time." I wrap my arms around me to ward off the mid-November chill. No one's around to hear me curse, not that I care either way. "You'd have liked Amber. She's a survivor like you were." I can almost hear Ryan asking, *Then why the hell did you mess things up?* Wish I had an answer. "Alejandro's involved with Carlos's gang. I made a mistake and took Amber with me while I was looking for him."

I should have left her at the youth center. Bringing her was a huge mistake. Ever since I received Amber's text yesterday, I've cursed myself a million times for not doing the smart thing. After sending me several texts and voice messages asking how I was doing, she shocked me by suddenly dumping me. I've tried calling her, but she hasn't responded.

"I don't know what to do. I can't imagine being without her. Not that I deserve her. Not when I can't be completely honest with her. But I swore I'd never tell your secret, and I won't." Maybe Amber was right to dump me. But knowing that doesn't take the ache away. It makes it a thousand times worse.

I snatch up a small stone, push myself up, and hurl it at a tree several yards away. A sharp pain stabs at my ribs, reminding me just how much I screwed up. *Shit.*

I don't want to lose Amber. I miss the way her smile brightens my day. I miss the beautiful sound she makes when she laughs. I miss how she makes me feel whole and wanted, and not in the same way most girls want me. The emptiness she once filled is returning. And I don't want to feel that way, again.

After saying bye to Ryan, I drive to Amber's dorm. If she won't answer my calls, then she has no choice but to talk to me face-to-face. I'm not letting her walk away so easily, as if the past two months meant nothing. I know it's not true, for either of us.

Luck is cheering for me when I arrive. I bump into a guy I know from engineering, and he gets me into the building and past security, without asking too many questions. It doesn't take too long to track down Amber's room. Flirt with girls, especially when you have a black eye, and they're willing to tell you anything.

I knock on Amber's door. No one was able to tell me if she's here, but I'll camp out in front of it if I have to.

The door opens to reveal a girl in black. Black dress. Black tights. Black boots. The only thing that isn't black is her hair, which comes pretty damn close. She's got on way more makeup than Amber ever wears. In a way, she reminds me of an emo version of Tammara. But whereas Tammara's appearance screams sex appeal, this girl's appearance screams "Mess with me and I'll mess with your face." Or at least that's the vibe she's sending. There's a wariness in her eyes that I recognize. A wariness I saw too many times in Ryan.

"I'm looking for Amber."

She gives me a once over, but not in the same way most girls do. She's judging me. "She's not here."

"You know when she'll be back?"

"Can't say I'm privy to her schedule, if that's what you're asking." She leans against the doorjamb. "I haven't seen her since yesterday morning, when she freaked out over some stupid letters."

"What do you mean? What letters?"

"Hell if I know. But one of them was delivered to the wrong mailbox and a guy dropped it off for her."

"What guy?"

"Geez, you're as bad as her." The girl shrugs. "Like I told Amber, I have no idea what his name is."

"Do you have any idea where I can find her?"

"No, but her friend might." She points down the hall, then shuts the door in my face.

I knock on the door marked Isabelle & Jordan's Room. The door opens but instead of Jordan, a tiny girl with waist-length black hair and Asian ancestry answers.

"Is Jordan here?" I ask.

She shakes her head. "No. She and her friend went away for the weekend."

My stomach drops several floors. "Which friend?"

"Amber. They're visiting Jordan's family."

37

AMBER

Jordan and I pass field after field as we drive along the interstate. After Paul's last messages, I contacted the cops. Now all I can do is wait while they investigate who sent them. So far the only thing they can confirm is that Paul is in the psych ward. I'm still safe from him.

With each mile Jordan and I travel, each field we pass, each second we're away from Chicago, tension drains from every cell in my body until I feel like I'm the same girl I was over a year ago.

Almost the same girl. I miss Marcus something fierce.

He's called me, but I haven't had the courage to listen to his messages, to hear his voice. Knowing I can never see him again, my heart feels like I played basketball with it, and it's hit the backboard too many times.

And my head's a panicked mess because now I'm screwed when it comes to math. There's no way I can pass the class without Marcus's help. We're covering new material and I'm already lost again. And the final exam, which makes up the majority of my grade, is rapidly approaching.

"You sure your parents are okay with me coming?" I ask again, for no other reason than to avoid dwelling on my math grade, Marcus, and Paul.

Keeping her eyes on the road, Jordan says, "Don't worry. They're excited to meet you." She briefly turns to me and smiles, her grin filled with mischief. Why do I feel like I'm missing something? "I'm gonna tell them the truth. And you're gonna help me by being the buffer."

Truth? Which truth? "What do you mean?"

"I'm going to tell them I'm studying to be a child psychologist, not a physician. It's my future, and it's about time I have a say in it. I mean, it's not like I'm getting my body pierced and joining a rock band."

I stifle a laugh at her heartfelt speech and decide not to point out that she's been doing what she wants for the past two months. They just don't know about the dancing and drinking and partying.

"So when are you gonna tell them?"

"Tonight at dinner. Can I ask you something?"

"Sure."

"What happened between you and Marcus?"

Okay, not what I was expecting. I thought she was going to ask something about her boyfriend or family. This was the question I was hoping to avoid, because the truth hurts, and I can't exactly tell it to her.

"What do you mean?"

"I saw Chase yesterday, and he told me you ended things with Marcus." Even though she does her best to hide it, her voice betrays her disappointment that she had to hear it from Chase and not me. "I don't get it. You guys are perfect together."

If there's one thing I've learned in the past year, perfect doesn't exist. Perfection is an illusion, nothing more.

I quirk an eyebrow. "Is something going on between you and Chase? You know, you guys would be cute together, and he really likes you."

She smiles. "I really like him, too."

"More than your boyfriend?" Who lives a million miles away.

Her smile turns into a frown, and she shoots me a quick glance. "Hey, no redirecting. We're talking about you and Marcus."

Darn it. I was hoping she hadn't noticed what I was up to. "Look who's talking. You're redirecting, too."

"I love Garrett, so end of that discussion," she says. "Now, you and Marcus..."

"It's really no big deal."

She flashes me a look to tell me she's not buying it. "You've been depressed since yesterday. Even now you're hurting. It's so obvious. Which means you didn't willingly dump him."

"I think you're reading too much into things."

"So, you can look me in the eye and tell me you don't want to be with him?"

"Sure, but then we'd get into an accident and die. And what's the point of that?"

Jordan shakes her head in mock irritation. "Nice try. I meant when we're no longer driving."

I want to tell her the truth, that I care about him too much to let him die. Enough people have died because of me. I won't let him be another one.

I want to tell her that, but I can't. Not without telling her what's going on. And I would if I thought for a moment she was in danger. "It's better this way. I need to focus on my schoolwork."

"But wasn't he helping you with your math? Who's going to help you now?"

I shrug even though her gaze is not directed at me.

"You could always ask Chase. I bet he'd love to help you."

I'm not too sure about that. He might not be too thrilled to help me—unless Marcus isn't all that brokenhearted about the breakup.

"I don't have his number," I say as an easy out. I'm hardly going to drive to their apartment and risk bumping into Marcus.

"That's not a problem. I have it."

"Oh, really?" I grin. "And why do *you* have it?"

Her face reddens, and she mutters that it doesn't matter. I'm about to ask more questions about her boyfriend when my phone rings. Mom. Relieved that the conversation with Jordan has moved away from Marcus and me, I answer the phone moments before realizing that was a dumb idea.

"The DA contacted me about the letters you've been receiving. Do you know how bad it looked when they didn't hear about them from me first?" she says, without so much as a "Hi. How are you?"

I glance at Jordan. She's paying attention to the road, but that doesn't mean anything. She can still hear everything I say. "Now's not a good time, Mom."

"It's the perfect time." She uses her lawyer voice, which means she's not interested in arguments or excuses. At least not from me. "We need to discuss your strategy with the DA."

What she means is *she* needs to discuss the strategy, and it won't be pretty. Those two have nothing but a strong dislike for each other.

"I'm going to ask Grandma for help. She knows what she's doing." She might not have been a defense lawyer, but she was a successful family lawyer until she retired from her practice.

"You're my daughter," Mom snaps. Glad to hear she still remembers that.

"I know, but..." *Grandma doesn't look at me and see my dead brother and remember that I never saved him when he was shot.* "You're busy..." *Getting drunk.* "Your clients need you." I need her, too, but not in the same way. Not that this is anything new. I've needed her since Dad walked out on us, but her job always came first.

"I'll call you later." I hang up on her before she can respond.

———————————

The weekend is better than I imagined it would be, and Jordan's parents aren't so scary. Actually, they're downright amazing. Despite what she had feared, they accepted her decision to pursue child psychology, even admitted she'll excel at it.

"What do you say, ladies?" Her father pulls into the mall parking lot. "You ready to shop till you drop?" He's nothing like I was expecting. He looks more like a linebacker than a surgeon, and according to Jordan, he used to be one during his pre-med days. But he's not intimidating, even though he is over six five.

"You're gonna love this," Jordan has yet to tell me anything, only that it's been a family tradition for the past few years.

We walk to the toy store. At the entrance, I pause, confused why we're here. Jordan was already smiling when we arrived at the mall. Now she's beaming. She gestures for me to grab a shopping cart, and she and her parents claim their own.

"Our trauma unit sees a lot of victims, many who are children," her mother explains. "They're victims of physical or sexual abuse, family violence, or other types of criminal activity. They come in scared and irreparably changed." She smiles at Jordan, pride clear on her face. "Jordan came up with a great idea a few years ago. She and the kids in her school raised money and bought gifts to give to traumatized children when they're admitted to the hospital. Something to give them hope and show them they're loved."

"Someone else is now responsible for the fundraising." Jordan's father pushes his cart to the side to let a mother and her two young kids pass. "But we love to do our part and buy gifts for the kids. With the holiday season coming, the incidence of violent crimes increases. We want to ensure there are enough toys."

Somehow, at his words, I manage to keep back the tears at how wonderful my friend and her family really are. And not for the first time since I met Jordan's parents, I wish they were mine. And Marcus's.

Just the thought of Marcus encourages the tears I was trying to restrain. Not because we're no longer together. But because he was the boy they were talking about, and Jordan doesn't even realize it. I can't tell her, though. It's not my story to tell.

"Are you okay, dear?" Jordan's mother asks.

I could tell them how I was that girl, the one who was a victim of a violent crime. But the mall isn't where I want to have this conversation. I wipe the tears away and do my best to smile without letting any more fall.

I say I'm fine and Jordan hugs me. But in that moment, I feel like she knows more about my situation than she realizes, more about what happened to me than I had intended.

"We'll talk after this," she whispers, and I nod.

We spend the next hour laughing and figuring out which toys will make a difference, even just a small difference, in a child's life. By the time we're finished, I feel better than I have in a long time. The toys are meant to give their recipients a taste of hope, but they've given me so much more in return. If only Marcus were here. Then he'd see how wrong he was. There are people, like Jordan and her family, who do care about what happens to victims, especially the kids.

Once we return to her parents' house, I tell Jordan about Paul and about the stalking and kidnapping. I tell her about the nightmares and the flashbacks, and how they're the result of what happened to me. I leave out a lot of details. She doesn't need to know everything.

I do, though, show her my tattoo, and tell her why I had to turn away from my best friend. Like Marcus, she points out that Trent's death isn't my fault. The only person at fault is Paul.

"I'm so sorry I didn't tell you sooner," I say. And I mean it. "I wanted to, but I also wanted to keep you separate from what happened. I wanted us to have better memories than the ones I want to forget."

Jordan smiles, then hugs me. "You're forgiven." She pulls away. "Does Marcus know?"

"Yeah. A friend of his figured out I'm dealing with post-traumatic stress disorder. Marcus eventually convinced me to tell him what happened."

"You guys didn't break up because of this, right?"

"No. It had nothing to do with that." I almost choke on the lie.

My cell phone buzzes from Jordan's desk. I check to see who sent me a text but don't recognize the number. I open it.

It's from Tammara.

38

MARCUS

I open the door. Tammara's standing in the hallway, streaks of mascara on her cheeks.

"Can I come in?" she asks.

Against my better instincts, I open the door wider and let her in. This better be quick. I was about to go to the youth center to talk to Dave about Amber.

Tammara sits on the couch. Her face crumples and she starts sobbing. I've never seen her eyes get even the slightest bit wet, never mind her breaking down into full-out sobs.

As much as I don't want her here, and as much as I want to see Dave, I sit next to her. "What's wrong?"

Her sobbing slows and she rests her head on my shoulder. Her arms snake around my waist. "I was at my sister's place." She shudders. "Can I have a drink? I need a drink. Do you have any beer?"

I nod and get us each one. When I return, I hand her the open bottle and sit back on the couch, this time putting distance between us.

"Thanks." She sniffs and looks through her purse. "I'm out of tissues. Could I have one, please?"

I nod, put my beer down, and return a minute later with a wad of Kleenexes. I grab my beer and gulp it.

She sips hers, making it clear she's in no rush. "I went to visit my sister this afternoon, but she wasn't home. Her fiancé was, though. He told me she wouldn't be long, and I might as well come in and wait for her." Her voice cracks. "Then h-he..." She can't talk after that as she breaks down, again, in tears.

I pull her into my arms. I don't tell her it's going to be okay, because these things never are. I just let her cry against my shoulder. Exhaustion seeps in and drags me into its depths. I haven't slept well since Amber dumped me, but I can't believe I'm this tired.

Unable to keep my eyes open another second, I let them drift shut.

39

AMBER

I stare at my math test, and the numbers swirling around in a blur. All I want is to lay my head on the desk and sleep. Something I haven't done much of for the past week, ever since I received the text from Tammara. Ever since I received more messages from Paul, all hinting the same thing: if I get back together with Marcus, he's dead.

I close my eyes for a second. When I reopen them, things aren't much clearer. *Come on, focus.* I'd feel more confident if Marcus had helped me study, but I haven't spoken to him in over a week. After seeing the pictures Tammara sent me of her and Marcus together in bed, kissing, and who knows what else, I couldn't ask Chase for help. I was too afraid of seeing the truth in his eyes. That Marcus and Tammara are a couple again, for good.

My hopes of passing the test fade with each ticking second. Now my only goal is to finish it so I can skip my next class and have a nap.

After the instructor announces time's up, I hand him the exam and trudge to my dorm. Brittany isn't due back for another two hours, unless like me she decides to miss her next class.

I lie on my bed and pray I don't have another bad dream. For once, I'd like to sleep without being haunted with memories of my real-life nightmare.

<hr>

I WAKE WITH A JOLT, THE VISIONS OF MOM AS PAUL'S DEFENSE lawyer—because she believes I'm the guilty one, not Paul—fresh in my head. I've slept maybe forty-five minutes. Not great, but good enough for what I need to do. Drive home and talk to Mom.

Outside, I glance at the massive gray clouds in the distance. I don't want to drive in bad weather, but I have to do this if I want the nightmares to end. It's time I face my fear of storms. A storm didn't kidnap or torture me. It didn't kill Trent or Michael. And it didn't take away my father. Humans, not the weather, were responsible for each of those events. I keep repeating this in my head. I'm not sure if it's helping, but at least I'm not dwelling on Marcus and the photos.

Over an hour later, I pull into the driveway of my house. On the way over, I practiced what I wanted to say, but as soon as the place looms in front of me, those thoughts vanish.

Mom and Grandpa, who was a former Marine, used to tell Michael and me that only the strong survive. Never show weakness in front of the enemy. Never show weakness in front of friends and those you love. No matter what happens, be strong and never show fear.

I guess I should thank them, in so many ways. Smoky wasn't the only one who saved my life.

But Mom hasn't been strong for a while. The alcohol only made her believe she was. Which means for once I'm the stronger of the two of us, the one who will have to save her.

I enter the house. Voices from the TV in the living room greet me. From the sound of it, Mom's watching the twenty-four-hour news station.

"Hey, Mom," I say as I walk into the room. She's sitting on the couch, wearing lounge pants, legs tucked under her. In her hand is a half-empty glass, filled with ice and the familiar dark liquid I've seen too many times in the past. Rye and coke.

"What are you doing here?" she slurs.

"I want to talk to you." I approach and point at the glass. "You need to stop doing this to yourself."

She glares at me. "I had a rough day. I don't need you telling me what to do."

"That doesn't make it right. You know what else isn't right? You treating me as though I'm one of your clients. I'm not. I. Am. Your. Daughter. Or have you forgotten that?" Even though I don't mean for it to happen, even though this isn't the speech I rehearsed in the car, my voice grows louder by a few degrees, barely covering the volume of my heartbeat.

Mom pushes herself off the couch, her face red, though I can't tell if that's from the alcohol or her reaction to my words. "Don't talk to me like that, young lady." The slur is gone, replaced by a tightness I rarely hear from her. The last time I heard it was when Michael cut down a small tree in the backyard when he was eleven. Our father had planted it just before he left.

"I'm well aware I'm your mother. I'm also the person who worked long hours so I could give you and your brother everything you needed."

"Yes, but we never asked you to do that. We didn't ask you to spend all your time defending rapists and murderers and criminals just so you could give us this..." I gesture at the room.

The glass in her hand trembles, sloshing brown liquid onto the beige carpet. "What you mean is defending guys like Paul Carlson?"

The heat of her words forces me back a step. "You're right. I do!"

Her hand slaps my face, hard, stunning me into silence. "I do what I do because I believe everyone has the right to a fair trial." Her voice is soft, broken. She storms out of the room.

I'm left here alone, my skin stinging from her touch, as I try piecing together what just happened. It's clear to both of us that I blame her as much as she blames me for what happened to Michael.

A door at the rear of the house slams shut. A minute later the sound of the garage door opening grumbles through the house. A car engine rumbles to life and then she's gone, reversing out the driveway to go who-knows-where.

My head droops forward. I screwed up big-time. I wanted to convince Mom to get help. I've just made things worse.

Although I want to return to Chicago before the storm hits, I drive to my grandma's house and cuddle with Smoky for a while on the couch. Grandma's not here and I don't know where she could be.

"What am I going to do about Mom, Smoky?" A tear drops on his gray fur, and I kiss his head. I leave Grandma a note and head out.

I've been driving for forty minutes when I feel the unmistakable pull of a flat tire. Rain splatters against the windshield and my heart speeds up. *Oh, God. Not again. Not again. Not again.* Hands shaking, I steer the car onto the shoulder of the quiet side road. *It's okay. It's not Paul. I'm okay. It's just a flat tire.*

For the next few minutes I sit quietly, trying not to panic, trying to rationally think what I should do. Except, it's hard to be rational when dealing with an adrenaline overload. In the end, I call Chase with the number Jordan programmed into my phone. Marcus is probably with Tammara, and I don't want to risk him bringing her here. And I doubt the cops would even come out here unless it's a real emergency.

Like my body found on the roadside.

40

MARCUS

"**W**here are you?" Chase asks, talking on his cell phone.

I go back to watching the football game on TV. It's not until I hear him say Amber's name that he has my full attention.

"I'm on my way." Without looking at me, he hangs up and grabs his keys from the kitchen table.

"What's going on?" I don't like the idea of Chase meeting up with Amber.

"It's no big deal. Amber's got a flat and needs help."

Shit. "Where is she?" If she gets flashbacks during storms, what the hell will she be like with a flat tire? And the last I saw, when I left campus, we were in for bad weather. That's bound to make things worse.

I grab my leather jacket from the hall closet.

"Dude, you don't have to come," Chase says. "I can handle it."

"I have no doubt you can handle the tire. It's Amber you don't know how to deal with."

His eyebrows pinch together. I'm not the only one who cares for her. "What do you mean 'deal with' her? She dumped you, Marcus.

What exactly is there to deal with?" Though as he says the last part, I can tell he's thinking back to the day she reacted to Jordan's roses.

"I'll explain everything in the car." And I do. Well, almost everything. I stick to the general stuff you would find in a newspaper. I don't mention she was raped and tortured, though I'm sure he can figure that much on his own.

The entire time I'm talking, I try getting through to Amber on her phone. She might not want to be with me anymore, but hearing my voice has to be better than being stranded alone. At least then, she'd know we're on our way.

"Well, that explains a few things," Chase says as we push the speed limit in the rain.

"Between the weather and the flat tire," I warn, "she might be a mess by the time we get there."

By the tenth attempt to call her, I'm ready to hurl the damn phone out the window. *Fuck*. What if she's having a flashback? She could get killed by running in front of a truck without realizing what she's doing.

Chase eventually pulls up ahead of Amber's car. The car has barely come to a stop when I jump out the door. The rain pelts me at a sharp angle, soaking through my jeans, as I sprint to her car. Water drips from my hair and into my eyes.

Amber's curled in a ball on the floor of the passenger side. Her face is against her knees, her arms wrapped over her head, and she's shaking violently.

I try the driver's door. It's locked. Knowing Amber, all the doors will be locked. After what happened with Paul, she wouldn't take any chances.

I bang the window. "Kitten, it's me, Marcus. Can you open the door for me?" She doesn't respond. She doesn't even look up. I bang louder. "Kitten, please open the door. You're safe."

Slowly, she raises her head to reveal her tear-soaked face. Her wild eyes make contact with mine, her body visibly shaking, though not as much as before. She gives a small nod and twists around to unlock the car. I run around to her side and carefully open the door, then gather her in my arms. I just want to hold her while I can, hold her before she remembers that she ended things between us.

She twists around and places her head on my shoulder.

"It's okay," I murmur in her hair. "You're safe now."

This seems to have the opposite effect to what I was after. She shivers in my arms. "No, I'm not," she whispers, voice rough as if she's been screaming for hours. I tighten my hold on her. "He's still going to come after me."

I frown. "Who's coming after you?"

"Paul." The name trembles from her lips.

"He's locked away, Amber. He can't hurt you anymore."

"He's locked away, but he has a friend."

"What friend?"

She shakes her head. "I don't know but he's been sending me messages."

All I'm capable of is blinking, and I'm barely doing that. What kind of fucking prisons allows their fucking psychopaths to write letters to their victims?

"What did he tell you?" I ask.

Amber pulls away and pushes herself onto the passenger seat. I unfold myself to a stand, the wind and rain whipping against me. She reaches behind the seat and drags a purse onto her lap. She opens it and removes an envelope, which she hands to me.

"Are we fixing this tire or what?" Chase approaches the car from behind.

I glance at the envelope. The desire to rip it open and read the messages burns in me. I hand it back to Amber. "Go stay in Chase's car. We won't take long. I'll read them once we're finished."

She looks like she's going to argue, but I stop her before she can. "Please, Amber. Then I'll take you to my place, and we can discuss this." And after that, we'll discuss the real reason she broke up with me. I need something more than what she gave me. I need to know she really means it, even if I don't want to hear that it's true.

She thinks about this for a second, nods, then runs to Chase's car and climbs into the passenger side.

Chase and I work quickly to replace the tire. Once we're finished, Amber returns to her car and waits for me in the passenger seat. I've already told her I'm driving, no argument.

"Thanks for your help," I tell Chase as he gets ready to climb into his car.

"Anytime." His gaze jumps to where Amber's sitting. "I'm gonna stay at my parents' tonight. You know, in case you two want to patch things up."

I thank him and jog to Amber's car, where she's waiting, her face paler than when I arrived. Which is hard to believe given everything that's happened.

Opening the car door, I wave to Chase as he drives by, and drop onto the driver's seat. After I start the engine to warm us up, Amber hands me the envelope and I remove the small stack of papers from it.

"They're in the order I received them," she explains. "You have to read them that way. It's part of his game."

I leaf through the pages, reading each quote. I know Paul is one fucked up psychopath, but this is beyond comprehension.

"He's planning to kill you," Amber whispers. "He's got a friend on the outside who's gonna do it. That's why I ended things with you. As long as we're not together, you're safe."

I stare at her, not knowing what to say. "*This* is why you broke up with me? 'Cause you thought a guy who's locked away would be able to kill me?" I'd laugh if Amber's face wasn't so distraught. *Shit*. She really believes he's going to hurt me.

"He did the same thing before he killed Trent. No one realized that's what the messages meant. No one realized what he was capable of. And no one took the threats seriously. Just like you're not taking them seriously."

"This is different, Amber. Last time he was free to kill. He's locked away. He can't hurt me." No, that honor goes strictly to Carlos.

"You don't get it," she says, voice rising, chest heaving in and out. Her wet T-shirt clings to her, her nipples erect through the fabric of her bra and top. "He's gonna kill you."

"Look, we'll go back to my place and talk to the cops." I work hard to keep my voice even. "They'll tell you you're perfectly safe. If you're not, they'll protect you."

"I've already talked to the cops. In all honesty, Marcus, they did a crappy job last time of protecting me." She's practically yelling, eyes shiny.

Not sure what else to do to calm her down, I do the only thing I can think of.

I kiss her.

41

AMBER

The moment Marcus's lips touch mine, my mind goes blank. I'd almost forgotten how amazing it feels when he kisses me. I scoot closer, so I'm practically in his lap, and run my fingers through his wet hair. I open my mouth to let him in, but as his tongue finds mine, the images of him and Tammara in the photos crash the moment.

I jerk away and glare at him. "What the hell do you think you're doing?" The rain continues hammering the car in reply.

A heart-stopping smile slides onto his face. "Distracting you. Is it working?"

I shift away from him so that I'm pressed against the passenger door. "I know about you and Tammara."

He frowns. "What are you talking about?"

"I saw the photos."

"Again, no idea what you're talking about."

I pull the phone out of my purse and locate the photos that for some idiotic reason I haven't deleted yet. I pass it to him. "These photos."

He takes the phone and flips through the pictures. With each

228

one, his face grows paler. "Fuck," he breathes. He doesn't say anything else. He just gapes at the screen.

"I..." he finally says, still focused on the phone. "I've no idea how she did this. All I remember is her coming over, 'cause her sister's fiancé tried to hurt her. She wanted a beer and a shoulder to cry on, I guess. The next thing I remember is waking up in bed."

"With Tammara?"

"No, alone."

He doesn't beg me to believe him, claiming it's all a lie, or say anything else I'd expect he would to cover his betrayal. He just continues to stare at the phone, lost and in shock.

"Did you...did you drink anything?" I ask, unable to believe where my thoughts are headed. But something about his reaction tells me he's genuinely confused. Not at how I got the pictures. But at how he ended up kissing his ex-girlfriend.

This can't be real. These things don't happen. Not to guys.

"Yeah, I had a beer."

"Did you leave it alone with her at any point?"

Still studying the photos, he shrugs. "She'd been crying and asked for a Kleenex. So I got her some from the bathroom."

No, this is crazy. Why would she drug him?

For the same reason she sent me the photos. She wanted me to think they were back together, which she couldn't do without any "evidence." She wanted me to dump him, not realizing I already had.

"Is it possible she drugged you?"

His head shoots up and a frown forms between his eyes as he contemplates my question. "You mean like the date-rape drug?"

"Maybe. It's the only thing I can think of if you're telling me the truth. It's that, or she got you drunk."

He shakes his head. "I would've remembered that." He bangs the back of his head against the headrest, as if that will help him remember.

"You need to report this to the cops."

He turns to me. "You've gotta be kidding me, right?"

"No, I'm serious."

"Do you really think anyone's going to believe me? The cops are gonna take one look at Tammara and think I'm making this all up 'cause I was screwing around with her and didn't want you to know the truth. That's what I would think if I were them." He looks at me like he can't believe I'm not thinking the same thing, like he can't believe I'm even considering he's innocent of what the photos suggest.

But when you study the photos, and I mean really study them, it's easy to see how they could be staged. If Marcus were unconscious because of a drug, these pictures would be simple to pull off. His eyes are closed and her lips are pressed against his. In all the photos. Even the ones where her naked breasts are squished against his chest. Nothing in the photos indicates he's kissing her back.

I was so upset when I first saw them, I didn't take time to analyze the pictures. Why would I? Which is exactly what Tammara had counted on.

Marcus shifts the car into Drive and pulls away from the gravel shoulder. He's right. It's been a week since the photos. If I'm right about him being drugged, the drug is long out of his system by now. He has no proof that he's the victim. If he says anything to the cops, they probably won't take him seriously.

He squeezes my hand. "Thank you for believing me."

I squeeze back. "I just don't want you blaming yourself for something that wasn't your fault."

"You mean like what you're doing? When are you gonna stop blaming yourself for Paul's actions?"

I peer out the side window but don't say anything for a while. "How are your ribs?" I eventually ask.

"Perfect."

He's exaggerating. I did research on bruised ribs. It'll take several more weeks, at least, before he'll be a hundred percent better.

"I've missed you," he says, eyes on the road.

"I've missed you, too."

"Good." The word's soft, as though he's saying it more to himself than to me. "Do you think we can try this again? You and me?"

My body screams *say yes*. My head is less sure. Seeing him again makes me realize how much I care for him. Really care for him. This goes beyond the things we have in common, such as the love of classic rock and chicken noodle soup and basketball. It goes beyond the way he makes me laugh with his goofy math jokes. And it goes beyond how he'll do anything for the people who matter to him most. Marcus gets me. Gets me like Trent did as my boyfriend and as my best friend.

I'm not sure I can go through the pain, again, of letting him go. But I know I couldn't go through the pain if I lost Marcus because of Paul. Or possibly even because of Carlos.

"Kitten?"

My heart melts at his hopeful expression. I swallow all my fears...at least for now. "Okay."

Relieved, he gives a happy sigh, smiles, and returns his attention to the road.

As promised, after we go to a tire store to have the damaged tire replaced, he drives us back to his apartment. I scan the parking lot but don't see Chase's car in his usual spot.

"He's gone somewhere else for tonight."

I smile, hoping Marcus can't tell how nervous I am. Although I know he has no expectations, I'm ready to move past what happened with Paul. I have to if I want to feel normal again. If I want to feel like Trent used to make me feel when we fooled around. If I want to feel alive and whole.

Tonight is about Marcus and me, no one else. Where Paul was cruel, Marcus will be gentle. Gentle and patient.

Marcus suggests we watch a movie. I borrow a T-shirt and sweat pants and change into dry clothes. We settle on the couch, my head on his shoulder, his warm muscular arms wrapped around my waist. It's like we've never been apart.

We cuddle for most of the movie, but Marcus's familiar smell of safety and spice proves too tempting. I glance up, having long since lost interest in the show. I don't get far beyond his strong jaw, with the light layer of stubble, before Marcus realizes I'm no longer watching the movie and turns his intense hazel eyes on me. My breath stalls in my chest.

We stay like this for several rapid heartbeats, savoring the sight of each other; then his mouth lowers to mine, and I reach up to meet him halfway.

Our tongues slowly mingle, tease, explore. Remember. Every aching nerve between my legs begs to be taken to the heights I know are possible again. Marcus has shown me that.

My fingers inch along the waistband of his jeans. They creep under the soft fabric of his T-shirt, feeling each defined ridge of his stomach. I continue moving my hand higher and higher, my mouth never leaving his.

Marcus pulls away, hooks the bottom of his T-shirt with his fingers, and yanks it over his head. The spot where Carlos's man booted Marcus in the ribs is marred by only a faded yellow bruise. My fingers skim over it as I marvel at his perfection. I was wrong. There is such a thing. This sweet and loving man, with all his scars both inside and out, is as perfect as you can get. And he's mine.

"Do you think you can...? Do you think your ribs are okay to, you know, to go all the way?"

His mouth moves into my favorite one-sided smile. "Don't worry about me. I'll be fine." His smile fades. "Are you sure? We don't have to do anything. I'm fine just holding you." He leans down and kisses me gently on the lips. "And kissing you."

"No, I want to," I say with more determination than I thought possible, given that my body is a battlefield for desire and fear. "I need to do this, to help me move on. I was a virgin when Paul kidnapped me." My gaze locks with Marcus's so he understands just how big a deal what we're about to do is for me.

His eyes search mine for a moment, and he nods.

His hand shifts from my waist and glides under my top until his fingers brush my bra and nipple. I inhale sharply. Every touch is a mind-numbing caress. Every touch strives to make me forget about my brutal first, second, fifth time. Every touch proves that he doesn't want to rush me. And each time he touches me, I want him oh, so much more.

I move off the couch and hold out my hand. He takes it and lets himself be pulled up. I lead him into the bedroom. Once there, I remove Marcus's T-shirt so that I'm standing in his sweats and my bra. His gaze roams over my body, hungrily taking me in, yet making me feel desirable and strong. Strong enough to make love to Marcus without any fear or regrets.

He envelops me in his arms and walks me backward, only stopping when the bed hits my calves. I laugh and Marcus covers my mouth with his, turning the sound into a soft moan. His hands slowly slide up my back, pausing whenever they brush the thick raised scars. He lovingly strokes each scar with his thumb, as if by doing that, he can erase the memories.

His hands continue up and with skilled fingers, he unhooks my bra, slides the straps off my shoulders, and tosses it to the floor. His mouth still on mine, he lowers me to the bed.

"Don't close your eyes," he tells me even though they're open. "Then you'll know you're safe. If you want to stop, no matter what, tell me. Okay?"

I nod.

He studies my face one more time before he's finally satisfied with my reply. His lips glide along my jaw, showering small kisses along the way, and down my neck to my chest. His breath is hot against my nipple, and it tingles in eager anticipation. He brushes his tongue lightly over it and suddenly I can't keep still.

"So beautiful." His mouth encircles the nipple and he teases me relentlessly, between the flicking of his tongue and the sucking. God, he's good. Better than good.

I can't keep back the moans, even if I tried. He grins at the sound, his mouth still on my breast.

Unsure what else to do, my fingers wrap themselves in his hair. *His* fingers wander over my stomach and pause at the waistband of my sweats. They slip between the fabric and my skin. I tighten my grip on his hair.

He lifts his head from my breast, gauging my reaction. Biting my lip, I nod. The intensity of his eyes leaves me speechless.

"You sure?" he asks, his voice a husky whisper.

"Yes," I reply, tone equally soft.

His lips return to mine, raining butterfly kisses on them. I open to him and he deepens the kiss. His fingers slip under the elastic of my panties and slide along the slick surface surrounding my entrance. They tease me in a way I've never been teased and drive me closer to the edge. I grip the sheets to keep from tumbling over. I'm not ready for that yet. This time I want to feel like *I'm* in control.

With tentative hands I undo Marcus's zipper, then tug on the waistband of his jeans. He gets the hint and clumsily removes his jeans and boxer briefs, releasing his erection, which is as beautiful as its owner.

I look up at his face. He's biting his lip, something I've never seen him do. I'm not the only one who's nervous. That thought fills me with joy. The guy who has a reputation of being a man-whore, who has slept with women more experienced than me, is acting as if this is his first time.

Marcus leans over the bed and my hand drifts to the base of him. I gently grasp him, marveling at his response to my touch. The erotic sounds he makes almost make me come right there.

I take in his expression as I move my hand along the length of him until I reach his tip. Not once do his eyes move away from mine, as if he's memorizing every one of my reactions.

He slides the sweat pants and my underwear off me and tosses them next to his clothes on the floor. He lowers himself back on the bed. With his gaze still on my face, he eases one finger inside me. It caresses and swirls against my inner core, and I gasp at the overwhelming sensation rocking my body.

Another finger joins the first one, gently stretching my soft heat. Marcus takes his time, slowly moving his fingers in and out, taking care to make sure I'm truly ready.

He doesn't say anything. He just keeps his eyes steady on me.

I reach for his length again and resume stroking him. Enjoying the velvet feel of it against my palm.

"You might want to stop doing that," he says after a moment, voice slightly strained.

"Am I doing it wrong?" I worry my lower lip.

"Far from it, Kitten. But if you keep that up, this will be over before you're ready."

I smile and release him.

Heat gradually builds between my legs, growing hotter with each stroke of his thumb on my clit, until an explosion rips through me. I moan and call out his name along with "Oh, God."

My body feels limp, sated, one with the universe as it floats back to earth, and I inwardly smile.

Marcus pulls away, opens his desk drawer, and removes a foil package. He rips it open and rolls the condom on. All I'm capable of doing, once again, is marveling at his perfection, and at how badly I want that perfection inside me, making me feel things I've never felt before.

He gently bites his lip again. "Are you sure?"

I can't help but smile at his sweet concern. "Absolutely."

Marcus positions himself so he's pressed against my entrance, and eases his way in, the entire time watching my reaction. Making sure he's not moving too fast, too soon.

When he's positive I'm not going to break, he starts moving in and out, faster and harder until my body shatters around him, in a good way, and I cry out. He cries out seconds later.

Tears slide down the side of my face. I can't help it. Trent and I had been waiting for the right moment. I never had that moment until now.

Marcus removes himself from me and discards the condom in the trash. He returns to the bed and pulls me into his arms. "Are you okay?" His voice is so gentle and sweet, it sets off another wave of emotions. More tears leak out.

He rolls onto his side and props his head up, bent elbow on the bed. He frowns, concern filling his eyes. "Did I hurt you?"

I give him a soft smile. "You didn't hurt me. It's just...it never felt like that with Paul." I hate saying his name after what Marcus and I just did. That was beautiful. What Paul did was cruel.

Marcus brushes my cheek with his thumb. "What he did to you was rape. He didn't share what we shared. He didn't make love to you." He kisses me tenderly on my lips.

"He didn't rape me." I swallow, knowing I can't keep up with the lie any longer. He needs to know the truth if we're planning for this relationship to work. I don't want any more lies between us. "I had sex with him. Willingly." Numerous people have told me it was rape. That I was coerced into having sex to stay alive, but there were times when it didn't feel like rape. When during those rare tender moments, it felt like part of Paul did care about me. It was the same tenderness I had seen in Paul when we worked at the animal shelter.

I want to say this all to Marcus, but the words remain stuck in my throat. Especially at the look of disgust on Marcus's face. It would be one thing if Paul had raped me. It's another thing for me to be a willing partner. I can see that on his face. I can hear it in his silence. I can feel it in my heart as it crumbles under the weight of his reaction.

I scramble off the bed and yank on my clothes. Marcus doesn't say anything. He's lying back on the bed, his bent arm covering his face.

I run. Run out of his bedroom. Run out of the apartment. Run down the stairs and out to the parking lot. I keep running until I'm in my car, and with tears joining the previous ones, I drive away.

42

MARCUS

uck. Fuck. Fuck. That's the only thing I can think of after Amber slams the apartment door shut.

I'd been so deep in thought, I hadn't realized until it was too late that she misunderstood my silence. I'd been thinking about what she had said and how Ryan used to let Frank abuse him just so our stepfather wouldn't hurt me. I hadn't realized it until Amber told me what she had done to keep alive. I hadn't realized until now that this was part of why Ryan never wanted the secret out—he felt like he'd consented.

Instead of telling her what was going through my head, I kept silent. God, how could I have fucked this up? How could I have fucked up the best thing that's ever happened to me?

It takes a minute or two before I'm physically able to scramble out of bed and into my jeans. I race out of the apartment, and practically hurl myself down the stairs and out the main entrance.

But I'm too late.

I chase after Amber, but she either doesn't see me or can't get away from me fast enough. She speeds off, leaving me standing there barefoot on the sidewalk, the air squeezed out of my lungs.

With the cold rain pelting my half-naked body, I bend over,

hands braced against my knees. My ribs cry out in pain as I fight to catch my breath.

I can't believe how much I screwed things up, and how I did it right after I told her I love her. Okay, I might not have said those exact words. But it was implied when I told her Paul didn't make love to her. I've never referred to it that way with another girl, but I've never made love before now. With other girls, I've only had sex.

I return to the apartment, uncertain what to do next. Throw something. Get drunk. Track down Carlos and let him finish me off. My heart feels as though I'm dragging it on the ground behind me. With each step, it becomes more damaged, to the point it's barely functioning.

First, I try phoning Amber, but all I get is her voice mail. All I can do is leave a message, telling her she's wrong. I didn't think badly of what she did to stay alive. And no matter what she thinks, Paul did rape her.

I spend the next hour pacing, waiting for her to return my call and text. When it becomes obvious that's not going to happen, I snatch an empty beer bottle from the coffee table and throw it against the wall. It shatters, leaving a shallow dent. Bits of glass hail onto the beige carpet.

Next, I grab five beers from the fridge and place them on the table in a single line. I plunk myself on the couch and drink from the first bottle. The sound of laughter from the neighbor's TV drifts through the wall, and for a second, I swear the laughter is directed at me. A reminder of how my life is nothing but a sick joke. The punch line's on me. Just when I thought I'd finally redeemed myself to some higher power, for everything I've done, my life becomes even more fucked up.

I finish the second bottle and then the third. I know I'm being reckless, but I don't care. Maybe Frank has the right idea about getting drunk all the time. It really does dull the pain.

Only, it doesn't eradicate it.

"DON'T TOUCH HIM!" RYAN YELLS, GLARING UP AT FRANK. HE MIGHT BE trying to act brave, but my fifteen-year-old brother is scared shitless.

Frank reeks of beer but he's still stable on his feet. He doesn't have enough alcohol in his system to help soften the blows.

Ryan realizes this. "Get out of here, Marcus," he pleads, eyes not leaving Frank for even a second.

I take a step toward the door. I'm not sure where I'm going, but I have to escape before it's too late.

"Where ya think you're goin'?" Frank grabs my arm and flings me to the side. I stumble and hit my head hard on the drawers. The world spins around me in a blur of blues, browns and white.

I collapse to the floor.

Frank grips my arm and yanks me to my feet. He pushes me to the bed, forcing me onto my back, legs dangling over the side. Before I realize what he's doing, he unsnaps my jeans and pulls down the zipper. His cold callous fingers grope inside my boxers and grab hold of my dick. Shame floods my body, but I'm too dizzy to do anything about it.

"You stuck that in a girl yet?" His cruel grin makes my stomach turn.

I want to kick him and try to get free, but I'm afraid, afraid he'll do something worse if I fight back.

"Get off him," Ryan screams, pounding his fists against Frank's arm. But he's not strong enough to do any damage. Not like the damage Frank has inflicted on us for years. Though this is the first time he's touched me there.

Frank sneers at him. "You want me to do you instead?"

I expect Ryan to scream, "Fuck, no!" but he doesn't. His face pales and he can't even look at me when he nods. "As long as you don't touch my brother." His voice is so small, I'm not even sure I heard him right. I pray with everything I have in me and then some that I heard him wrong.

Frank removes his hand from my boxers, yanks me up by the arm and shoves me to the floor. I lie there, too stunned to move, and helplessly watch as Frank turns to Ryan. He orders my brother to undo his jeans *and pull them and his underwear down. He then gestures for Ryan to bend over the bed.*

My stomach churns in anger; my eyes snap open. I roll off the couch and stagger to the bathroom. I barely make it in time before I heave into the toilet.

Even in my current drunken state, I feel the pain in my ribs from the strain. And for once, I welcome it.

Puking the contents of my stomach does nothing to erase the image in my brain of Frank raping Ryan. And not just that one time. Even though I never saw Frank touch Ryan that way again, I wondered if it was still happening, to keep me safe, but I was always too afraid to ask Ryan. Too afraid to find out the truth.

I hurl into the toilet again. Once my stomach has had enough and there's nothing left to heave, at least for now, I collapse onto the cool tile and lie there, unmoving.

I've never told anyone my secret. Not even Chase. After what happened that night, after I realized Ryan was probably letting Frank continue to violate him—just to protect me from Frank—I hooked up with any female willing to spread her legs for me. Anything to prove I wasn't Ryan.

And I'm still not. Ryan risked his life for me. The night Frank shot him, Frank had come home drunk like usual, carrying a gun. He took me by surprise and threatened to kill me if I didn't let him screw me. I've never been more terrified. Ryan came in at that point, after Chase told him where to find me. Ryan shot Frank in the leg. Frank shot Ryan in the chest. And just like that one night many years ago, Ryan made me promise never to tell anyone what happened when we were teens. To not let him die in shame.

I wipe the tears away with the back of my hand and sit up. I can't even feel angry for puking so much. I deserve it. I didn't stop Ryan from being hurt. I didn't stand up for him and tell the authorities what Frank had done to me. Like Ryan, I was too ashamed to admit it. If only I had been as strong as he was and Amber is. I hurt Amber when I hadn't meant to. I don't deserve her love. The only thing I deserve is exactly what I'll get—a hangover to rival all others.

CHASE COMES HOME THE FOLLOWING AFTERNOON. I HAVEN'T MOVED from the couch all day, other than to puke in the toilet a few more times. "Dude, you look like shit."

Feel that way, too. "I think I have the flu," I mumble. From the way he takes in the sea of beer bottles on the table, it's obvious he's not buying that.

He frowns. "You wanna talk about it?"

I shake my head, the movement aggravating an already bad headache.

I stay on the couch for the rest of the day, not talking. Chase pulls up the armchair and we watch mindless TV. He doesn't push anything, but I can feel him watching me more than he watches the TV. He doesn't even comment on the new dent in the wall. The pieces of glass have since been removed, when I was sober enough to pick them up this morning.

He eventually gets up and sighs loudly. "Call her." He doesn't say anything else before disappearing into his room, and I'm glad I'm not privy to his thoughts. I'm sure he's calling me an idiot, even though he has no idea what I've done.

THE NEXT DAY, I RETURN TO MY CLASSES. MY HANGOVER IS GONE, though I still feel like shit. The memory of what happened with Amber and the memory I've tried to repress for so long are both warring inside me, and I'm not sure how to escape.

I also wish I knew how to escape Tammara. "Hi, Marcus," she purrs as I get ready to leave campus, my hand moving to the car door handle.

I freeze for a second before turning on her, voice tight. "What do you want?"

"You." She smiles, a seductive tigress going in for the kill. "After the other night, I'm surprised you haven't called." She takes a step closer. I take one back, purposefully keeping the distance between us. After what happened, after what she did to me, it's taking everything I have not to kill her.

"I don't make it a habit of calling girls who drug me." My voice is smooth like the sharp edge of a knife.

She doesn't so much as flinch, but the icy intensity in her eyes tells me everything I need to know. I turn away.

"I don't know what you're talking about, Marcus. Why would I drug you? That's ridiculous." The sincerity in her words surprises me. She's a better actress than I realized.

"So you're telling me you have no idea why I don't remember that night, other than you coming over 'cause your sister's fiancé tried to hurt you? And you're telling me you have no idea how Amber ended up with those photos of you and me in bed?"

"I didn't drug you." Her exasperation is as fake as her fingernails. "We were drinking and you must have drunk too much. That's why you don't remember. But everything in those photos... that really did happen."

"Neither Amber nor I believe any of that. So whatever you thought was going to happen between you and me, you can forget it, Tammara. I already told you it's over between us. And I meant it. What I want to know is if you"—I swallow hard, struggling to get the words out—"if you touched...violated me."

Tammara frantically shakes her head. "No. It was nothing like that. I would never—"

"What about what you told me about your sister's fiancé? Was that a lie too?"

She turns her gaze to the ground and nods.

"I don't get it. I've told you before there's nothing between us, other than the friends-with-benefits thing we agreed on. Why are you so desperate to be with me?"

"Because you're different, Marcus. You're the first guy who's pursued me that I was sure wasn't interested in my family or my money. Plus I'm supposed to settle down with a respectable guy, so it'll look good for when my father runs for the senate. God, do you know how boring that is?"

I frown. "So you're pulling some sort of high school rebellious crap? What, I'm the bad boy your parents will disapprove of?" Not wanting to hear any more, I open the car door. "Keep away from me, Tammara, or else I will press charges." I climb behind the wheel and slam the door.

Tammara stands motionless for a moment, seeming lost.

No longer caring whether she's still here or not, I check my phone. Amber still hasn't returned any of my calls or texts. If she hasn't by now, she never will. It really is over this time.

She was one of the few good things in my life, and I've lost her.

I hurl the phone against the passenger door and watch it shatter.

43

AMBER

Brittany's in our room when I return from classes. Her head is slumped forward, her back pressed against the wall in the small space between the closet and her desk, and her knees are pulled tight to her chest. Her shoulders jerk rhythmically while small sobbing sounds fill the cramped space.

I've never seen Brittany like this before.

I'm not even sure she's aware I'm here. Usually the first thing she does when I enter the room is glare at me, but this time she doesn't even glance up.

"Are you okay?" I crouch in front of her.

Scattered around her feet are what appears to be anime drawings. When she doesn't reply, I pick one up and examine it. It's a black-and-white sketch of a girl with long black hair and big eyes. She has no mouth but still manages to look sad. In one hand is a knife dripping with what I guess is blood, as it's been colored in with a red pencil. In the other hand is a red heart. Above where her heart would be located, a piece of her long-sleeved T-shirt is missing and the spot around it is also colored in red pencil. Next to the young girl, who could almost be Brittany, are the words "Some-

245

body take my heart. Cuz I don't want it," which are written in black Goth-like letters.

I pick up the next picture and gasp. This one contains what could easily be cute little-kid versions of Marcus and me. He's sitting on the ground, wearing jeans and his black leather jacket. I'm kneeling slightly behind him, hugging him with my arms around his neck. Above the kids are the words "I love you."

In front of me are the words I've known for a while but have been too afraid to admit. I love Marcus. Only now it's too late.

I haven't listened to his messages. I'm not going to. I know what he's going to say, and I'm too scared to hear the words. The words that confirm he and I are over.

Scrawled in the corner of each picture is what appears to be a signature. It takes a few seconds to make out Brittany's name. As in, she drew them. I glance back and forth between the pictures. Is that what this is all about? She had a secret crush on Marcus, like every other female on campus, and now she's upset because she thinks he and I are an item?

I stare at the girl, unsure what to do. Do I tell her Marcus and I aren't together, so she thinks she has a chance with him after all? The idea of them together, kissing, causes my heart to ache. The idea of *any* woman kissing him causes my heart to ache.

But Brittany doesn't come off as the type who would cry over a relationship that never existed. She might glare at me more, but never openly sob or cower in a corner over something like this.

I rest my hand on her knee. "Brittany, has someone hurt you?"

She lifts her head. Blood from a small cut below her left eye mixes with her tears.

I suck in a breath. "What happened?"

Brittany wipes the damp mascara trails with her hand, smearing them and the blood. "I don't want to talk about it," she mutters.

"It might help."

"What would a princess like you know 'bout anything?"

I snort. "What? You think I get several nightmares a night because I'm a princess? You think I wake up screaming 'cause I left my tiara at Prince Charming's house?"

That gets a small smile out of her. Her gaze moves to my forehead. "How did you get that?" She touches her forehead in the same spot where I now have a scar.

I know what she's really asking. "I didn't get it 'cause someone hit me. I stumbled and lost my balance..." I avert my eyes, trying to figure out how much to tell her. I need to gain her trust if I want to help her. She might not want to admit it, but she does need my help.

Or maybe I need to help her as a way to help me.

"I get flashbacks," I blurt.

Her eyebrows scrunch in confusion.

"Someone hurt me earlier this year. He almost killed me. That's why I have the nightmares. When I'm not asleep, anything can set me off and make me remember things I'd rather not remember." I swallow back the pain of telling her the truth, of opening myself up to the girl who dislikes me.

Brittany stares at me, as if she's digging deeper, finding another way to make me feel even more fragile. Between what I've told her and the knowledge that Paul is out there, and after what happened last night with Marcus, she doesn't have to delve too far.

I already feel exposed and raw.

"I was raped," she whispers, voice hoarse.

My insides squeeze into a tight ball at her words. The words I wish I could take away and make less real. "Do you know who it was?"

She looks down and nods. "Jack. My boyfriend."

"Have you told the police?"

Still looking down, she shakes her head.

"You really should. They can lock him away and—" I want to say, *you can feel safe again*, but I'm still waiting for that to happen. Even if Brittany's rapist is locked away, will she ever feel safe?

"I can't do that. I don't want to be poked at like I'm some crappy science experiment."

"I know. But I'll stay with you if you want."

She looks at me, and I don't see the girl who has disliked me all semester. I see the girl who wants to trust me, the girl who needs a friend, the girl who wants someone to be there for her, to help her get through this nightmare.

"Why the hell would you do that for me? I've been a bitch to you all semester."

"Yeah, well, it's not like I didn't deserve it. I kept waking you up with my nightmares. I'd probably be bitchy too if our places were reversed."

Her gaze drops to the drawings. I pick up the one of the two kids who resemble Marcus and me. "These are great. How come we've been roommates for so long and I never knew you could draw like this?" I figured she liked drawing. I've seen her supplies. But until now, I'd never seen her artwork. I never knew if she was any good, and I hadn't bothered to ask.

She fingers the picture of the girl with the bloodied knife. "My father thought my drawings were a waste of time. He used to get angry when he saw me draw, so I got good at hiding them." She runs her finger over the knife. "You promise me you'll stay with me...at the hospital?"

"Yes. Unless you want me to leave. I know what it's like to be checked for signs of rape. And I know what it's like to have no one there for you. So yes, if you want me there, I'll stay."

Because Brittany doesn't want anyone to notice her, I lend her Trent's hoodie, which swallows her up. She cleans the mascara and blood off her face with a tissue and slips on a pair of sunglasses. She presses a tissue against the cut, though it doesn't seem to be enough to stop the bleeding.

I drive her to the hospital, but I don't press her to tell me what happened. I let her know I'm here if she wants to talk. We mostly just listen to the rock station on the radio. Every so often, I look at her to check that she's all right.

At the hospital, I reach for her trembling hand as she leans in to talk to the triage nurse. She almost squeezes the life out of my fingers when she tells the nurse that she was raped.

Much to Brittany's obvious relief, the nurse doesn't make us sit in the waiting room. We're sent to an exam room where we wait, still not saying much. Brittany retreats into her own world, and I pretend to be fascinated with the various pieces of medical equipment in the room, while I sit next to her on the exam table. Every now and then, the distant wail of sirens approaches the hospital.

"Did they catch the guy?" she says at one point, while I'm trying not to think about Marcus, while I'm trying not to think about when the doctor examined me after my kidnapping, while I'm trying not to think about the upcoming court case. While I'm trying not to think. Period.

"He's in a psych ward."

A doctor and nurse enter the room, keeping me from elaborating, which is fine by me. Even though they're both women, Brittany still clutches my hand, the pressure on my fingers even tighter than in triage.

The doctor cleans the cut and places Steri-Strips below Brittany's eye. Once she's finished, she asks Brittany to lie back and examines her while I focus on my roommate's face and stroke her silky hair. Brittany stares at the ceiling. A tear runs down her temple and she sniffs.

Once the doctor's finished, she and the nurse leave, and a female cop enters and asks questions. Brittany answers the best she can. She's still scared, but the cop tries to make the process easier for her.

"If he's caught, he'll end up in a psych ward?" Her confusion over my earlier comment clear.

The cop shakes her head. "No, he'll go to jail."

Her confusion deepening, Brittany looks at me.

"My—the man who hurt me has mental issues," I explain. "He's in the prison's psych ward." I leave it at that.

After the cop leaves, a rape counselor comes in. She and Brittany talk for a few minutes, and the woman tells her about the resources available to rape survivors.

"It wasn't your fault, no matter what anyone tells you," she says. "You didn't ask for this to happen. The only person responsible for what happened is the man who hurt you."

As the woman answers Brittany's questions, I dwell on how Paul may have been responsible for his actions, but the system failed me, and it failed Trent and Michael. It didn't do enough to protect us.

Can it protect me from Paul, even though he's supposed to be locked away? Or will it fail me once again?

44

MARCUS

Chase and I are sitting in the Marketplace when my phone rings. I don't recognize the number, but I'm expecting an important call. I lift my finger to let Chase know I have to answer this.

"I need to talk to Marcus Reid, please," a man says on the other end of the line.

"Speaking."

"This is Detective Goodwin. I have some information concerning Paul Carlson. Is this a good time?"

"Did you find out who his partner is?"

"I contacted the facility where he's staying. Mr. Carlson is under a high-security watch based on the nature of his alleged crimes. It'd be impossible for him to contact Miss Scott or anyone else on the outside via mail or email. According to his records, only his lawyer has visited him."

"Could the lawyer have sent the messages on the creep's behalf?"

"We're investigating him, but I checked the videos of their interactions, and there was no exchange of materials between the two individuals. In all honesty, I don't believe the person who is sending

251

the messages to Miss Scott has anything to do directly with Mr. Carlson."

"Could it be a copycat?" I ask. "Someone who read about her case in the newspaper?"

"It's possible, but during an investigation certain details are kept from the media, to help us make a case against the suspect later on. In the case of Miss Scott's stalking, none of the details about the messages were ever released. The only way anyone would know about the contents of the original messages would be to have heard about them from another source, or they've seen them. Sorry I can't be much help beyond that."

"Have you told Amber yet?"

"Yes." We talk for a minute or two longer and end the call.

"Good or bad news?" Chase asks. I haven't told him about the messages. The only person I told was the detective, whom I contacted after I screwed up with Amber. I wanted to learn if they had made any progress in the case. Since it was believed I might somehow be involved, the detective was more than happy to talk to me.

"I'm not sure." I spot Jordan on the far side of the food court. Amber isn't with her. "Give me a second."

I dodge around people as I make my way toward her. She turns from the Mexican food counter and walks in the opposite direction of me. I pick up my pace and bump shoulders with someone.

"Hey, watch it," the guy yells. I'm too focused on Jordan to respond.

If it were anytime but lunch, the place wouldn't be so packed, and I'd catch her in no time. But as it is, it takes me several minutes before I'm close enough so she can hear me call her name.

She pivots and the smile on her face vanishes the second she realizes I was the one who called her. Her eyes narrow. Clearly Amber told her everything.

"How's she doing?" I ask.

Jordan crosses her arms over her chest. "What's it to you?"

I've always liked Jordan, but right now she's pissing me off. "Because I care about her." Because she means the world to me.

"From where I am, it doesn't sound like it." Jordan makes a move to leave.

I step in front of her. "I made a mistake, but I don't want to discuss that with you. What I want to know is if she's still receiving any letters that are upsetting her." I don't know how much Amber has told her, but I take a gamble that Jordan might know something. But I leave things vague enough so that I don't betray Amber's secret.

Jordan releases a long slow breath that I sense has nothing to do with me, and drops her arms to her side, revealing the rainbow design on her T-shirt. "They're coming almost daily. She barely sleeps at night because of the nightmares. She failed two tests last week. I don't think she's gonna last much longer before she has a breakdown."

"Have you read the letters?"

She nods. "It's pretty much the same as the other ones, but now some are quotes from classics. Whoever's sending them thinks you two are still together. But they're no longer threatening your life. They're threatening Amber's."

Fuck. No wonder she's having so many nightmares. Things aren't going to get better as long as the cops have no idea who's sending them.

"Look, I have to go," Jordan says. I don't stop her this time. Detective Goodwin's words are on repeat mode in my head. *The only way anyone would know about the contents of the original messages would be to have heard about them from another source, or they've seen them.*

I know one person on campus who fits the description, and I scan the food court in case she's here. When I don't see her, I tell Chase I'll see him later and head to Emma's dorm.

Fortunately I don't have to figure out how the hell to get inside this time. Emma is talking by the steps to a guy who could be on the men's basketball team. He's at least my height.

I march up to her. "We need to talk."

Without so much as a glance at me, she says coolly, "No, we don't."

"This is important."

"Doubt it," she fires back.

"C'mon, man, she's not interested. Get the hint." The guy's voice is even, but there's no missing that I'm pissing him off.

I level him with a dark expression. "I'm not interested in her, either. But unless she wants to be dragged to the police station, she's gonna find time in her busy schedule to talk to me. So what's it going to be, Emma?"

Her eyes widen. "Police station? I haven't done anything wrong." She briefly looks at the guy, who's staring at me, unsure what to make of any of this. "Okay. But is this going to take long?"

"Depends on how much you have to tell me." I tell the guy she'll call him later, and wave her forward, toward the engineering building.

As expected, the building isn't busy. I point for her to take a seat at a table away from everyone else.

She does; her eyes scan the area as if searching for the nearest exits. "So what do you want?"

"Some information."

She taps her foot on the floor. The sound of it reminds me of a basketball bouncing against the hardwood of a basketball court. And that makes me think of Amber.

"Could you be maybe a little more specific?" she huffs.

"It's about the messages the psychopath used to send Amber."

"Why are you asking me about them? Ask her."

"I'm asking *you*. You two were best friends. I'm betting you saw them, didn't you?"

"What's it to you?" she grumbles.

I fist my hands, fighting the urge to shake the answers out of her. "Like I said, you have a choice. Talk to me or I'll call the cops."

"Yes, I saw them. I saw every one of them. Including the ones we later realized were his twisted way of saying he was going to kill my brother." Her voice splinters, and the pain I know she's been struggling with flickers on her face before she glances down at the table.

My tone softens. "Have you told anyone else about them? Someone on campus, maybe?"

"My brother was killed. I lost two of the most important people in my life because of what that murderer did." She looks at me. "Do you know what that feels like?"

"I do. My brother was killed, too." *And it's my fault he's dead.*

Emma's eyes tear up. "But your best friend didn't turn his back on you because of it, did he? Mine pushed me away when I needed her the most."

"Amber's not trying to hurt you. She's punishing herself because she blames herself for what Paul did. And she's punishing herself for hurting you because of what happened to Trent. You need to talk to her. But first you need to tell me if you told anyone about the letters."

She nods, clearly confused at what that has to do with anything. "I told your girlfriend."

45

AMBER

Some people say friends and family give us the inner strength we need to deal with our demons and help us find the will to keep going no matter what challenges face us. But as I check the bulletin board in the Student Services Building, I realize the right poster can have the same effect.

I remove the brochure from the display below. *Self-Defense Class for Beginners*. Perfect. I slip it into my backpack and enter the Counseling Center.

A few students are waiting in the plastic seats along the wall. Some spare me a glance when I enter. I gasp at the sight of one girl. She's tall and athletic and has familiar long blond hair curtaining her face.

I don't know if she heard me or felt me watching her, but her head turns in my direction. It's not Emma. The heaviness residing in my chest since last spring stirs. I push it aside and walk to the front desk.

A female with purple chunks in her short dark hair looks up from her computer. "Do you have an appointment?"

"No, but I'd like to book one. To see a counselor."

She taps at her keyboard. "We had a cancelation for this after-noon at two. Can you make that?"

Accepting help is a sign of weakness, Mom's voice says in my head.

Is it? Until I reached out and helped Brittany, she was scared and uncertain. A week later, she's strong and determined never to give another guy power over her.

Mom was wrong. Accepting help isn't a sign of weakness. It's a sign of strength.

I've already failed two of my exams in the past two weeks because of the nightmares, insomnia, and flashbacks. I can't keep living like this.

"That will be great. Thanks."

I leave the center a tiny bit lighter than when I went in, and return to my dorm room as Jordan is leaving hers, wearing her favorite T-shirt to study in. It's black with the word HOPE in rainbow colors on the chest.

"Are you and Brittany studying now?" she asks.

When Brittany discovered I was struggling with math, she offered to help me study for the final. Although she's not Marcus, she's not a bad tutor after all.

I nod. "But I want to show you and Brittany something first."

We enter my room. Brittany's at her desk, working at a math equation. I remove the brochure from my backpack and place it on her textbook.

"We're signing up for this," I tell them.

With Jordan glancing over her shoulder, Brittany picks up the brochure and reads it. "You want us to learn to kick some major ass?" She nods. "Yep, I can live with that."

"I don't know," Jordan says slowly. "We could get hurt."

Both Brittany and I look at her, eyebrows raised.

She removes the brochure from Brittany's hands. "Do you really think knowing this stuff would've helped you two?"

"You're right," I say. "It wouldn't have helped me. When Paul kidnapped me, he had a gun. There's probably nothing I could have done. But not every situation is going to be like that."

"Amber's right," Brittany chimes in. "If I had known how to defend myself, I could have escaped."

"It'll be fun," I promise. "Don't you have ass-kicking somewhere on your bucket list?" I wrap my arm around Jordan's shoulders. "I promise you won't regret it."

"Okay," she sighs. "But only if you promise you'll talk to Marcus."

I drop my arm from her shoulders and step away. "Why would I do that? I told you it's over between us."

"Is it? You're miserable and from what Chase told me, so is Marcus. Marcus won't tell him what's going on and you haven't told me anything, either. But I saw him yesterday and he told me he made a mistake. I swear, Amber, he still cares about you."

"It's complicated."

"Just talk to him. I get the feeling you two have unfinished business, and you won't get closure until you talk things through."

"You have a psychology final tomorrow, don't you?" Brittany says with a smirk.

"How did you know?"

Brittany and I can only laugh, even though Jordan has a point. But whatever I decide to do will have to wait for a few more hours. I have a math final tomorrow that I have to study for before my counseling appointment this afternoon.

46

AMBER

I sink farther into the black leather couch, the weight of my phone with Marcus's messages heavy in my hoodie pocket. I haven't listened to them yet. First, I was too afraid to. Too afraid to hear the disgust in his voice. But after Jordan told me what Chase said, I decided to listen to them before coming here. Except I was too busy studying and lost track of time. As it is, I barely made it here in time for my appointment.

"What is it that you want, Amber?" the therapist asks from the matching couch. Behind her is a large painting of a young girl reading under a tree filled with cherry blossoms. A golden retriever puppy sits next to her, listening intently to the story.

"I want to feel normal again." Like that girl.

"What does normal mean to you?"

I have to think on that one. It's been so long since I've felt normal, I don't know what it means anymore. "I guess it's no longer having nightmares and flashbacks. To not feel scared all the time. To feel whole."

"Why do you want the nightmares and flashbacks to stop?"

"Because I want to forget what happened. Because they're affecting my classes. I can't sleep. I can't do anything."

She smiles, the sight of it reassuring. "It's your desire to forget, Amber, that's causing the nightmares and flashbacks. I want you to try the opposite. I want you to accept what happened. You can't go back and change it. You need to accept that it happened and move on. While you've been blocking out the painful memories, you've also been blocking the good ones that happened during the same period. Those are the memories that are important to help you heal and be emotionally healthy again."

She warns me it won't happen overnight, but I will start to feel better over time, and eventually the nightmares and flashbacks will no longer be an issue. I might still have them, but I'll be able to cope with them better.

It's like a hundred-pound weight has been shoved off my shoulder. Unfortunately, the other one is still pinned down with the weight of knowing the cops have no idea who's been sending me the quotes. It's not Paul. That's all they know.

I leave the therapist's office and find a quiet spot on campus, where no one is hanging out. I claim an empty bench overlooking one of the snow-covered sports fields. Before I listen to Marcus's messages, there's one thing I have to do. The one thing I've put off too long.

I need to apologize to Mom.

Usually she'd be at the office, but when I call her, her assistant tells me that Mom phoned in sick. I know why she's sick, and it has nothing to do with a cold or flu.

I dial my home number. Mom doesn't answer. I get her voice mail instead. It's not what I want, but it'll have to do—for now.

"Mom, it's Amber." My pulse pounds loud and fast in my ears at what I'm about to tell her. I shouldn't be this nervous. But I am. "I just want to tell you that I love you and that I'm sorry for what I said. I love you very much and I miss you. I miss the mom who doesn't drink. The one who once told me she loved me more than anything." A small sob escapes, but I don't let that get in my way of telling her how I feel. "I wish you would come back to me, Mom. I want you back, but I want the mom who doesn't drink. And the mom who would have never looked at me and blamed me for Michael's death." I hang up and take a deep breath, knowing it's too late to grab the words back. Not that I want to.

I'd have preferred to tell her everything to her face, but the way my grades are dropping, I don't have time to go home. Finals start tomorrow. I didn't want to wait another week to talk to her. Now I just have to hope she listens to the message—the entire message—and that it will make some sort of difference, no matter how small.

With my head down, I walk to my dorm. And accidentally bump into someone.

"Sorry," I say as I look up, only to discover I've run into Emma. Before she can say anything, I fling my arms around her shoulders and hug her. She stiffens at first but then returns my hug, holding me tight. The heaviness in my chest that has been there since spring fades.

"I'm so sorry, Em. For everything." I pull away, even though I never want to let go of her again. "Can we go somewhere to talk?"

She nods, a soft smile on her face. That alone is enough to ease some of tension that's been building in me with everything that's going on.

We walk to The Coffee Shack, where we order drinks and find a quiet corner by a large window with the view of the courtyard.

Loud laughter breaks out from a group of students several tables away, but they're far enough from us to prevent them from overhearing our conversation.

My heart pounds against my ribs as I sip my coffee. I wouldn't be surprised if the force of my heart fractures one of my ribs. "I'm sorry about what Paul did to Trent. And I don't blame you if you hate me. I deserve it."

Emma's lip trembles and she chews it for a second. "How could I hate you, Amber? You were my best friend. And you had nothing to do with what happened to Trent. You were as much a victim as he was. I just don't get why you didn't want to talk to me anymore. I thought we were best friends. I needed you, but you wanted nothing to do with me, or any of our other friends."

She sniffs. "When you were found, I tried to visit you so many times, at the hospital and then at your house. But your mom kept telling me you needed time, that you weren't ready to talk to me. Then you came back to school and avoided me. You avoided everyone. Why?"

I close my eyes briefly. When I reopen them, the world is a blur of colors. "I was so messed up when the firefighters found me. I was barely holding on. Paul hurt me in ways you could never imagine, but knowing how much he hurt you when Trent died"—my voice shakes—"was worse than anything Paul ever did to me. I knew seeing me would only cause you more pain. I couldn't do that to you, Em. You had lots of friends who would help you. I thought you were better off without me."

She just stares at me, barely breathing. "What about you? You had no one." She wipes away a tear. "I saw you at school, looking half-dead. I wanted to help you but when I tried, you'd disappear. I even talked to your grandmother. She was worried about you, but she was afraid if she pushed you, you would pull away further. Neither of us knew what to do."

I shift my gaze to the window and sigh. "I know. She tried to get me to return to therapy, but I couldn't." I glance back at Emma and smile. "Until today. I realized I couldn't deal with everything on my own anymore." Not that I was dealing with it. "I've started to see a therapist."

Emma's face lights up. "Does that mean we can be friends again?"

I nod. "I would love that." We talk about what we've been up to for the past few months. I avoid the topic of Marcus.

"I talked to your boyfriend today," she says at one point. "He really cares about you. You're so lucky."

I almost choke on my coffee at her words, but I smile as if I already knew this. "I miss Trent and I'll always love him." I remove my hoodie and place my bare arm on the table, tattoo side up. Scars and all.

She gasps; then her eyes widen and she grins. Though there's no missing the moisture in her eyes due to the scars on my wrist and the meaning behind the tattoo.

"I'm betting your mom doesn't know about this?" She runs a finger over her brother's name. "Where did you get it done?"

I tell her.

"And here I thought you weren't the tattooing type." She laughs, and I realize how much I've missed the sound of it.

"Grandma loves it," I say, grinning.

"I bet she does. I wouldn't be surprised if she has several tattoos you don't know about." Her smile vanishes and her expression grows sober. "I'm sorry about what I told Tammara. I had no idea she was going to use that information to hurt you."

I frown. "Tammara? What are you talking about?"

Emma's face pales. "I thought you knew. That's why I was talking to Marcus. He didn't tell you?"

"I haven't talked to him"—*for over a week*—"today."

"I was upset and Tammara pretended to be my friend, and I kinda told her about the sick notes the murderer used to send you. I never realized she'd use that to hurt you."

I stop breathing and gape at Emma. It's all I'm capable of after hearing that Marcus's ex-girlfriend is the cause of my recent downward spiral.

"You okay?"

I nod. More than okay. Everything now makes sense. Tammara's been trying to drive me away from Marcus and drag him back into her life. And she almost won. But it also means Marcus and I are no longer in danger. No one's going to hurt us.

More than ever, I want to listen to Marcus's messages, but this isn't the right time. Not with Emma and I finally talking again.

I get the chance a few minutes later when a very tall, very cute guy walks over to our table. He flops onto the seat next to Emma and smiles at her before asking if it's okay if he sits with us. It doesn't take long to clue in that not only do they know each other, something's going on between them. I've never seen her smile like that at a guy. He means more to her than the short-term flings she had in high school.

"Go ahead," I say. "I need to check my messages."

The only messages I've received are from Marcus. The first one is from the night I had sex with him: *"Amber, I'm so sorry. You got things wrong. I didn't think badly of what you did to stay alive. No matter what you think, that psychopath did rape you...."* I listen to the message, which is followed by another one. *"Kitten, I'm sorry about... what happened. It's not what you think. I need you. Please call me."* There's a similar message after that.

God, how could I have been so stupid? He's done nothing but try to help me, and I turned my back on him without giving him a chance to explain his reaction that night.

Deep down I know why I ran and why I've avoided listening to his messages. And why I've come up with every reason why I needed to push him away. I've been afraid. Afraid of my growing feelings for him. I loved Trent and he was stolen from me. I was afraid to love again and have that person taken away as well. I was afraid that by loving Marcus, I would be betraying Trent's memory. But I've already been betraying his memory by trying to forget. The therapist was right. I have been trying to block out everything to help me move on, except I haven't moved on at all.

I call Marcus's number but end up with his voice mail. Emma and the guy are laughing, their attention focused on each other.

I grab my jacket and backpack off the seat next to me, and after a quick good-bye, I run out of the building.

There's somewhere else I need to be.

47

MARCUS

My cell phone rings from the cup holder as I drive down the street toward Tammara's apartment. Thinking it might be Amber, I check the name. It's Alejandro's mom.

A bad feeling in my gut warns me something's wrong. I answer the phone.

"Is everything okay?" I ask.

"Is Alejandro with you, Marcus?" Her voice sounds like she's trying to be calm but it's not working. Her words are too rapid to hide the truth.

"No. I haven't seen him since Thursday." And when I did see him, he still seemed pissed at me. When I asked him about that, he pointedly ignored me. I sigh. What the hell am I supposed to do? Everything inside me is screaming he's in trouble. "You want me to go find him?"

"Yes, please. He never showed up for school, and no one seems to know where he is."

After I hang up, I head directly to Carlos's lair. I know what I'm doing is stupid, especially since I have no one watching my ass. But right now it doesn't matter. I need to get Alejandro away from Carlos.

I pull ahead of a car that looks like it got into a fight and barely came out the winner. I've no idea how many men are with him, but based on the number of cars parked in front of Carlos's house, there are at least five guys.

I'm fucked. Big-time.

I'd call Chase, but it won't be enough to even the odds, and I don't want to get him involved. He's got everything to live for.

I park my car farther down the street and take a deep breath. It does nothing to calm my out-of-control heart rate, but as long as Carlos can't sense my fear, I should be fine.

Loud music blares from a neighbor's house. Silence blankets Carlos's place. If it weren't for the cars, a few of which I recognize, I would have figured no one is here.

Before I can walk up the path, the door opens and one of Carlos's men steps out. At first I think he's expecting me, which is why he opened the door, but the flicker of surprise on his face suggests otherwise.

He calls out something in Spanish. I don't understand most of it, other than a few choice curses directed at me, but I'm sure the men inside are chuckling if his joyful tone is anything to go by.

I take a step forward, ignoring the ache in my ribs and its not-so-subtle reminder of what happened last time I confronted Carlos and his gang. "I'm looking for Alejandro Rodriquez."

The bald man with winter-white skin steps out of the house, followed by Carlos, a delighted sneer on his lips. He stays in the doorway while the two men flank it. "What are you, his mummy?"

The men chuckle, the sound void of humor.

Carlos folds his arms across his chest in what appears to be a relaxed stance. I know better than to fall for it. He's as tightly wound up as his men. Make the wrong move and I'm dead before I can say Amber's name.

"I take it my message wasn't clear enough last time," he says. "You mess with Alejandro, and you mess with us."

That's not quite the gist of it as I remember. I seem to remember it more along the lines of "You mess with us and you're fucked," but whatever. The outcome's the same either way.

"I'm not looking for trouble. All I want is to take Alejandro home." I hold my arms out to the side. "That's all."

"What makes you so sure he's here?"

" 'Cause I saw the bike you bought him. 'Cause it's obvious you're trying to recruit him."

Carlos laughs with an edge of humor that causes me to stiffen. "I'm not fucking Santa Claus." His men chuckle again. I ignore them.

"So you're saying you had nothing to do with the bike?"

He takes a step forward. "That's exactly what I'm saying." His eyes narrow but stay steady on me. "Maybe you've got the wrong gang. Maybe he decided to join the Blood Crappers." His men laugh at the purposefully messed-up name. "Did you ever consider that?"

He rattles off something in Spanish, which clearly amuses his men. One of them replies, also in Spanish. "I was asking them what we should do with you. Ludwig thinks you're stupid enough to bang down the Blood Crappers' door and let 'em kill you. I'll have to agree with him there." He snaps his fingers and Ludwig pulls out his semi-automatic and levels it at me. My already fast heart rate spikes. "Now, unless you have some more pressing business with us, I suggest you run along."

Instinct tells me to leave. And for once, I have to agree with it. Without turning my back on them, I return to my car, aware Carlos or Ludwig could change their mind at any second and shoot me.

I start the engine and speed away.

Shit. If Carlos isn't the problem, then I don't even know where to begin looking for Alejandro.

I drive around the neighborhood, checking all the places he

could be, before making my way to the youth center. I haven't heard from Alejandro's mom since I last talked to her, which means he isn't home yet.

It's dark by the time I get there. Dave's car isn't here, but the lights are on inside.

I park my car and jog to the main entrance. Maybe whoever is here has seen Alejandro. Otherwise, I'll have to do what Carlos predicted would happen; I'll have to pay a visit to their rival.

I pull open the door and enter the building. An odd silence settles around me, giving the place a strange morgue-like feel.

Light streams out from under Dave's office door. As I walk closer, I hear voices coming from inside but can't make out what they're saying.

I reach for the doorknob and almost sag with relief when I hear Alejandro's voice. But the next voice sends a cold finger of fear down my spine: Frank.

<h1 style="text-align:center">48</h1>

<h2 style="text-align:center">AMBER</h2>

Marcus could be anywhere.

I check the engineering building, in case he's hanging out there late. I even ask a few people if they've seen him. Either they know who I'm talking about and haven't seen him, or they have no idea who Marcus is. I even try calling Chase, but I get only his voice mail.

After exhausting every possibility, I head to the dorm parking lot, calling Marcus as I walk. When I still get only his voice mail, I hurl my bag into the passenger seat of the car. Why isn't he answering?

Maybe he changed his mind about me after leaving the message? Maybe Jordan and Emma got things wrong. Either way, I need to talk to him and find out where things stand between us.

His car isn't at his apartment building. Chase's car is, though. I miss Marcus, but there's one thing I should find out before risking my heart again.

After Chase buzzes me into the building, I knock on the guys' door. Chase opens it wearing only jeans. He's hot and works out, yet unlike his roommate, he's never used his sex appeal to entice girls into his bed.

269

Then again, maybe there's a girl currently in his bed and I'm interrupting. My face heats up at that possibility.

But instead of glowering at me, Chase cocks his head to the side and gives me a half smile. "You looking for someone?"

"I need to talk to you."

The hopeful gleam in his eyes drops away. He steps aside and lets me in. "You want anything to drink?"

"No, I'm fine, thanks."

Chase walks over to the tiny kitchen and returns with a beer.

I accidentally glance at the couch. The image of what happened last time I was here on that couch sneaks into my mind and a tingling warmth spreads throughout my body.

Swallowing the ache at the memory of what happened after that, I turn away. And notice a dent in the wall that wasn't there before.

"What can I do you for?" Chase asks, waiting patiently for me to pull myself together.

"I need to know the truth." I look him squarely in the eyes. "Is Marcus sleeping around again?"

Chase lets out a hard breath. "Not yet, but..." He pauses, visibly conflicted.

"But what?"

"I've been friends with Marcus since elementary school. He's always been restless and reckless, till he met you. But since your breakup, he's been sliding back to the guy he used to be."

"You're worried he'll do something stupid." He already has, and that left him with an injured rib.

Chase nods. "Can I ask a question?"

"Sure, what?"

He levels his gaze at me. "Are you here to hurt him again, or what's the deal?"

"I made a mistake. I thought he didn't want to be with me anymore. I know now that's not true. I've been trying to get hold of him to talk to him, but he's not answering his phone."

"Try the youth center. He's been hanging out there a lot lately."

Of course.

I thank Chase and hurry to my car. Hope has let me down before. But this time I'm willing to put my heart on the line for Marcus—and do whatever it takes to get him back.

And do whatever it takes to make it up to him for not having more faith in him, in us.

49

MARCUS

My first thought when I hear Frank's voice is, *What the hell is he doing here?* My second thought is, *Fuck.* Everything makes sense: The mysterious bike. Alejandro's behavior and sudden anger toward me. I thought Ryan and I had been Frank's only victims. I was wrong.

The urge to slam my fist into the wall—or better yet, Frank's face—hits me full force. I don't wait to hear what they're talking about. I shove the door open and it bangs against the wall.

Surprised at the sudden intrusion, both Frank and Alejandro spin around. They're standing several feet apart, but the discomfort at being so close to Frank pours off Alejandro.

At the sight of me, anger and guilt pile onto Frank's unshaven face.

"What the hell are you doing here?" I snap, eyes focused on him. Ryan and I learned the hard way how quickly he can sink his deadly fangs into you, the poisonous reptile that he is.

Frank raises his hands in front of him. "It's not what you think."

I edge closer to Alejandro. "What exactly is that? You're not touching him like you touched me and Ryan?"

Until then, Alejandro had been watching Frank, body tense. At my admission of what Ryan and I had endured, he whips around to face me, shock and betrayal written all over him. He's right. It *is* my fault. If I hadn't kept silent about what happened, Frank would be in jail, and Alejandro wouldn't have suffered the same fate as Ryan and me.

A startling, gut-twisting thought jabs me in the stomach and almost knocks me to my knees. "How many boys have there been, Frank?"

He was forced to stop molesting my brother when Ryan finally had enough and left home. Except for the night Ryan died, when Frank held a gun to my head, he hasn't touched me since. And he hadn't touched me since the night he raped Ryan in front of me. But Ryan, Alejandro, and I can't be his only victims. There must be others.

"How many boys have there been, Frank?" I yell.

He flinches.

I've been silent for too long. It's too late to have him charged for what he did to Ryan and me, but his most recent victims can testify against him. He knows one way or another, he's going to jail for a long time. I can see it on his face.

"It's not like that." A drop of sweat drips down the side of his face. He looks at Alejandro. "Tell him," Frank begs. "Tell him he's got it all wrong. Tell him I've never touched you."

Alejandro keeps silent, eyes still on Frank.

Frank tears his gaze from Alejandro and locks it on me. "I recently won a lot of money," he says, words rushed. "I'll buy Ryan his damn gravestone. I'll buy him the best one money can buy. All you have to do is walk away and forget everything."

50

AMBER

Marcus's car is in the parking lot, but he's not on the courts playing basketball. No one is. The place looks pretty deserted. If it wasn't for Marcus's car and the soft glow coming from a window, I'd have left, thinking no one's around.

But I don't.

From several blocks away, an emergency vehicle siren speeds past and fades in the distance. I park next to Marcus and walk to the entrance. I don't know why, but I have a weird feeling something's not right.

I check that I have my cell phone and quietly enter the building. The temperature feels chillier than outside. Part of me, a very small part, tells me to turn back and go home. But after what happened with Marcus, when he talked to the gang about Alejandro, turning away is the last thing I can do. He might need help. He could be bleeding to death. He could be...

I silently tell my brain to shut up. I don't need my overactive imagination working overtime. That won't help anyone.

Relief floods through me at the sound of Marcus's voice coming from Dave's office. I'm about to sprint down the hall and into the room, fling my arms around his neck, and kiss him, when he speaks. His icy voice stops me cold.

A man replies but the words are too quiet for me to hear. I move closer, careful not to make a sound.

"I recently won a lot of money. I'll buy Ryan his damn gravestone. I'll buy him the best one money can buy. All you have to do is walk away and forget everything."

I peer into the room, but not far enough to be seen by anyone. All I can see is Alejandro and Marcus, both looking angry and sick. I can't see the owner of the voice.

"Forget it," Marcus snaps. "Ryan and I made a mistake by keeping quiet." His voice shatters on the last word. "You touched me and raped Ryan. We should have told the cops, but we didn't."

My heart crumbles at his words, and my stomach rushes up to meet it. My hand flies to my mouth to keep the sob from escaping.

"Ryan let you keep hurting him just so you wouldn't hurt me. Isn't that right?" Marcus screams the last part.

He has always been strong and cocky. I've never seen him so vulnerable and beaten, not even after Carlos's men attacked him. All this time, I've been suffering from survivor guilt, as the therapist explained to me, but I wasn't the only one. It's been tearing Marcus apart, too. And now his reaction after we made love makes sense. It wasn't disgust at what I did. It was pain at what his brother endured.

I fight the urge to run into the room and hug him. He won't appreciate it. Not now. I doubt he wanted me to know the truth about his past. Especially not this.

I'm about to leave when I see Marcus notice me through the doorway. Sadness crowds every inch of him.

An intense heat builds inside me at the man who hurt him, and I have to hold myself back before I rush in there and slam my fist into the man's face.

51

MARCUS

"**R**yan let you keep hurting him just so you wouldn't hurt me. Isn't that right?" I scream the last part. Frank doesn't answer, not that he needs to. I already know the truth.

And now so does Amber.

The secret Ryan begged me to keep is no longer a secret. I've betrayed my brother's dying wish, but I've betrayed Alejandro's trust in me even more. He'll never forgive me for what I've done and for what I didn't do.

And I don't blame him.

Amber looks as though she's going to storm in here and hit Frank, and I silently will her to stay put.

She mouths, *I'm sorry*, and I know that she is. She's sorry for what Frank did to me and Ryan, and she's sorry for finding out this way, instead of me being the one to tell her—when I was ready.

I lean down and whisper in Alejandro's ear, "Amber's in the hallway. Go outside with her and wait. Whatever you do, don't let him know she's here."

He gives a small nod and leaves. I don't have time to dwell on what Amber now thinks about me. I just relish the warmth surging

276

through me that she cared enough to come looking for me. For now, it'll have to do.

"Hey, where's he goin'?"

"This is between you and me, Frank." I don't wait to hear the main door click shut. I launch myself at him. He's used to beating me up without my fighting back. I learned at an early age that there was no point in trying. It only made things worse.

The benefit of that is, he's not prepared for my attack. He stumbles back and I punch him in the jaw. Fortunately he doesn't have the foresight to dodge out of the way and my fist makes contact.

"That's for what you did to me and Ryan." My knuckles throb, but it's a pain I more than welcome.

Before he can retaliate, I punch his gut. He doubles over, breath ragged. "And that's for Alejandro and everyone else you've hurt."

He recovers and charges at me. I sidestep out of his way. Years of basketball have made me quick on my feet. Years of beers have turned him into a slug.

He spins around. "Should've tossed out your sorry ass when your mom and I hooked up. It's not like she ever wanted ya."

"Tell me something I don't already know." I swing at him. My fist slams into his eye. "It's over, Frank. I might not be able to press charges against you, but once I talk to the cops, they'll investigate, and all your dirty secrets will be out." Including mine.

Shame crashes through me, but instead of making me weak, it fires up my anger.

Frank moves to the side, placing a metal folding chair between us. As if that's going to stop me. A satisfied smile spreads on his lips.

What the fuck?

"Last chance to accept my offer, Marcus. Just how badly do ya want that gravestone for Ryan?"

He slips his hand into his jacket pocket.

52

———

AMBER

"Who's the man you two were talking to?" I ask Alejandro once we're outside. My fingers repeatedly tap my thigh. I don't bother to stop them.

Alejandro leans back against the wall, arms crossed. "Frank Wilson. Marcus's stepfather."

I don't even know what to say to that. The man was supposed to protect Marcus and Ryan and love them. Not physically abuse them or demean them in the worst possible way.

Once again, I wonder what kind of mother would marry a monster like that and do nothing to protect her sons. Even my mom, with all her faults, would never be so cruel.

The pain on Alejandro's face leaves me numb. Marcus and Ryan weren't Frank's only victims. Alejandro is one, too.

"If Marcus had known what Frank was doing to you," I say, "he would have stopped him."

"What do you know about anythin'?" The way he says it confirms what I already suspect.

"I know what it's like to trust someone and have them hurt you to the point where you wish you were dead. I know what it's like to wait for someone to save you, but no one comes. I know what it's

278

like to live as a shadow of who you used to be, too afraid to trust again. And I know what it's like to be broken and wonder if you'll ever feel normal again."

He looks at me with renewed curiosity. "What ha—" A sharp noise, like a backfiring engine from inside the building, interrupts him.

I suck the chilled air into my lungs and feel it spread through my body. We spin around and stare at the door, unsure what to do.

Seconds later, the door flies open and slams against the brick wall. Frank spares us a moment's glance, face white, blood splattered on his royal blue jacket. At first I think it's his, but then I remember what Marcus told me about Ryan's death. His stepfather shot Ryan. Which means Frank probably has a gun.

Before I can register what that means for Alejandro and me, Frank takes off. He scurries across the street. I don't wait long enough to see where he's going. I shove my phone at Alejandro and yell for him to call 9-1-1 as I yank open the door.

I run back to Dave's office. Marcus is sprawled on the floor, a hand pressed below his left shoulder. Blood covers his T-shirt and seeps from under his hand. A wave of dizziness rushes over me. I bite my lip hard. No matter what, I've got to keep myself together and not have a flashback.

I drop down beside him and touch his arm. "Marcus, it's going to be okay. An ambulance is on the way." He moans.

I rush to the file cabinet, grab the first-aid kit, and return to his side. He's lost so much blood. I'm not sure how coherent he is anymore. I flip the catches open and lift the lid, praying it contains more than just Band-Aids.

After riffling through the kit, I snatch up two individual packages of large gauze pads and rip them open. "Here, I've got something for the bleeding."

Marcus is barely able to apply pressure to the wound, his energy rapidly draining. It doesn't take much effort to peel his hand away. I push up the sleeve of his blood-soaked T-shirt and press the pads on the wound.

Marcus groans.

God, where's the ambulance? He won't last much longer before he bleeds out.

That thought drowns out the effects of the adrenaline that's been keeping me going until now. Tears cloud my vision.

"I..." Marcus whispers. "I didn't...accept his offer." I can just make out his words. "Tell...cops what you...heard." He winces at the effort it costs him to talk.

I'm not sure if I'm supposed to tell him to stop talking, so his condition doesn't worsen, or keep him talking so he doesn't slip into unconsciousness.

"He needs to be...stopped."

"I will. I promise." With my free hand, I interlace my fingers with his. "I'm sorry I didn't listen to your messages sooner."

Marcus's eyes drift shut and he whispers, "I love you, Kitten." The tears I've managed to restrain break free. One lands on his hand. I sniff.

"I love you, too." I should feel lighter saying those words, but I feel the opposite. Every time I open my heart to someone, they're ripped away. But even knowing that, I repeat the words for Marcus's sake. He hasn't experienced much love in his life. The people who were supposed to love him turned their backs on him. And he never gave any other girl a chance to love him. To really love him. Not like he gave me.

I kiss his cool lips. A tear splashes onto his cheek. "Stay with me, Marcus. Please don't leave me."

After what feels like a million years, sirens approach and blue-and-red lights flash behind the closed blinds. The main door bangs open and a few seconds later a cop followed by two EMTs enters the room.

"He's been shot," I say, my hand still pressed against Marcus's wound.

One of the EMTs kneels next to me. "You need to move away so I can work on him."

Still on my knees, I back away and use the desk corner to help me stand. Now that the EMTs are taking care of him, my body starts shaking violently. I keep hold of the desk so I don't collapse.

"I need to ask you some questions," the cop says as I watch the EMTs work.

"Okay," I whisper past the lump wedged tight in my throat.

"Can you tell me what happened?"

"I didn't see everything."

"That's okay. Tell me what you did see."

I tell him about finding Marcus and Alejandro in the office, talking to Marcus's stepfather. I tell him how Marcus admitted that Frank sexually assaulted Marcus and raped Ryan. I tell him how Frank had offered to pay for Ryan's gravestone if Marcus kept quiet about everything. I tell him Alejandro and I were outside when we heard the gunshot. And as the EMTs roll Marcus away on the stretcher, I tell him how Frank ran out, covered in blood. The only thing I leave out is that Alejandro has also been victimized by that monster. Alejandro has to find the courage to tell the cop his truth.

The cop keeps me here long after Marcus is taken away, asking me more questions, many of which I don't have answers to. After a while, I don't care anymore. I just want to be with Marcus.

Once the cop finishes, I drive to the hospital in a daze.

I park and sprint into the ER and ask the nurse about Marcus. I'm redirected upstairs, to the surgical waiting rooms.

The cop told me Marcus's mother will be contacted. From what limited information Marcus has told me about her, I'd be surprised if she shows up. Secretly, I hope she doesn't. I'd rather see Tammara here. At least in her own twisted way, she cares more about Marcus than his mother ever did.

Chase comes hurtling into the waiting room forty minutes later, breathing hard. All I can do is throw my arms around him and cry against his shoulder. He wraps me in his arms and hugs me tight.

We're not the only ones here. It's been a busy night. Two other families sit in their own corners, stuck in their own private hell.

"What happened?" Chase asks once my sobbing slows enough for me to catch my breath and answer.

I don't want to tell him everything. Not here where the families can hear us. None of them need to hear the horrifying details of what Marcus and his brother suffered through. And it's not my place to tell Chase. Marcus only gave me permission to tell the cops the truth.

I repeat what I told him on the phone, adding a little more detail this time, about how Frank shot Marcus. Chase clenches his hands, ready to punch the wall. Several times.

"Do you think his mom will come?" My fingers tap-tap-tap my thigh. I stop them midtap and pick at the small thread sticking out of the tear in the padded chair I'm sitting on.

Chase shakes his head. "You and I are all he has, Amber."

It kills me to hear that, even though it's true. Marcus has spent most of his life building walls to keep people out. At least now I know why.

I lean my head on Chase's shoulder. He keeps his arm around me as my eyes drift shut. At some point he shifts slightly, jarring me awake.

"You should go home," he says, his voice low. "Don't you have a math final tomorrow?"

"How did you know?"

"Marcus told me. He's been worried about you and blames himself for not being there for you. In case you haven't noticed, he's quick at blaming himself for everything." Pretty much like me. "Go home. I'll call you once I know something."

I smile at him, grateful for his concern. "Thanks, but I'd rather stay." It's not like I'll be able to sleep or study anyway.

"You sure?"

"Yes." More than ever before.

An hour or two later, a guy in scrubs comes into the room and approaches us. One family has already left after receiving bad news. I hold my breath, hoping the guy isn't going to tell me what another surgeon told them.

"Are you Marcus Reid's family?" he asks.

"He doesn't have any family," Chase says.

The surgeon checks the file in his hand. "It lists his parents here as next of kin."

Chase grunts. "No one knows who or where his biological father is. His stepfather's the one who shot Marcus." He gestures at the room. "And as you can see, his mother doesn't give a damn about him, even though I'm positive the cops told her hours ago that Marcus is here. So you tell me. Do you think he has family?" He pretty much growls the last part.

I put my hand on his knee, knowing how much this is killing Chase, like it's killing me. What if they won't tell us anything or won't let me see him because we aren't his family, even though we're more family to him than his parents ever were?

The surgeon looks at the chart again. "He's out of surgery and is recovering."

"Is he gonna be okay?" I ask.

"Barring complications, he'll be fine."

"Can we see him now?"

"It's late and he's sleeping. You should go home and rest. You can see him in the morning."

"Please," I breathe. "Just for a minute."

I don't know what he sees in my face. Maybe a girl who's scared he's not telling the truth because she's been lied to too many times before, or a girl who struggles to find hope when it's been stolen more times than she cares to admit. Whatever it is, it's enough for him to cave in and tell me I can see Marcus. But only me. And only for five minutes.

He directs me to the ICU. Chase waits in the hallway while a nurse leads me to Marcus's bed. His eyes are closed and his skin is as white as the sheets, but he's still the same guy I love. And more important, he's alive. The beeping heart rate monitor by his bed is all the proof I need of this.

Tears prick my eyes as I smile at him. I don't say anything. I just watch him sleep, hoping he doesn't have any nightmares, knowing I will. But maybe the therapist can help me with those, too.

The nurse comes to tell me it's time to go.

"I love you," I whisper, my heart fluttering at the words.

I drive back to the dorm and tumble into bed. But tonight it isn't nightmares that follow me into sleep. Tonight I dream of strong arms, a crooked smirk, and the belief that normal might actually be possible.

53

AMBER

"**A**mber!" Someone shakes my shoulder.

I open my eyes and blink the room into focus. My head is resting on my arms, which are folded on top of a textbook. I sit up and spot Brittany's drawing of Marcus and me on the wall.

Memories of last night swarm me. My chest feels as though someone jumped on it, forcing air out of my lungs.

"Isn't your math test soon?" Brittany nods at my alarm clock. Crap, it's already 10:50. My exam begins in ten minutes.

"Thanks." I grab my backpack and bolt from my room without bothering with my jacket, and sprint across campus, through the falling snow, to the classroom. A few last-minute students scurry into the room as I approach. I enter the room with a minute to spare and locate an empty seat with a test booklet facedown on the desk.

My lungs burn as I fight to catch my breath. Snow melts in my hair and drips down my face and Trent's hoodie.

"You may begin," a man at the front of the room announces.

Just remember to breathe, Marcus's voice says in my head. My throat tightens. *Focus.* Just three hours; then I'll be finished with the exam and can hold him and make sure he knows how much I love him.

I flip the test over.

On the way to the classroom, I didn't have time to think about Marcus, but now that I'm sitting, the memory of the gunshot, the memory of seeing Marcus barely conscious, the memory of so much blood, and the memory of Marcus pale against the hospital sheets spills into my mind, and shoves aside everything I knew for the exam.

I try pushing all non-math-related thoughts from my head and focus on the test. I finish the first twenty questions, but my mind keeps drifting. The memories I'm struggling to forget, and the fear that something's happened to Marcus since I left the hospital, keep bombarding my brain.

Focus. Focus. Focus. FOCUS.

I work through the questions, but my pace is dragging. I yawn and round my eyes in an attempt to prevent them from shutting. The moment I do, it's over.

The person in the next row over coughs. I look up and spot a guy who could easily be Alejandro in five years. He's working away at his test, hopefully never having experienced the same horrors as Marcus and Alejandro.

Tears prick my eyes at what Frank did to them and Ryan. Marcus once said the world doesn't give a shit what happens to victims, especially kids. It only cares about the people who count. Jordan wants to make a difference. So do I.

And right now, I want to be at the hospital with Marcus, to be there when he wakes up. So he's not alone.

I finish the question I'm working on and walk to the front of the room. I hand the unfinished test to my instructor. "My boyfriend is recovering from surgery he had last night. As much as I want to finish this test and the course, I can't stay here anymore. I need to be there for him."

The man gives a curt nod, his expression unreadable. I shoulder my backpack and leave.

54

MARCUS

I open my eyes to the sun shining in my room. It takes a minute or two to remember where I am, and for the memories of last night to surface through the haze in my head. I vaguely recall waking up several times during the night, but this is the first time I've felt this coherent.

"Afternoon," a short curvy woman says, smiling next to my bed. The top of her uniform is covered with cartoon cats that make me think of Smoky. "How's the pain?"

"It's good." They must have me doped up on some pretty strong meds. I can't feel too much right now, though I'm sure that won't last forever. "What time is it?"

"One thirty. Your girlfriend should be back soon. She went to get coffee."

"Amber's here?" Didn't she have her math final this afternoon? I strain to remember what time it was scheduled for. Maybe it was for this morning. Or maybe I've been out of it for a few days, and she's already had it.

"She's been here for a while. Poor girl looks exhausted. You sure know how to show a girl a good time." She laughs and checks my IV, then peels back the dressing from my wound.

She's just finished redressing it when Amber enters, carrying a brown paper bag and wearing the sexy black dress she wore that first night at Nightshade. The night when I first realized, deep down, I never wanted to let this beautiful, damaged girl out of my life. Only, thanks to me screwing up several times, I almost did.

Unlike the nurse, she blushes at the sight of my half-naked body, even though she's seen a lot more of it than the nurse. Or maybe that's why she's blushing. She's remembering just how much of it she's seen. That thought makes me grin.

After retying my sling, the nurse gathers her supplies and smiles at Amber. "All right, young lady, he's all yours. Just remember to be careful with his wound. We don't want it to start bleeding again."

Amber blushes a deeper shade of red at the comment. My grin widens at where her thoughts might have gone.

The nurse adjusts the bed so that I'm sitting and leaves.

Amber places the paper bag on the moveable table near my bed and sits on the chair. "I brought you some chicken noodle soup."

"Thanks." Not that I'm hungry. There's only one thing I'm interested in holding right now, and it's not food.

I pat my bed. No way is she sitting on that damn plastic seat when there's a comfy spot—well, as comfortable as a hospital bed can be—next to me.

She looks at it, uncertain, then smiles and moves out of the chair. Leaning over, she gives me a sweet kiss on the lips, setting off the heart rate monitor next to my bed. I laugh at her smug smile when she realizes why the monitor beeped.

She pulls away and sits next to me. I crave more than a sweet kiss, but I don't think the nurses will appreciate walking in and finding out exactly what I want to do to Amber now that she's finally back in my life.

"What time's your math test?" I don't want her to leave, but I know she'll have to go. Too bad she doesn't have her math books with her. I could help her study. Though I'm not sure how good a tutor I'll be with these drugs in my system.

She bites her lip. "It was this morning."

"How did it go?"

She glances at the heart rate monitor, which started beeping again even though she didn't kiss me this time.

She smiles and shakes her head. "It doesn't matter anymore."

I frown. "It doesn't? Why not?"

"I've decided not to be a veterinarian."

"I thought that's what you've wanted to be since you were a little girl."

"I did. But that was the old Amber. I'm not that girl anymore, and I never will be." The corners of her lips slide down briefly before she smiles, again. "I want to help other victims of crime. I've been seeing a therapist." Her smile widens at my surprise. "I want to help other victims realize that to win, you have to stop blaming yourself for something that wasn't your fault, that only then can you be a true survivor. Otherwise you let the criminal win." She looks at me pointedly as she says it.

"You have to stop blaming yourself for what happened to Ryan," she adds softly. When I don't respond, she says, "How old were you when it happened?"

She doesn't say the words, but I know what she's referring to. "Thirteen."

"You were only a boy, Marcus. Frank was a full-grown man. You couldn't have protected yourself and Ryan against that. You didn't let your brother down. Frank did, and so did your mother. Don't let them win by blaming yourself for their actions."

I thread my fingers through her hair and bring her head close to mine. "Have I told you how much I love you?" I murmur. I vaguely remember telling her after I was shot, but I'm not sure if she heard me, or if I just imagined saying the words.

She smiles against my lips. "I love you, too. More than you

could possibly imagine." We kiss, and the monitor goes all kinds of crazy. I'm surprise the nurse isn't rushing in with a crash cart.

My fingers slide under the hem of her dress and glide across her soft skin, making up for lost time. The door opens, but the meaning of it doesn't register until a female voice interrupts our moment. "Is everything all right in here?"

I move away only far enough so that Amber's forehead rests against mine. "I'll say."

The nurse chuckles and leaves us to enjoy the rest of the kiss. Unfortunately, Amber decides to switch to chaste pecks on the lips. I groan. How much longer do I have to stay here before I can have her in my apartment and back in my bed?

55

AMBER

"**D**o you want me to come in with you?" Marcus asks from the passenger seat of my car. I'd planned to see my mom today, for better or for worse, and Marcus came with me, saying he had a surprise.

I still don't know what it is.

I smile at him, thankful he's here, even if I want to face Mom on my own. "I'll be fine."

"Okay, call me when you're finished." He leans over and kisses me on the lips. I'm tempted to deepen the kiss and stay in the car with him, but I know I have to get this over with. And I know Marcus needs to stretch his legs after the drive. It's been a week since he was shot. He needs to take things easy for a while and continue to wear the sling. But that isn't stopping him from taking a short walk in the freshly fallen snow.

"Be careful," I remind him. "The sidewalks might be slippery."

"You're sexy when you worry." He chuckles and kisses me, again. His tongue trails along my lower lip, hinting he wants more. I give in to him, because let's face it, I'm willing to do almost anything for this man.

Before things get too steamy, and Mom catches me making out

292

with him on the driveway, I pull away.

I use my key to get into the house. I'm about to call out to see if Mom's home, when I hear a light bang from the kitchen like someone's putting a glass on the counter.

As I walk through the house, I notice the absence of Christmas decorations. We used to love decorating the house. It was a family tradition. Mom would make hot chocolate and play cheesy Christmas music and we would spend the day decorating. Now more than ever, the place feels forgotten.

Pushing away the heartache at how much Paul altered our lives, I enter the kitchen. Mom's standing at the counter, lost in thought. An empty glass rests on the granite surface.

My heart lurches. "Hey, Mom."

At first she stares at me as if she's hallucinating; then her mouth glides into a smile. She rushes to me and throws her arms around me, squeezing me tight. "I've missed you, Amber." She pulls away and wipes a stray tear. "How's school?"

I'm only able to open and shut my mouth, a fish in a bowl, unable to make a sound. I eventually find my voice after Mom gives me a peculiar look. "It's fine." Other than the D I'll probably get in math.

I eye the glass on the counter.

"I was drinking milk. I'm attending weekly AA meetings again and seeing a therapist. And I left my position at the firm."

"But you love your job."

She shakes her head. "Maybe once. Before Paul Carlson killed Michael and hurt you so badly, I thought I'd lost you forever. I struggled with the job because I couldn't defend to the best of my abilities like I'd sworn I would do. So I started drinking. It was the only way I could make it through the day, knowing I was helping people like Paul, who willingly destroyed without regret.

"It didn't help that I thought you hated being around me, because I failed you by not protecting you. I didn't handle Michael's death well at all. But no matter what you might have believed,

Amber, I never blamed you for what happened to him. It wasn't your fault. I hope you know that."

I do, but hearing it from her makes it even more real. "Why would you think that I hated being around you?"

"Because you avoided me once you were released from the hospital. You spent more time at your grandma's house than you did here."

I can only blink. "I stayed at Grandma's because you wouldn't let me keep Smoky. He'd been through so much, and he was so scared. I needed to be there to help him heal. I was the only one he trusted to do that until he realized Grandma wouldn't hurt him."

Mom brushes a strand of hair behind my ear like she used to when I was little. "I'm sorry, Amber. I should have just asked you. I let my stupid pride get in the way. Anyway, it was your phone call that reminded me just how important you are to me. That, and your grandmother told me I'm an idiot and needed to smarten up. I thought she was going to ground me like she did when I was a teen." We both laugh at that. "I'm not giving up law. I'm just changing the side of the fence I'm sitting on."

We talk for a while longer, and I tell her about my change of career plans. She's more excited about it than I thought she would be. Then I call Marcus and introduce them when he shows up a minute later.

I'm a little nervous at first, but she accepts him just like she accepted Trent. Fortunately she doesn't ask about his sling, though she doesn't seem surprised by it, either. Maybe Grandma told her what limited information I shared with her on the phone last week. I mentioned he had been in the wrong place at the wrong time and was shot. They don't need to know all the details. And not all are for me tell.

Marcus and I are still deciding what to do about Tammara. Despite what she did to both of us, neither of us is interested in destroying her future. We're going to talk to her after Christmas, once we've decided what to do.

Mom makes hot chocolate, and the three of us hang up Christmas decorations. She doesn't have a tree, but she explains she doesn't need one. She's spending Christmas with us at Grandma's house when we come back next week.

Afterward, Marcus and I head to Grandma's, where Marcus explains my surprise is waiting. We walk to the front door, holding hands.

We don't have a chance to ring the doorbell. The door opens and Grandma hugs me and then Marcus, taking care not to hurt his shoulder.

Inside, I breathe in the familiar spicy smell of spruce and gingerbread. No fake Christmas trees for Grandma.

"You two want some milk and cookies?" she asks.

"Sure." I scan the area for signs of Smoky as Marcus replies, "Yes, please."

Grandma flashes me a knowing smile. "He's on the couch, waiting for you."

I grin and let go of Marcus's hand. He follows me into the living room.

"So what's the surprise?" I plunk myself on the cushion next to Smoky.

Marcus sits next to me, our bodies touching, and reaches over to stroke Smoky. Smoky purrs in response, stands, and relocates himself so he's sitting on both our laps.

"This is your surprise," Marcus says.

I feel my eyebrows head north for the winter. "Smoky sitting on our laps is my surprise?"

Marcus laughs. "No. I know how much you miss him, and it's obvious how much he misses you. So if you want, he can stay at my place. Chase is fine with it. Then you'll have a reason to visit more often."

I blink several times while his words sink in. This is a huge step for Marcus. For both of us.

I cup his face in my hand and give him a long, deep kiss, which he's more than happy to return.

Sighing softly, I pull back and rest my forehead against his. His warm, rapid breath caresses my face.

"I already have a very good reason to visit you often," I say. "But thank you. It means everything to me." I can tell from the smile on his face that he already knows this. I have time to give him one more lingering kiss before Grandma returns. One more lingering kiss to show him how amazing I think he is, and to show how much I love him.

"YOU KNOW WHAT YOU WANT?" THE MAN ASKS EMMA.

She smiles and points to a small basketball picture on the wall. "And I want it to say Trent below it." After I showed her the tattoo on my arm, Emma asked me where I got mine done. She wants her tribute to her brother to go on her ankle.

"What about you?" Kathy asks me. I show her the picture I brought with me of a purple lotus flower. She directs me to the room I was in last time. Marcus comes with me, still laughing that I'll be more inked up than him.

I take off my T-shirt and suddenly feel shy standing in front of him in only my bra and jeans. Seeing my discomfort, he winks. You'd think, with the way my face heats up, he's never seen me like this.

I sit on the tattoo table and describe where I want the tattoo: on the back of my shoulder, near the worst of my scars.

"Did you know the lotus flower symbolizes courage and awakening?" Kathy says. "The flower starts off small at the bottom of the murky pond and it grows toward the light. By the time it reaches the surfaces, it's the beautiful flower that we see."

Sounds like the last year of my life.

I smile at Marcus, who's smiling at me. "I know." And I do. We're both ready to surface, ready to let others in. Ready to find normal.

EPILOGUE
MARCUS

I enter the Student Services Building, the freezing late January air still clinging to me. I survey the open area and spot Amber. I'm about to call her name, to stop her before she disappears into the Counseling Center for her weekly appointment with her therapist, when I spot a guy checking her out from several yards away. He pretends to read a brochure he picked up some-place, but his spy skills need a lot more work.

Something about this guy unnerves me.

Amber strides down the hallway, oblivious to him. The guy places the brochure on a table and walks after her.

And I follow him.

He stops when she gets close to her therapist's office, and he whips out a small camera. What the fuck? I grab hold of his arm, not giving him a chance to take a photo.

Amber pulls the Counseling Center door open and steps inside without once turning around.

"What the fuck do you think you're doing?" I ask, glaring at him. He's a good several inches shorter than me and his muscles have never been introduced to weights.

"It's none of your business." He yanks his arm from my hand.

"Well, since that's my girlfriend you were planning to take a photo of without her consent, I'm making it my business."

"I wasn't gonna take a picture of her. I-I was going to take a picture of the Counseling Center."

"Bullshit. I saw you back there." I point in the direction we came from. "I saw you check her out and I saw you stalk her. Now tell me the truth, or she'll be filing for a restraining order. And that's gonna make your life real tough if you really are a student here." I'm bluffing. I have no idea if Amber can get a restraining order unless she can prove this isn't a one-time event. But since she complained the other day that she felt as though someone was stalking her, I suspect this isn't the first time he's followed her.

The guy holds his hands up. "Okay. Okay. I'll tell you. I'm a journalism major. She's a hot topic right now, and I figured a different angle on the story would be great for my portfolio. It's not like I'm hurting her."

"She's a person, not a hot topic," I growl, my face inches from his. I can smell the fear seeping from him. "And you don't have the right to harass her."

"You're wrong. I have the First Amendment backing me."

"The First Amendment doesn't give you the right to harass her, asshole."

"I'm not harassing her. The public has the right to know if an innocent man is being convicted for a crime he never committed."

Something inside me detonates in a series of explosions, and I shove the jerk into the wall. "The psychopath is not an innocent man. He killed two people and nearly killed her."

"Some people don't believe that. They believe your girlfriend is guilty, not Paul Carlson."

I slam him into the wall again. "You don't even know what the fuck you're saying." I'm ready to keep smashing him against the wall until he finally realizes Amber's the victim.

"Let him go, son," a man says behind me.

Still holding on to the asshat, I glance over my shoulder and groan. My hands drop away from the guy, and I turn to face campus security.

"He assaulted me for no reason," Asshat whines.

"He's stalking my girlfriend," I counter. "And taking photos of her."

The man looks from me to Asshat. "I don't have time for this. If you're serious about the stalking, you can file a report with campus police."

Asshat blanches, and I weigh my choices....

To Be Continued in LET ME KNOW...

ABOUT THE AUTHOR

Born in Brighton England, Stina Lindenblatt has lived in a number of countries, including England, the US, Finland, and Canada. This would explain her mixed up accent. She has a kinesiology degree and a MSc in sports biological sciences.

In addition to writing fiction, she loves photography, and currently lives in Calgary, Canada, with her husband and three kids.

For news about her books, social media sites, and to sign up for her newsletter, check out her website at stinalindenblattauthor.com. Newsletter subscribers will receive several bonus gifts.